THE DEEP STEAL

A Novel by
Blair Barrows

Bookman LLC
Publishing & Marketing
Providing Quality, Professional Author Services
www.bookmanmarketing.com

This book is a work of fiction. Names, characters, places and incidents are either products of the authors imagination or are used fictitiously. Any resemblance to actual events or locales or persons, living or dead, is entirely coincidental.

ISBN: 1-59453-359-8

This book is dedicated to submariners and divers
who serve worldwide.
We are all brothers under the sea.

ACKNOWLEDGEMENTS

I would like to extend my gratitude for the help, encouragement and sound advice for this book which I received from Sharlene Allen, Val Dobruskin, John Devaney, Job A. Sandoval, Marilyn Comrie and Pat Northrup.

CHAPTER 1

1961

The Bay of Pigs was eerily calm and slick as the huge U.S. cruiser turned slowly and silently to seaward from the distant coast of Cuba where rocket and artillery flashes could be seen through the predawn mist and darkness. To those on the bridge of the warship, the far-off rumble of war was a sure indication that the Cuban patriot troops, who had just hours before been put ashore to rid their island-nation of communism, were running into stiff opposition.

The Captain of the cruiser stares incredulously at the *Flash* message handed to him just minutes previously by Admiral Hayes, the flag officer in charge of the invasion support task force who stood on a wing of the bridge just a few feet from him. The terse message read:

"IMMEDIATELY CEASE CURRENT OPERATIONS x ALL UNITS PROCEED TO INTERNATIONAL WATERS x FURTHER TRANSIT ORDERS TO BE SENT ASAP…"

Standing next to the Admiral, CIA Special Agent Brady Carmichael, who was the U.S. government liaison to the invasion troops, threw his freshly lit cigar over the side as he glared at the same message…

"Christ! Admiral, they're leaving all those men to the wolves…what the hell is going on here?"

"I can't explain it Brady, but obviously Washington knows something that we don't. But we shouldn't discuss it up here on the bridge, for right now I've got to get things moving to properly form up these ships as we secure from battle stations and head to the southwest. Lets meet in my quarters in about 15 minutes where we can talk about this."

As the shocked Carmichael left the bridge, the Admiral entered the inner-bridge of his flagship and gave further orders to his operations officer.

"Signal all ships to proceed on this present course at a speed of 22 knots. After the carrier completes aircraft recovery, have her and her escorts join in the same ASW formation we used coming down here. We should receive new orders within the hour. I will be in my quarters with the CIA liaison man."

"Aye aye sir."

Now, as the cloudless sky to the east turned a pale orange with the first light of day, Hayes went to the starboard outer wing of the bridge and with his binoculars took a long, final look at the now distant beachhead while hoping to himself that necessary air and sea support for the invading force was being called off due to some last-minute diplomatic agreement that may have been reached with Castro's communists. He found it hard to believe that the President would just leave all those men on the beach with no support as suggested by Brady Carmichael. With other probabilities roaring through his head, and using a trained seaman's eye, the Admiral slowly but methodically searched the horizon with the large, black, navy-issue binoculars, mentally checking the positions of the other ships in the invasion-support flotilla. Satisfied that all was in order and that the entire flotilla was now heading away from the conflict as ordered, he left the bridge through the pilothouse and headed aft toward his quarters.

In navy tradition, whenever the ship's captain or an officer senior to him arrive on or leave the bridge the word is announced loudly so the officer of the deck will know such an officer is present or not.

"The Admiral's leaving the bridge," the boatswain mate of the watch hollered out for all to hear. The officer of the deck and the captain both responded with a "very well." A marine corporal walked behind the Admiral as he went aft in the passageway to a large door marked "Flag Officer Quarters" and took up his position outside the door as Hayes entered. After lighting a cigar, the admiral saw his steward emerge from the galley. Chief stewards mate Murano, who had been with Hayes for eight years, smiled and greeted his boss.

"Good morning sir. Are you going to have breakfast now?"

"No thank you Murano, just a cup of coffee please. I'm expecting a visitor shortly. Offer him coffee too when he gets here, and then I need you to take a break for an hour or so, as we're going to have some discussions here."

"Are we going home sir?"

"Right now it looks that way, but I don't want you to repeat that in the chief's quarters."

* * *

Brady Carmichael became an elite member of the fledgling and highly selective U.S. Central Intelligence Agency in 1949. His background during World War II as a U.S. Army intelligence officer combined with post war college degree in political science, Russian language skills and Washington pull from a congressman friend of his father facilitated his appointment. After a week of indoctrination at the Virginia office he was sent to a remote training area where the modern methods and gadgets of espionage were drummed into him and the handful of other new recruits. After three months of what Carmichael would later describe as "eye-opening, shocking, but fascinating techniques," he was placed in the Soviet Intelligence Division that was formed out of necessity due to the threat to Western nations caused by the ongoing Soviet expansion in Europe and elsewhere.

Carmichael's interest in law enforcement and information gathering came about naturally. The son of a big-city policeman and the nephew of a detective on the same force, throughout his youth he constantly barraged both men with questions and theories about on-going criminal activity. During college, before he went into the army, he took some courses in law enforcement and international politics, and it was during his sophomore year that he pulled off his first successful sleuthing adventure.

Although short and stocky, his determination enabled him to play for the football team in high school, but despite an all-out effort, his size prevented him from making the college team. He did, however, maintain a keen interest in the game by scouting future opponents for the coach. Besides just observing these teams during actual games, Carmichael would also snoop at practice sessions if the team was located reasonably close to his school. On one occasion he found the following week's opponent, a rival school in the same conference, practicing in secret behind a closed-in, fenced field. Undeterred, he found a nearby deserted building, and using the fire escape and a borrowed spyglass, was able to determine that the team was planning to come out with the then new "T" formation. Diagramming everything he saw, he delivered a thorough and accurate package to the astonished head coach who put the spy work to good use, the result of which was a big victory for his school before a huge homecoming crowd.

"A helluva good job Carmichael," barked a smiling, backslapping coach who sought him out in the locker room after the game.

After his sophomore year, he left college and entered the service as World War II roared on into 1943. From boot camp he was sent to officer candidate school, and after being commissioned a 2nd lieutenant was sent to an army school that specialized in teaching the methods of gathering military intelligence and how it could be put to good use. Sent to England after compiling the highest grade average in his class, he was put to work studying aerial photographs of German defenses along the coast of France in anticipation of the Normandy landings. Completely engrossed in the project and invasion planning, the young lieutenant worked day and night studying a wide variety of data, and many of the conclusions he passed on proved to be most accurate and extremely valuable to the allied forces. His commanding general thought so highly of him that when he was sent to France after the invasion he arranged for now Capt. Carmichael to accompany him as his staff intelligence officer.

After the war he remained in Europe and was stationed in the allied section of Berlin. Witnessing the build-up to the east-west crisis in Germany, he developed a loathing for the Russians, but found a new respect for the defeated Germans. During a 30-day leave back to the states, he became engaged to a former high school sweetheart whom he hoped to talk into staying with him in the army after the marriage and making it a career.

"I like the army Brenda. My work is interesting, you and I can live in many different parts of the world," he predicted.

Uninterested, Brenda offered two alternatives:

"It's me or the army," she declared. "I don't like war or the military and I wouldn't want to ever be in a position where I'd have to cow-tow to some general's wife. I'm sorry Brady but that's the way I feel about it."

After the leave, Carmichael returned to his post in Berlin and told a disappointed General that he was leaving the army in the fall of '46 when his time was up. Returning to the states, he was all set to get married and go to work in New York City with a private investigation firm when Brenda called him on the phone late one night and informed him that even though he obeyed her wishes and left the army, she'd now "truly found Christ," and that the marriage was off and she was to become a nun.

"I know this will hurt you, and I know you're gonna think I'm wacky, and you also know I love and respect you…but I have had my calling…and must now devote the rest of my life to the Lord. I'm gonna become a nun…I'm sure you'll find another mate, but from what I've seen, most of your future time and devotion will be put into a career. I think we're both gonna be better off this way."

It took a few weeks, but a badly shaken Brady Carmichael rethought his options, including going back into the army, but at the urging of his father and uncle, decided to go back to college, earn a degree and then re-enter the world of intelligence and espionage as a civilian. He told his now retired father that the breakup with Brenda was a blessing in disguise.

"I like my women dad, but the work I want to get into isn't gonna be conducive with family life. It's probably a good thing that Brenda's going into the nunnery."

* * *

Upon completion of his CIA training he was sent back to Germany as a special agent, where he moved about as a traveling U.S. businessman. Putting his Russian and German language skills to good use, he dealt with dozens of undercover agents who operated in East Germany, Poland and the Soviet Union itself. He also was introduced to the British Intelligence Service and worked with both MI5 and its rival, MI6 divisions. Although he rarely overdid it, it was during this time in Europe that he took a liking to Scotch whiskey, and on many occasions when he had a relaxed meeting with other agents, they would share a bottle. One of his closest associates who also liked aged Scotch, a German national who worked in East Berlin, was found out, arrested and executed by the Russians. Carmichael's hatred of the Russians intensified when a contact from East Berlin told him, "They tortured that poor bastard for three days before he died." This agent was neither the first nor the last that would suffer a similar fate at the hands of the Soviet KGB…Others simply disappeared, further causing a vengeful rage to surge within Carmichael, who kept trying to tell himself that what was going on was "all part of the dangerous game we are embroiled in." He also concluded that the Russians had the most extensive, elaborate and effective espionage and security systems in the world.

In early 1955 he was engaged in the joint MI6/CIA tunneling exploit that went from West to East Berlin to clandestinely place communication intercept sensors directly under the Soviet headquarters. When MI6 reported to Washington that they believed Carmichael was being tailed and about to be grabbed by the East Germans, the CIA took no chances and wisely recalled him to Washington. Once back in the states, he was reassigned to a desk job and labored studiously for two years in a Soviet bloc "think-tank" group that made recommendations to the Senate Foreign Relations Committee and to the Secretary of Defense and the President himself.

In the late fifties he went under another disguise to England and Scotland to study the feasibility and impact of placing an American submarine tender and a squadron of the newly developed polaris missile-carrying, nuclear submarines in the British Isles. In his final report to the CIA head, he commented that:

"Holy Loch in Scotland, as recommended by the Royal Navy and agreed upon by our Navy, should be a good location strategically. The biggest threat that I see to putting a base there is that some of the fanatic, left wing commie radicals from England may come to the scene and try to cause some problems. The good part though is that the Scots have no stomach for these people, and they will welcome our Navy there. MI6 Internal Affairs also agrees with this, I say we go for it."

A bright, upcoming agent named Jose Roque made the Scotland trip with Carmichael, who was breaking him in to the European scene to broaden his background. A native of the Philippines, Roque more than impressed his mentor with his motivation, intelligence and overall investigative smarts. After they returned to Washington, Carmichael commended the man for his assistance, made out a grade "A" performance report that recommended his promotion to the next higher grade and concluded with the recommendation that he be utilized solely as a field operative.

"This man is ideally suited for field (foreign) service versus being placed in a stateside administrative position," Carmichael advised in his report.

To himself, he made a mental note of the trip with Roque and with a smile, recalled that last night in Glasgow they spent with two lovely Scottish lassies and some good, local, unblended Scotch, the brand name of which escaped his mind, but somehow he knew that he and Roque would cross paths again.

Next came a shift in Carmichael's career to the Latin American scene. Having worked his way up within the CIA organization, he was asked to conduct an investigation into the possible connection between the Soviets and a man named Fidel Castro, who was leading a revolution in Cuba to oust the current regime. After much research, several trips to Cuba and countless interviews with escaped Cuban "patriots", Carmichael accurately concluded that "When Castro gets in, Cuba will go communist." After this became fact, and thousands of Cubans fled the country to Florida, the CIA worked with the Department of Defense to come up with a plan to help organize and train an invasion force of those among them who wished to return to their island and rid it of Castro and communism. Brady Carmichael was made the U.S. (CIA) liaison to this force that underwent intensive combat training in Florida and other places. The plan called for them to be landed in the Bay of Pigs and supported by the U.S. Navy ships and aircraft and the U.S. Air Force.

* * *

Arriving at the Admiral's quarters, Carmichael gave his name to the marine Corporal who knocked once on the door, opened it and spoke in a crisp voice, "Sir, Mister Carmichael."

Admitting Carmichael to his office with a nod and a wave of his hand as he spoke on the phone, the Admiral pointed for him to take a nearby chair, but the clearly upset CIA liaison man shook his head and paced back and forth until the Admiral finished his conversation.

The Chief steward poured Carmichael a cup of black coffee, picked up his hat and left the quarters as the guest lit his third cigar of the morning.

"What's goin' on…are we just gonna back out of this thing Admiral?"

"You're not going to like this Brady, and neither do I, but they've called off any and all U.S. involvement in the invasion. We're now returning to our homeports."

"Admiral, this is nonsensical. Unless all of Cuba rises up and supports them, and I don't think Castro will let that happen, those men don't stand a chance at victory without air and gunnery support. We never shoulda trained and brought 'em back here if we had no intention of supporting them. This opens the door, not only for Castro, but for the goddamned Russians too, and I'm tell you sir, somehow those bastards will take advantage of this."

"I don't know about the Russians, but I agree with the rest of what you say…but lets face it, neither of us can do anything about this sad and distressing situation but follow our commands from above. And speaking of above, I just got word they want you back in DC asap. I'll have my chopper take you to the carrier, and they'll fly you to Key West where another flight will be arranged for the rest of the trip."

* * *

Far away in the Soviet Union, 10-year-old Alexei Plavinsky left school for the day and sloshed his way home through and around banks of heavy, wet snow as the spring thaw turned the streets of Rostov into a watery quagmire. Halfway to his step-parents' apartment two older boys from his school taunted him from the other side of the street.

"Hey zhid (kike) where you going?"

Having heard these slurs for years, the young Plavinsky had hardened to the Jew barbs, but now was reaching the point where his young maleness urged him to retaliate. Big and strong for his age, he learned to defend himself early on, and more than held his own on the rough streets of Rostov against boys of like age, most of whom now stayed away from him. Now two 12-year-olds yelled insults as passing trucks sprayed melted snow to both sides of the thoroughfare. Looking out of the side of his eye without moving his head, Alexei noted that one of the boys was taller than he and that the other was the same height but fatter. Now the fat one made a soggy snowball and hurled it in his direction. Alexei ducked as the wet snowball splattered against the brick wall behind him. Pretending to tighten the strap on his boot, Alexei made a quick snowball of his own and threw it at the two, striking the taller boy in the shoulder. Surprised and angered, the two antagonists made more snowballs and threw them at Alexei as they crossed the street in his direction.

"That was a big mistake you zhid and *Christ killer*, we're gonna whip your ass," they yelled.

Dropping his books in a snow bank, Alexei waited with clenched fists, and when the taller boy stumbled coming at him out of the gutter, Alexei punched him in the eye with his right fist, knocking his heavy hat to the sidewalk. The fat boy hesitated when he saw the younger boy could fight, and while he glanced at his partner rising from the snow bank, Alexei faked a punch then kicked fatso in the groin and made him double up in pain, but Alexei lost his footing with the kick and fell to the ground, and as he did so, the tall boy jumped on him and began to pummel him in the head while sitting on his chest. The other boy then tried to hold Alexei's arms while the fists flew both ways. Getting the worst of it and bleeding profusely from the mouth and nose as the two boys pinned him to the sidewalk, Alexei was suddenly saved from further damage when two grown men arrived at the scene, jerked the older boys to their feet and told them to "Get outta here and pick on someone your own size."

Arriving at his step-parents' apartment, Alexei tried to sneak to the bathroom to clean up, but his stepmother Deborah spotted him before he got there and sprang up from a large group of people crowded around a black and white tv set, which happened to be the only one in the neighborhood. The set displayed a picture of Fidel Castro and Nikita Khrushchev hugging at the United Nations in New York City in 1960 as the Moscow commentary talked on and on about the Bay of Pigs.

"What happened to you Alexei?" she asked, bending over to look closely at the wounds. "You've been fighting again, haven't you?" she said, as other concerned women in the room crowded around, all voicing sympathy. After being doted on, cleaned up and bandaged by three of the women, he asked why all the people were there. A middle-aged woman who was cleaning the last of the blood from his face responded.

"There's news from the island of Cuba that comrade Castro's people's army have fought off the capitalist invaders. The Cubans want communism not imperialism."

* * *

Deborah Salisbury fled to the Soviet Union from England in 1955 with her husband Roland who was under investigation there for spying for the Russians. Roland had in fact functioned for over seven years as a Soviet mole while employed with MI6 in the British Intelligence Service. A habitual gambler, the KGB kept his losing habits alive in return for classified information.

Alerted by the KGB that the Brits were on to him and that he would soon be arrested, he accepted a Soviet offer for he and his wife to "live free" in Russia for the rest of their lives. The Soviets kept their promise and the childless Salisburys were secretly flown from England to Russia via Denmark just days before he was to be nabbed. Once in Russia, the Soviets provided them with a nice five-room, first-floor apartment in Rostov and a monthly pension for "service to the USSR". All that was asked of Salisbury was that he continue to work for the KGB in an advisory capacity when called upon, and he frequently made the three-hour trip to Moscow for that purpose.

Roland Salisbury was surprised and disappointed in the boring, stagnant way of life he found in Russia, but accepted it as a more fitting alternative then spending his remaining years behind bars as a traitor in his native England. On the other hand, Deborah quickly learned to detest the Soviet way of life and deeply regretted making the escape with her husband.

"Loyalty to Roland, plus the fact that I'd be hated back in Britain were the two reasons for this damn hopeless exile. I have made a colossal mistake," she constantly reminded herself.

Despite the fact that the KGB told Roland, "It would never happen," he feared the possibility that the Russians would someday "swap" him back to Britain as part of some political deal.

Originally from Liverpool, Deborah went to Paris as a young woman during the 30s and hung out in the arty left bank section of the city with the adventurous, socialist-minded companions who also lived there. Although she never became a member of the communist party, she had many friends who did, and she shared some views with them, particularly the anti-capitalist rich versus poor scenario. Returning to England when the war in Europe started, she met and married Roland while he was an officer in the Royal Navy stationed in Gosport, just south of London. Working in naval intelligence, Roland remained in Gosport for the duration of hostilities. Despite the Nazi bombing raids and other wartime deprivations, they had an active and enjoyable social life which they shared with a wide variety of men and women from many allied nations who worked and played in southern England for the duration of the war.

Soon after the war ended, both became reasonably well off financially with the passing of parents from both sides of their families. In 1946, they traveled to the United States, Canada and Australia, where Roland began his addiction to gambling, mainly on sporting events such as rugby and soccer. While staying in Brisbane, he was amazed to find that a fairly small city not only had two racetracks, but every corner store offered betting sheets on athletic matches taking place all over the world. When they returned to England, he couldn't get away from it and one thing led to another... Although his treachery began three years after becoming a member of MI6, an unsuspecting Deborah never knew of his disloyalty until just weeks before they fled. Her deep love for him and her proclivity for globetrotting had more to do with her fleeing to the Soviet Union with him than her past flirtations with left wing ideologies.

"It'll be an adventure for us both dear," she told Roland. "And besides, if I stay back here in England, they'll hate me just as much as they'll hate you for spying for the Russians."

Alexei came into the life of the Salisburys in 1958 after his mother died of cancer. Anna Plavinsky had become a close friend and confidant of Deborah's when she did housework and other chores for the Salisburys as a means of picking up extra rubles to help her and her fatherless son survive in the run-down housing slum where they and thousands of other poor people lived in squalor. Anna toiled eight hours a day cleaning indoor and outdoor toilets at the extensive Rostov railroad center and worked weekends and nights at private dwellings. She met Deborah through one of the Salisbury's neighbors and she hired her for part-time housekeeping work and took an immediate liking to Anna Plavinsky and the beautiful young boy who accompanied her.

After the first evening's work at the Salisbury apartment, Deborah offered Anna and Alexei some refreshments before they left for the walk home. Deborah was amazed at the intelligence level that a housekeeper such as Anna possessed and wondered why such a woman could not find more meaningful employment. Learning the Russian language had not been easy for Deborah, but she was now proficient enough to hold an enlightened two-way conversation, as long as the other person spoke slowly. Anna was not as good at English as Deborah at Russian, so that is how they conversed. But when Deborah and Roland were alone they always spoke to one another in English. That first evening Anna talked of her situation:

"They know I am Jewish and that I want to leave here and go to Israel…and for that reason they closed all the doors to decent work on me. I could easily have become a prostitute, but that is something I would never do, for I wasn't brought up that way."

"Anna, I have lived in many parts of the world, and I can assure you that if you could get out of this country you could find decent work and live better."

As they talked, Anna reminded her friend that any conversations they held criticizing the Soviet system must be kept secret between the two and never should they talk of such things in front of others.

"The KGB will come after people who criticize the communist system…we must be careful," Anna warned. "But you don't have to worry about Alexei here, for despite his young age, he knows how to keep his mouth shut."

The following year Anna was diagnosed with pancreatic cancer and was told she had only two to three months to live. Before they placed her in the hospital, she asked the Salisburys if they would take in Alexei and raise him after her death. A sobbing Deborah agreed, and Anna died six weeks later. Although no formal adoption papers were signed, Alexei Plavinsky began a new life. He learned English from the Salisburys and developed a great curiosity about life outside the Soviet Union. As time went by, the Salisbury's became more and more estranged. Roland knew that Deborah was constantly talking to Alexei about the western world, and he was afraid her harsh, anti-Soviet attitude would somehow become known to their friends and neighbors, any of whom could snitch on her, and big troubles would start. As time went on, Deborah and Roland moved to separate rooms as their relationship completely fell apart. Finding no outlets for her frustrations, Deborah began to drink heavily, and with the exception of daily chats with Alexei and an occasional book or newspaper from the west, she continued to fall into an alcoholic depression. Without hope of ever leaving Russia the bouts with vodka became more and more frequent until in 1965, she actually drank herself to death. Her body was found by a housecleaner, crumpled in a corner of her bedroom with an old copy of *The London Daily Times* still clutched in her hands.

All of these tragedies created a most unusual and brutal upbringing for Alexei Plavinsky. He never knew his father, but his mother always told him he was a navy man and a Jew, like her. Although she told him that his father died before they were to be married, the truth of the matter was that at the age of 17 she had an affair with a young Russian sailor who happened to be Jewish, which was important to her because she wanted to marry a Jewish man. Just before she discovered she was pregnant, her lover disappeared from Rostov, and try as she could, she was never able to find him again. When she contacted the Navy, they told her that they had no one in their service who went by the name she submitted. With no family, the state shuffled her off to a facility for unwed mothers. After Alexei was born, Anna devoted herself completely to the raising of him, but for reasons of her Jewish heritage and being an unwed mother, she never found another man she could trust and her life slipped directly into poverty.

After Alexei's mother died, and he was taken in by the Salisburys, life became easier, but he sensed that there were problems between the step-parents, and he gradually began spending more and more time away from the apartment which he devoted nearly entirely to athletics such as boxing and soccer. He managed average grades in school, but lacked the incentive to further his education at a university. Through reading, movies and, before her death, endless conversations with his stepmother, Alexei developed a deep yearning to see other parts of the world. He knew his mother always wanted to take him to Israel, and he resented the discrimination he encountered on a daily basis, but Israel was not a dominant goal for him, as his daydreams included many other places such as Hong Kong, Australia, Paris, etc. Through his teen years he excelled in soccer, swimming and boxing. He also excelled with the young ladies, who found him strong and handsome. He also worked part-time and developed skills as an auto mechanic. In the late '60s, he was drafted into the Soviet Navy and was not disappointed, as it was something his real father did and it also opened possibilities of seeing some of the rest of the world. Upon hearing the news, Roland told him, "The only thing against you is the same thing you've grown up with…and that is your Jewish heritage. It isn't fair, but there will also be those in the navy who will use it against you."

In the spring of 1970 Alexei Plavinsky started his basic Navy training at the big base in Leningrad. Next was five months of intensive submarine training in Murmansk, and finally orders to his first vessel, the Soviet nuclear powered submarine *Morozov,* homeported in Petropavlovsk on the east coast of the Kamchatka peninsula in faraway Siberia.

CHAPTER 2

THE SWORDSMAN

1972 was a year when both the "hot war" in Vietnam and the so-called "cold war" between east and west dominated the TV tube and newspaper headlines everywhere. The resultant repercussions of both conflicts triggered political convulsions in the United States and caused global rethinking in many other parts of the world. 1972 was also the year when Herman Wouk's novel *"The Winds of War"* remained on the best-seller list, and in Washington, D.C. the "winds of Watergate" started as a mere whisper, when on June 17, five men were arrested for breaking into the National Democratic party headquarters.

That same year in another headquarters, this one in the Soviet Union, Captain Second Rank Boris Stepakov had just returned to the Naval Base at Baltiysk after a three-day exercise in the storm-swept Gulf of Danzig aboard the newly commissioned Nuclear Attack Submarine *Dmitri Sobolev.* A submarine officer on the staff of Submarine Flotilla Two, he was responsible for submarine crew training, including political indoctrination. Every one of the 16 submarines in the Flotilla had an officer designated as "Political Officer," and one of Stepakov's assigned tasks was to ensure that these political officers were doing their jobs and that political indoctrination on board every submarine in the Flotilla was ongoing and effective.

Although bone-weary from lack of sleep and rough seas that caused him to "hold-on" during the bumpy surface transit into port, Stepakov was generally pleased with what he had seen aboard *Dmitri Sobolev,* and was relieved that the written report would not take him long to prepare.

"This will be an easy one, and I'll be out of here in an hour," he predicted to himself, as he laid his briefcase on his desk and hung his heavy, salt-encrusted, leather sea-jacket on a wooden peg near the only window in his modest office. Gazing out at the waterfront submarine finger-piers through the freezing, wind-blown mixture of snow and sleet that pelted the window, Stepakov lit a welcome cigarette while observing another submarine returning to port and mooring outboard of the *Dmitri Sobolev.*

It was the last Friday in March, and as he turned to the Flotilla Scheduling Chart on the wall next to his desk, Stepakov calculated that the submarine now in the process of mooring was the last, and brought to eight, the number of Flotilla boats that were in Baltiysk for at least the weekend. He also observed that another three were deployed on "Special Operations" in the Norwegian and Barents Seas, two were in transit either to or from those areas and that three units were in shipyards, either for repair or overhaul. His thoughts were interrupted by a knock on the door, and a subordinate who entered and stiffly announced, "Comrade Captain, Admiral Zhiltzov wants to meet with you in his office in ten minutes."

Stepakov acknowledged with a simple *da* and then quickly picked up the phone and dialed the office of Captain First Rank Alexei Fatayev, the officer he reported to in the Submarine Flotilla chain of command. Fatayev greeted Stepakov over the phone and inquired about the training on the *Sobolev.* As is the custom among friends and relatives in Russia, he called him by his middle name.

"Well Petrovich, how did things go?"

"It seems that everything is coming along satisfactorily aboard *Sobolev* comrade," Stepakov replied, "but I wanted to ask you if you know what the Admiral wants to see me about?"

There was a slight pause, then Fatayev said, "It is good news for you comrade, but he's the one who should tell you about it…Stop by my office after the meeting, we need to talk about a few things."

Stepakov weighed the possibilities of what was in store for him, and concluded that the Admiral more than likely had some sort of "special" temporary job for him in mind… probably a few weeks in Moscow or Leningrad. Something like last year, when he was sent to the exotic port of Sevastapol in the Crimea, to straighten out some "political problems" at the Naval Base there. His mind wandered to *Natalya,* who had more than adequately occupied his leisure time on that particular trip. Maybe the Admiral, who most assuredly knew of his dalliances with the voluptuous woman, was sending him back to the same place.

The old bastard had cracked a half-smile on his face when they met upon his return, and he had said, "You are to be commended Petrovich for taking care of things in Sevastopol, and I take it you also had some relaxation there."

* * *

Born in Leningrad in 1935, Boris Petrovich Stepakov was the son and only child of a Soviet Naval Officer from the "old" Soviet Navy. The senior (Petr) Stepakov had been an enlisted man prior to the German invasion in 1941, but was made a commissioned officer just days after the Wehrmacht stormed over the border from Poland. He subsequently served with distinction and bravery aboard submarines and minesweepers in the Baltic Sea. Thanks to a big push from Josef Stalin himself, who called Stepakov "the toughest son of a bitch on the Baltic," he rose rapidly through the ranks, and was made a Vice Admiral just before the "Great Patriotic War" ended.

Although young Stepakov survived the war years at a youth *Pioneer* camp far from the fighting, his Mother Raisa, perished in 1943 during the long and horrific siege of Leningrad where more than a million Russians lost their lives.

After the war, Boris Stepakov received all the privileges accorded a son of a war hero and prominent member of the Communist Party. He was entered in a *Nakimov* secondary school at the age of 11, then went on to the prestigious M.V. *Frunze* Naval School (Academy) in Leningrad, where he graduated in 1956 as a Junior Lieutenant with an engineering degree. He then went into basic submarine training, followed by assignment to a Baltic-based "ZULU" class diesel submarine, where he served as torpedo officer then navigator, until 1959, when his father's guiding influence and connections, called *"blat"* in Russia, again came into play, and resulted in his assignment to the Soviet Navy Political School in Kiev. Upon successful completion of this school in 1961 and his acceptance as a full member in the Communist Party, Stepakov's naval career continued to spiral upward with his selection to Nuclear Power training, and early promotion and then orders to a new Nuclear Submarine of the "NOVEMBER" class, where he was the boat's political officer for three years, missile officer for two then Executive Officer for three more years before assuming his present duties on the staff at Baltiysk in 1969. But for all his professional prowess and political *blat* that allowed him to swiftly climb the Navy professional ladder, Stepakov had a disturbing trait…he was an insatiable womanizer, and this reputation was well known throughout the Baltic Submarine Fleet, where fellow submarine officers called him *"The Swordsman."*

Finding family life a bore (he had been married and divorced twice) and inconsistent with Navy life, he spent most of his free time, when not at sea, partying at clubs, bistros and apartments, where the predominant and ultimate name of the game was the pursuit and bedding of women.

Neither discreet nor selective in his whoring, Stepakov merely sought to get warm female bodies into bed, and took full advantage of his good looks, trim body and smooth talk to accomplish that goal. One of his most recent and still ongoing conquests was the wife of a Polish Army Colonel who was stationed on a joint military staff in Kaliningrad, 25 kilometers east of Baltiysk. This particular tryst was now causing problems, for unbeknownst to Stepakov, the disgruntled, cuckolded Pole found out what was going on, and complained to his commanding general that a Captain Stepakov was "bothering" his wife and "threatening his marriage." The General, in turn, reported the affair to the Soviets, demanding that Stepakov "be dealt with."

Although the KGB kept an eye on the behavior of naval officers when on leave or liberty, they paid little attention to routine sexual liaisons between men and women, and merely recorded the names of those involved, and where the liaisons were taking place. Their main effort was to find and report military personnel involved in homosexual perversion or associating with blackmarketeers or westerners. In Stepakov's situation, the KGB dutifully reported his trysts with the Polish woman to the Admiralty because of who she was and who he was. While Stepakov had been at sea aboard *Sobolev,* discussions regarding his involvement with the

Polish Colonel's wife had taken place at the Admiralty in Leningrad, in Moscow and in Baltiysk. Fleet Admiral Matevlov, who was the head of the entire Soviet Navy, decided to end this "nonsense" and scheduled a meeting with his old friend, Leonid Nikolaevich Stepakov.

Now a retired admiral, the elder Stepakov had made the most of his naval reputation and lifelong membership and devotion to the communist party by becoming a high municipal official in the city of Leningrad and enjoying direct connections to many ruling members of the Central Committee and even the Supreme Soviet in Moscow. As a *Hero of the Soviet Union,* he was known and respected by many in the *Politburo,* including the Chairman himself, and thus became a *Comrade of Nomenklatura* ~ a brotherhood of the privileged rulers of the Soviet Union. Because of this respect, the senior Stepakov was invited to Moscow for dinner and drinks with Matevlov, who was the Deputy Minister of Defense as well as Commander in Chief of the Soviet Navy.

After several rounds of vodka in Matevlov's private quarters, the two old friends got down to discussing young Stepakov's womanizing, and the ticklish problem it now posed to Soviet/Polish army relations. Matevlov related that the stories of his son's activities had even reached the ears of the Soviet Premier, who chuckled in private about "Stepakov the Swordsman."

"Despite the chairman's lack of sympathy for the cuckolded Polski Colonel, he gave me a straight-faced command to immediately work something out that satisfies the Poles, but keeps Captain Stepakov's career intact," Matevlov emphasized.

"It appears my son has become famous in high places comrade!" said a tongue-in-check Stepakov.

Matevlov smiled and gestured with an upward lift of his glass as he spoke. "Nikalaich, both the comrade Chairman and I have the highest respect for you. We also admire the excellent naval skills your son possesses. I have worked out a solution to this problem, and I want you to hear it first before I put it in motion, because we must act swiftly."

"What have you worked out comrade?"

It seems we have an urgent need for a new captain of a nuclear submarine in the North Pacific out of Petro (Petropavlovsk). The Flotilla and the KGB have a captain that they want relieved because of his failure to politically indoctrinate the crew, and other deficiencies they did not elaborate upon. They want a strong man on this boat, and they want him out there within a week. I think your son would be a good choice. It is an upward career move for him, as it will give him his first command and it will also solve the Pole problem, as Petrovich will be home-ported way out on the big Siberian peninsula, and scheduled to go to sea on a special patrol within a few days of reporting aboard. With half the Amerikanski fleet fooling around off Vietnam, the opportunities for submarine surveillance are unlimited, and a bright, young officer as your son can certainly enhance his career by making a name for himself where the action is. It is far better than making his name as a swordsman."

"But what do you tell the Poles?"

"All we have to tell them is that Captain Stepakov will be transferred to Siberia within a week. That is all they need to know, and it will be the truth!"

"I am honored that you talked to me about this, and I greatly appreciate and agree with your solution of this matter. It is a positive opportunity for the boy. He needs to go to sea, and stay there for awhile. By the way, what is the name of the submarine?"

"The nuclear attack missile submarine *Morozov.*"

* * *

Stepakov left his office and headed down three flights of stairs in the Flotilla headquarters, all the while wondering what the admiral's news would be. He had no way of knowing that a week earlier, a KGB arrest in the Ukranian city if Kharkov would have a direct and dramatic impact on his future. This arrest, combined with his affair with the Polish colonel's wife were about to lead to an extraordinary chain of events.

CHAPTER 3

THE WORLD

For more than a year, a clandestine, underground newspaper had been mysteriously appearing on a weekly basis in Moscow, Leningrad, Kiev, Odessa and several other major cities. The *Real World,* contained remarkably accurate reporting of current events in the Soviet Union, the West and Third World nations. It also contained gossipy, embarrassing tidbits about Soviet and Eastern Bloc political bigshots. To the Politburo's dismay, the *World* was eagerly awaited each week by thousands of citizens and ravenously devoured from front to back by those lucky enough to come across a copy. The Kremlin and the KGB were enraged not only by what the underground paper contained, but by their inability to find and punish the culprits who dared write, print and distribute a paper they described as "anti-communist propaganda," right under their noses. Things got so bad that the KGB organized a new section of its Internal Affairs Directorate just to handle this problem.

The KGB finally got a break when a young female chemist named Emma Riavin was arrested in Kharkov for possessing contraband. She apparently got careless, and was caught when a woman "friend" (who, unknown to her, was also a paid KGB informant) from her laboratory workplace turned her in after spotting a copying machine in a closet while visiting Emma in her apartment. IN 1972, the Soviet Union considered illicit possession of such machines to be a far greater threat to their society than other taboos such as narcotics and black marketed goods from the West. Anyone unfortunate enough to be caught with this kind of equipment was severely dealt with, and in most cases sent off to spend time at one of the infamous "ice-farms" in Siberia. Even copying machines that were legitimate, those used for official purposes, were secured with sophisticated locks, and in some cases guarded by police or dogs.

Upon learning of the copying machine, the KGB conducted a quick and thorough search (*obysk*) of the woman's apartment, and found not only the machine, but documents, photos and other incriminating miscellany to indicate that the small apartment was most certainly a part of the *World* operation. Emma Riavin was immediately taken into custody and flown to Moscow for interrogation by several of the KGB's most vicious but highly effective "persuasion" specialists.

Before the questioning, and eventual drugging and torture of the defiant woman began, interrogators knew from her dossier that she was not only a chemist, but a Jewish intellectual who despised the Soviet system and who longed to immigrate to Israel, but had been denied her request to do so. The dossier also revealed that Emma's only other known relative was a brother, *michman* (senior petty officer) Yevgeny Riavin, presently assigned to the guided missile nuclear submarine *Morozov,* based at the far North-Pacific port of Petropavlovsk.

The whole affair caused severe convulsions within the KGB and the highest echelons of the Soviet government. The KGB wished to wipe the underground publishers from the face of the earth, but the Russian hierarchy urged caution so as not to appear to be faltering in their promise to the West to maintain human rights as a part of *détente.*

The merciless job of break-down and truth extraction, which can involve the most sadistic of techniques, began with "semi-friendly" open discussions with a female interrogator who faced Riavin across a clean table isolated in a quiet room. The KGB woman, who, like Riavin, was in her late twenties, spoke softly, but looked anything but amiable to the captive. She was flat-chested and quite skinny with a vivid scar across one cheek, gold false teeth and short brown hair cut like a man's. Her starched brown shirt had one pocket, which contained questioning notes and a package of cigarettes, which she opened and offered to Riavin before any questions were asked. Riavin refused the cigarette and refused to utter a word in response to anything said to her. Finally, the KGB woman slammed her fist on the table and gave Riavin a harsh warning as an armed guard led her from the room to a cell.

"You have made a big mistake miss *zhidovka* (female Jew insult) by not cooperating with us, and now you will suffer, because one way or the other, we will find out just what you know about this abdominable, so-called newspaper!"

After 6 hours alone in a dark cell without food or water, Riavin was visited by two men. Without a word, one held her while the other slammed a long needle containing "truth serum" into her arm. After an hour, they dragged her semi-conscious from the cell to another interrogation room where two experts probed her delirious mind for over three hours. The KGB head interrogator was not pleased with the results, and he spoke to his cohorts prior to calling for the final stage of the truth-extraction process.

"She gave us little or nothing from the serum…but, as you heard, she did let on that she knows more…one hell of a lot more. Don't let her sleep, but give her another hour for the serum to wear off then put her on the table in the electric room."

The groggy Riavin was stripped naked then strapped to a steel table under bright lights. The interrogator directed that an electrical connection clip be attached to one nipple before he growled at the still defiant woman.

"You had better tell me all the names of those involved with the paper or I will get it from you the hard way!"

Riavin rolled her sleepy eyes then turned her head and spit in the direction of her torturer. The next thing she felt was a sharp pain that increased to a point where she screamed and shook from head to toe with pain beyond anything she had ever experienced. After several more clips were attached to other parts of her body, a barely coherent Emma Riavin began to talk, but the torturers kept it up for another seven hours until they were satisfied they had gotten all they could from the wreathing victim who steadily coughed up blood as she was finally and mercifully dragged to her cell.

In finality, the semi-conscious and near-death victim gave the KGB the names of many other Soviets involved in editing and publishing the *World*. They learned that many of the country's best-known writers, artists, dancers and members of the so-called intelligentsia were in the ring. After much debate and argument, the leadership decided to take a soft approach, letting the culprits remain at large for now, but with a stiff warning that if they ever got involved with an illicit publication again, they would be immediately arrested and severely punished. Despite much fist-banging and vindictive verbal rage from Soviet hard-liners, that the Kremlin was "giving in to the filthy zhid intelligentsia," the threat tactic worked, and the *World* never appeared again.

Emma Riavin was not as fortunate as her colleagues. After the brutal ordeal with the ruthless but efficient KGB in Moscow, what was left of her broken body and spirit was swiftly dispatched to an insane asylum where she died within three days. Her brother was not notified of her death. The Jewish situation in general though, continued to be the cause of concern and lively discussions within the Kremlin.

"Why do we coddle these goddamn zhids?" asked KGB Internal Directorate boss Soslov. "If the bastards don't like it here, why don't we ship all their zhid asses to Israel with good riddance? If we'd have let this Riavin bitch and others like her go to Israel two years ago, we wouldn't have had this problem in the first place!"

KGB chairman Pavel Gurenko gestured straight at Soslov's face with a plump, shaking forefinger.

"It matters not comrade whether I agree with you or not! The leadership has decided how to handle this matter, and all of us have a duty to fall in line with that decision. Also, you must know that as of last year we are letting some of the zhids emigrate. We just can't let them all go at once."

"What about the *zhidovka's* brother who's in the Navy? Shouldn't we nail his ass too?" Soslov pressed.

"The KGB has already dispatched someone to look into that and Admiral Matevlov has assured me that our navy will do a follow-up," a clearly irritated Gurenko growled and then concluded the discussion by slamming his fist to the table and blasting Sozlov:

"You have had your say comrade, but now your major responsibility in this matter is to continue tight surveillance of all the people on the newspaper list…every time one of them shits you should know about it!"

* * *

Captain Stepakov was met in Admiral Zhiltov's outer office by his good friend and fellow classmate at Frunze, the admiral's chief of staff, Captain 2nd Rank Mikhail Butenko.

"How are you Petrovich? I heard the Gulf was not too pleasant a place to be last week!"

"Well it's that time of year when the seasons are changing. We had high seas and zero visibility for five days running out there. But what does the Admiral want to see me about? Do you know?"

"I can't tell you the details Petrovich, but it shouldn't disappoint you…and I can tell you quite honestly that I think you're one lucky bastard!" Then, gesturing toward the entry to the Admiral's office, Butenko knocked once, opened the door and announced to the admiral, "Captain Stepakov, sir."

After exchanging greetings, the Admiral wasted little time in getting right to the point.

"I have orders for you to take command of the *Morozov* next week out in Petro. They have had some personnel problems on this boat, and we think you are the man to straighten things out. Your replacement on the staff here will arrive tomorrow, and you and Fatayev will have to turn everything over to him in a two-day period. The tight time frame is unfortunate but necessary."

An astonished Stepakov responded, "Sir, I am certainly pleased with the opportunity to command at sea, and there is no problem meeting the time frame for both the turnover and for me flying out of here, but can you tell me any more about the problems aboard *Morozov?"*

"I only have sketchy details," the Admiral said. "You will be fully briefed at the Pacific Fleet Headquarters in Vladivostok, both about the personnel situation and the forthcoming mission of the submarine, which is scheduled to sail within a week. After the briefings, they'll fly you up to Petro. What I do know, is that the Captain of the *Morozov* by the name of Ivanov, was relieved last week for failures that apparently were more of a political than technical nature.

The KGB insisted upon his removal, and you know full well who wins when they recommend something!"

Still standing, Stepakov was ready to convey his thanks and leave the office when the Admiral said, "There's one more thing, Petrovich."

Stepakov remained expressionless, but a sense of foreboding came over him as the Admiral motioned for him to sit down.

"As of right now, this damned affair with the Polski army wife is over. You must not see her or call her. This latest conquest of yours is causing a lot of problems politically, as news of you and this Colonel's wife has traveled to the highest echelons of our government. You should have realized that not only were we watching you, but the Poles were too, and they're the ones who told the Colonel husband that you were putting it to his wife. Then he told his General, and all hell has broke loose since then. It is over… *Konchevno!*…and that Captain Stepakov, is a direct order!

An abashed Stepakov remained silent and somewhat red-faced as the Admiral continued: "If it wasn't for the deep respect we all have for your father and the fact that you have a superlative professional performance record and great potential for the future, you would not be given this exceptional opportunity for command at sea in a very active theater of operations."

Like all aspiring naval officers, Stepakov considered command at sea the ultimate assignment. No matter where it is or what kind of vessel is involved, command at sea means you have succeeded in the mastery of all the disciplines required for such a position. It is a privilege that is never turned down. Getting one's ass chewed out by the Admiral was of little consequence. He was getting kicked upstairs!

Gathering his wits and keeping himself under full control, he answered the Admiral in a slow, calm voice.

"I fully understand comrade Admiral and apologize for the problems I have caused in this matter. I had no idea this thing would ever cause such repercussions. You have my word that I will not contact this woman again."

The Admiral nodded, and then put on the same semi-grin expression he displayed after the trip to Sevastapol, as they both rose and shook hands.

"I wish you good fortune Petrovich, but you must remember that there are times when it is wiser to keep it in your pants. You have reached a level in the navy where one must know when and where discretion must be observed."

Stepakov marveled at Admiral Zhiltzov, and how the old bastard could dole out a first class tongue-lashing but still have you liking him when it was over…he was a good man to work for.

Fully exhilarated over the prospect of commanding his own nuclear-powered, guided-missile submarine, Stepakov's mind nonetheless found time to wander, and he told himself, "There wouldn't be time to see her even if I wanted to. Besides, there's plenty more like her out there. I wonder what I'll find in Vlad or Petro? Will there be time before I go to sea?"

It was after dark and approaching meal time when he finished discussions with Captain Fatayev concerning the *Dmitri Sobolev* report, other paperwork and the turnover schedule for the officer who was to start relieving him the following morning, and Stepakov decided to go sit down somewhere, pour himself a stiff drink and collect his thoughts. Although he ached to get off the base and find a woman, he managed to convince himself that it would be best to go no further than the officers' club on the base and behave himself for just a few more days. Besides, he knew that a clear head and rested body would be necessary to provide a detailed and intelligent turnover before leaving for Vladivostok three days hence.

CHAPTER 4

SIBERIA

Stepakov relaxed in a rear seat of the large *Ilyushin* military jet as it headed east on its long, twice-weekly "courier" flight to Vladivostok. The plane carried only classified military mail, high ranking officers, KGB operatives and senior government officials. Reflecting upon the hectic events of the past three days, he found himself glad to be rid of the ponderous amount of administrative reporting that entailed a great deal of his time at the Flotilla. "Now, as Captain, I will have someone else to do the paperwork," he mused.

Upon arrival in Vladivostok, Stepakov was taken in a Navy car directly to the Soviet Pacific Fleet Headquarters and escorted to a room where three naval officers and a man in civilian clothes with several bruises on his face greeted him. They were introduced as rear Admiral Panov, Fleet Political Officer; Captain 1st Rank Kursky, Fleet Operations; Captain 2nd Rank Bogordny, Pacific Fleet Staff Nuclear Weapons Specialist and Aleksandr Tarobrin, a Senior KGB Agent from the Naval Branch of the Armed Forces Directorate.

Admiral Panov started the meeting by commending Stepakov. "You have an excellent performance report from Admiral Zhiltzov. He and I go way back, and we sailed together on an old diesel boat out of Murmanski in '47. I also served under your father's command just before he retired, and I have the deepest respect for him and his magnificent record during the Great Patriotic War.

The Admiral continued, "We know you must be very tired after the long journey, but *Morozov's* op-schedule is short, and we must sail her within a few days. I want to complete this briefing today so we can get you out to Petro by tomorrow afternoon. I will start by telling you the reasons we relieved Captain Ivanov."

Panov said that Ivanov had dissention among the crew and ignored the advice of his political officer, who is still aboard. Feeling weary and ill at ease not knowing how bad a situation he was walking into, Stepakov had decided that this meeting was a place to keep his eyes and ears open and his mouth shut. In pure Russian fashion, he would pay close attention to everything said, but not reveal his emotions or opinions until the right time and place. "If they're looking for a strong Captain here, they're going to get one…but I will do it on the *Morozov,* and not say or do anything until I have all the facts," he told himself.

Panov continued: "He (Ivanov) had problems allowing his michmen and junior officers to discipline their men when it was needed. He had no time for crew political training, and we are told by the boat's political officer, Captain Lieutenant Vavilov, that he coddled the few zhids on board. Tarobrin here was sent all the way from Moscow, primarily to investigate a crew member, but since he was also aware of other problems onboard, he investigated the allegations against Ivanov as well. He investigated a zhid michman by the name of Riavin, whose sister has been arrested for subversive activities in the City of Kharkov. Although we know now that Riavin had nothing to do with his sister's crimes, we have cancelled his orders back to Leningrad, where he had been selected to go next week for commissioned officer training. When Tarobrin told Ivanov that he was taking Riavin back to Moscow for interrogation,

Ivanov lost all control of himself and attacked Tarobrin, knocking him against the wardroom bulkhead and then ordering two of the crew to drag him from the boat and throw him off the gangway."

Senior agent Tarobrin next spoke, "Comrades, I have a job to do just as you do, and in this case, the decision to relieve Ivanov was the correct one. Whether he drank too much or just didn't give a shit anymore, or both, he was an accident waiting to happen. Although I don't like being the victim of the accident, far worse could have occurred if he lost his marbles at sea. He is now undergoing psychiatric evaluation in Irkutsk."

Panov nodded to Captain Bogordny to speak next.

Looking directly at Stepakov, Bogordny had some surprises:

"Not many know that the *Morozov* carries guided nuclear missiles as well as nuclear torpedoes. This boat was built at the *Krasnoye Sormovo* yard in Gorky, and commissioned two years ago. Although the other boats of this class have a nuclear weapons capability, this is the only one that has both the live weapons on board. These are added reasons why there must be stability and discipline on the *Morozov*. As you know, we must also have competent technical people to maintain these complex weapons systems. This michman Riavin is a problem because he is one of the highest trained and most efficient submarine nuclear weapons systems technicians in our fleet. If you combine his background with his sister's subversion, it is little wonder our friends in the KGB are concerned. We now believe Riavin should remain on board for this patrol. I think that comrade Tarobrin will agree that the best place for this man is at sea. The investigation can continue, and if they're still concerned that he is or could be disloyal, he'll certainly will be in safekeeping while on patrol under the sea. Also, if we took him off now, it would be impossible to get a competent replacement on board prior to *Morozov* getting underway. This is because the man who was supposed to replace Riavin when he went to officer training was seriously injured in an auto crash, and will be unavailable for full duty for at least six months. This boat has a one-of-a-kind missile system design, and Riavin has been aboard and deeply involved since *Morozov* was constructed at Gorky."

At this point, Stepakov used all his will power not to comment or shake his head. But he wondered to himself how the Soviet Navy could be so stupid as to not have more michmen highly trained and ready for duty. He knew that this was one of the big differences between western navies and the Soviets. The Americans and British, particularly, relied heavily upon career enlisted technicians. These petty officer ranks were provided with extensive training and enhanced with good career opportunities, adequate pay and other incentives. It was not until 1971 that the Soviets finally established the michman rank, but they still did not have enough of them to keep up with rapid technological advances in Naval weaponry and equipment...They still seemed to worry more about political training than teaching them about the new systems!

Now I must pay the price for our Navy's foolhardiness, Stepakov lamented to himself. "The *Morozov* has a dozen nuclear weapons on board, and only one completely qualified man to maintain the systems that launch them?" he thought with incredulity. He also wondered how competent his torpedo and missile officers were. "There will be no one-man operation on this boat," he determined.

Captain Kursky spoke next and told Stepakov that the mission of the *Morozov* would be explained in greater detail by the Flotilla staff in Petropavlovsk, but that his primary mission was to gather intelligence from the American fleet operating off the east coast of Vietnam.

"Some special communications technicians will go aboard *Morozov* tomorrow. Their code name is *Riga One.* They bring electronic monitors, recorders and some portable antennae with them. Senior Lieutenant Nesenkin is in charge of this group. He has three *michmani* under him, and these men are quite experienced and competent, having already made at least four patrols to the Vietnam area aboard other submarines. This group must be given full cooperation and left alone to do their job. They will take over both the radio room and sonar room for days at a time. Make sure your communications and sonar officers understand and comply with this arrangement as the data that *Riga One* collects is extremely valuable to our navy."

Stepakov had considerable experience when similar technical teams embarked on submarines where he was serving. He knew that all of these groups were from the Naval Intelligence Directorate and that the information gathered was shared with the KGB, who also kept very close tabs on all men selected for these groups and all those exposed to the kind of data they were collecting. Still sensing he should say little at this meeting, he merely responded by stating he had "worked with such groups in the past and that he foresaw no problems in this regard. I will ensure their mission is enhanced," he added.

* * *

Once the briefings were completed at the Vladivostok Fleet Headquarters, Stepakov got a good night's sleep, as all flights to Petropavlovsk were cancelled due to blizzard conditions from an early spring storm that raged into the area. By the next morning the blizzard roared to the north into the heart of Siberia, and the day dawned bright and clear. Flying low in a *IL'yushin 18* turboprop naval antisubmarine aircraft, Stepakov was able to observe the cold waters of the Sea of Japan below, dotted with fishing boats and occasional small icebergs. Up ahead he made out a tundra-like Sakhalin Island and then the frigid, dark green Sea of Okhotsk. The plane continued on a northeasterly course with the Kuril Island chain visible below. When the southern tip of the Kamchatka peninsula came into sight, Stepakov gasped at the spectacular view of huge volcanoes, some of which were spewing fire and smoke.

Because active volcanoes cause unstable air above them, the navy plane did not attempt to fly over them, but turned farther east around the tip of the peninsula and then north to parallel the eastern coast, providing the submariner with a breathtaking vista of a towering volcanic mountain chain and one of the most unforgiving coastlines in the world.

Petropavlovsk was soon in view, and as the plane circled low over the port to land at a large airdrome just north of the city, Stepakov noticed that the Petro waterfront and harbor were teaming with a wide variety of merchant and fishing vessels and that two icebreakers were plying and grooming two channels leading seaward from the port and all the way out to Avacha Bay.

Never having been in this part of the world, and as a means of familiarizing himself, Stepakov put the clear weather to good use and followed the aircraft's progress on a series of naval charts he carried on his lap. Now low over the harbor itself, the plane zipped above waters coated with a stark gray-white ice cover, neatly sliced here and there by narrow, shimmering blue, ribbon-like open water channel slots. The final sight he took in before landing was *Morozov's* home base in Talinskaia Bay, adjacent to Petropavlovsk. From this huge base, the Soviets operated more than a hundred submarines of different sizes and classes. He knew that this Base was of tremendous strategic importance, for although the Bay was frozen solid for six months of the year, the big, powerful ice-breakers insured year-round, direct, unimpeded access to the North Pacific Ocean, whereas other Siberian Pacific ports on the "inside" Sea of Japan, required all vessels to transit one of three narrow straits to gain access to open water. In time of war, this would cause the Soviet Navy major problems in getting their submarines and ships in and out of port, for such narrow straits could easily be mined or targeted by a wide variety of weaponry. He realized that this problem for the Soviets was not unique to the Sea of Japan, for despite its immense land-mass, the Soviet Union lacks direct-ocean access ports, a fact that, like an inferiority complex, Soviet Naval officers and war strategists are always acutely aware of.

While Stepakov was being briefed at the submarine base, the officers and crew of the *Morozov* were preparing for his arrival and for their voyage. Since the former Captain had been unceremoniously relieved, morale had sagged and tempers were short. A majority of the crew had liked Captain Ivanov, for he seemed to genuinely care for them and took an interest in their welfare. Also, he had brought many "sailor athletes" aboard the *Morozov,* whose teams regularly won soccer, basketball and hockey matches against other navy, army and civilian teams in the area. The sub also had several good boxers among the crew. On the soccer field, which Ivanov coached, huge crowds came to watch the *Morozov* team that had a high-scoring and spectacular player by the name of Plavinsky. Himself an excellent athlete and physical fitness enthusiast, Ivanov believed that young men with "athletic spirit" made for good sailors who understand the meaning of teamwork and sacrifice. He also knew that having athletic competition was good for morale and provided a break from a strict military atmosphere. Ivanov did not receive quality athletes aboard his sub by accident, but used his influence with several fellow officers who were stationed at various Soviet navy training centers, such as the basic submarine school, to weed out good athletes and have them ordered to *Morozov.*

A typical deal was arranged when seaman Alexei Plavinsky was ordered to the sub. Ivanov received a phone call from a fellow officer he once served with who commanded a submarine training facility in far away Murmansk.

"You won't believe the man we're about to send to *Morozov* for you! His name is Plavinsky, and yes, he's a zhid, but he is one hell of a soccer player. *'Dynamo Kiev'* have already given him a tryout, and they want to look at him again after he leaves the Navy. For this one you owe me a big night out on the town when we get together again."

Ivanov showed his enthusiasm for sports by attending all the sub's matches and eagerly rooting for his men. His involvement was a plus with most of the crew, particularly the young seamen, who saw him as a man who truly supported them, both on and off the athletic field. The only resentment came from a few senior michmani and officers who didn't like to see their Captain act in anything but an official/military capacity with any of the men.

Ivanov's philosophy for the running of a ship fit right in with his passion for competitive sports. He wanted the best man for the job, regardless of whether he was a Jew, a Mongol, or a member of any of the other races serving in the

Navy. He once told the political officer how he felt about zhids in the navy.

"If a match is going on, the last thing you think about is what race or religion are your best players members of! The same thing is true at sea and at war…I want the best men for the job they're performing. I could care less as to whether or not they are Jews or what their political philosophy is…the best man for the job!"

Most of the crew were leery of the new Captain coming aboard and the word was out that he was a "hand-picked hot-shot from the Baltic fleet," a "strict disciplinarian" and that he was "politically connected right to the top of the navy and the government." The next patrol will be two months in hell," one crewmember predicted.

* * *

Michman Yevgeny Riavin probably suffered the biggest loss of morale of any of the crew. First he heard about his sister being arrested, and he knew somehow that they'd make her disappear, as they refused to tell him if she was dead or alive or where she was located. Then his mentor, Captain Ivanov, was relieved of his command for standing up for his men and giving the KGB slimeball a well-deserved thumping. Next he was informed by the executive officer that the whole situation with his sister was still under investigation and that he would not be going to Leningrad for officer training until everything was resolved.

"You will make this patrol," he was ordered.

Riavin was admired and respected by Ivanov. For although he wasn't an athlete, he was extremely competent technically and Ivanov witnessed his abilities on many occasions when missile and torpedo control equipment broke down. Each time, Riavin was the man they sent for, because in most cases, he was the only one aboard capable of making the necessary repairs.

"This man is invaluable!" Ivanov once remarked to the executive officer. "We need a few more like him, or at least some back-ups. It is not good to have all our missile technical eggs in one basket."

Riavin was informed that the reason for his making the patrol was mandatory.

"Your replacement is in the hospital and unavailable. Also, you must remain on board after the patrol until he or another michman can be found and ordered here. Then you will have to train him…there will be a transition period."

Deep down, Riavin knew that, because of his sister, even after the patrol, he would never be sent to officer training. His naval career was over.

"But these bastards still find my abilities indispensable, don't they!" he silently cursed. "Maybe **I** should have an automobile accident!"

The other part of michman Riavin's life was also in shambles. His wife Yelena lashed out at his sister, all zhids (which she was not), the Navy and the KGB after Yevgeny broke down and told her why they wouldn't be leaving for Leningrad.

"They're forcing me to make another patrol. I'll be gone for many weeks…"

The next day the KGB took Yelena from her place of work and brought her to a local office for questioning.

"How well do you know Emma Riavin?" she was asked over and over again. She told them that she had only met her once, and that was two years ago when she and Yevgeny were married. They also pressed her about the *World* newspaper and if she or Yevgeny ever saw a copy or know what was in it. After two hours of this, the interrogators became convinced that like her husband, the woman knew nothing of the newspaper operation and that she was not a threat to security. They ended the session with a warning.

"We know all about your after-dark activities when your michman husband is not around, and this behavior is further reason why he will never be sent to officer school."

After this most unpleasant and humiliating event, Yelena returned to the apartment cursing the day she and Yevgeny got married, but she knew it was her own fault. Like many Russians who wanted to leave the country, Yelena purposely married a Jew when the Soviets began letting some of them immigrate to Israel in 1970. She now knew it would never happen and went straight for the bottle of vodka waiting for her on the kitchen shelf. Roaring drunk when Yevgeny arrived that evening, she kicked the door shut after he entered and proceeded to attack him with slurring screams as she staggered in front of him.

"Tttthat bull-dyke sister of yours has ruined it all, hasn't she? And I have stood living in thisss ssstinking hell-hole as long as I can…and I assure you that if the goddamn KGB leaves me alone, I'll be long gone when you get back!" Slumping to the floor, she hissed some final venom, "This navy of yours has now screwed both of us haven't they?" before passing out.

Unbeknownst to Yevgeny, who now sought what was left of the vodka bottle for himself, these slashing, drunken words were the last she would ever utter to him.

Yevgeny seated himself on the old couch in the corner of the room and tried to gather his thoughts. He had known for a long time now that his marriage was a disaster, but he just went day to day without doing anything about it. He knew Yelena had become an alcoholic and more. Her promiscuity had become obvious for several months now, but he somehow managed to blank out the suspicions and tell-tale signs from his mind. Her drunkenness and easy virtue were also common gossip among many of their navy friends who shared the squalid, cramped building where they lived. One anonymous neighbor sent him a note alerting him that "his wife was a drunken whore!" and that he "should get rid of that Ukranian slut!"

Unbelievably, even to him, that despite all of these problems, he still wanted her. In his eyes she was all he wanted physically in a woman. She was just under six feet tall and the same height as he. Like a fashion model, her face was startingly beautiful, with prominent cheek bones, deep blue eyes, curly blonde hair, full lips and a natural complexion that made it unnecessary for her to apply rouge. Her figure was such that regardless of her dress, men would turn and stare as she walked by. Their marriage was mainly a sexual one with little else to base their relationship upon. But he felt fortunate to have access to such a creature, for in his mind it was far better than spending every night aboard *Morozov* or in the michman barracks on the base, and furthermore, he knew if he wanted a woman he wouldn't have to spend a lot of rubles for a prostitute from the streets of Petropavlovsk. He remembered what his father once told him as a boy:

"It doesn't matter whether you're married, single or divorced, you will pay for each time you lay with a woman… one way or another it will cost you."

Due to his circumstances, Yevgeny preferred the marriage option, and he held out hope that things would get better for them once they got out of Petro. He had thought his future promotion to officer would settle Yelena down and they both would become more content.

"We could have children and start a family after officer training," he once said to her.

Now it was gone…for ten years in the elite Soviet submarine force he had worked hard, studied hard and become an extremely proficient nuclear weapons technician. At each and every navy school he attended, he had come out at the top of his class. After serving aboard a guided missile destroyer, he attended submarine school and then nuclear weapons school prior to going aboard his first submarine based in the Baltic Sea. Like the athletes aboard *Morozov*, Riavin was highly recommended to Ivanov by an officer with whom he had previously served. Ivanov then "pulled strings" to get him aboard. Once there, Ivanov was greatly impressed with the young michman and promised him a shot at becoming a naval officer.

"You should go places in this new, technical navy of ours," he told him.

Now the word was out on *Morozov* that Riavin was under investigation, and some crewmembers started using the zhid word to describe him. Hopelessly trapped in a situation he could no longer control, Riavin's mind wandered to desperate and dangerous alternatives.

Captain Stepakov was briefed on the upcoming patrol and ordered to take command of *Morozov* the following morning and sail the boat after dark at 2000 hours (8 pm). He also met at headquarters with *Morozov's* executive officer, the political officer and Senior Lieutenant Nesenkin from *Riga One.* He told them he would take command of the boat at 8 am and to muster the crew topside at that time.

"I will address the crew at 0800 and then meet in the wardroom with all officers," he ordered.

"We will sail tomorrow night, and I will discuss our patrol order in detail in the morning when we meet."

He closed the brief meeting by telling them "to get a good night's rest, for tomorrow will be a long day".

Stepakov met with several other staff officers at the headquarters, then checked into the base officers quarters. After the evening meal he went to his room to organize his thoughts, rest and prepare mentally for the next day, probably the most important day of his life. Then the old urge returned, and on an impulse, he called the quarters steward and asked if he could have a woman sent to his room.

"Sorry comrade Captain, they are considered a security risk here and not allowed on the base," the steward replied. "But an officer of your rank can check out a car, and I can tell you where to go for what you want," the steward offered.

Stepakov drove along the icy streets of Petropavlovsk knowing full well he was taking a chance, "But what the hell," he said to himself, "I'm going to be gone for two months, and what's wrong with getting laid, returning to the room by nine, have no booze and following my own advice and get a good night's sleep before the long day ahead?"

Yelena Riavin's lifestyle and state of mind had driven her beyond indiscriminate sexual trysts and random affairs, and she had now become a highly talented and much-in-demand prostitute. When she needed money for vodka, cigarettes, clothes or choice items found only on the black market, she sold herself, as the meager naval pay and the few rubles she received from the 30 hours a week worked at a local fish-packing plant were not nearly enough to satiate her vices.

Catering mainly to high-ranking military officers and political bigwigs, Yelena worked discretely when Yevgeny was at sea or on duty. Frequenting an exclusive club on the outskirts of Petropavlovsk, she had an agreement with the proprietor of the place who liked having her show up there now and then because of her good looks, large breasts, long shapely legs and nicely curved buttocks that she always accentuated by wearing tight-fitting skirts or winter slacks. Like some of the other women who frequented the place, she was good for business as she attracted customers who had time and money to spend. On her part, she agreed to dress nicely and behave properly while inside the club.

"What happens outside this place is your business," she was told.

Tonight was to become a "club night," for in no mood to spend the evening alone in the apartment, she prepared to leave as soon as it got dark.

Fearful of being followed, she dressed muslim style, as there were many of that faith who lived in the area. She wore a long, hooded coat and a facial scarf that covered all but her unmade-up eyes. She left the apartment by the back window fire escape that led to a back alley. Then taking the bus to town, she entered another alley, removed her disguise, applied make-up and then walked to a store where she bought vodka and cigarettes with the last of her rubles and placed them in her shopping bag with the muslim garb.

Yelena then walked two more blocks to the club, but decided not to enter, again fearful of KGB snoops within. Despite the cold, she decided to ply her trade strolling the street in front of the club, hoping to remain unseen among the evening shopping crowd. This way she could keep an eye out for possible agents while also watching for a past customer entering or leaving the club.

With a half of the pint bottle of vodka already under her belt and with pent-up anger and frustrations boiling within herself, she wanted to forget, even for just a few hours, what had occurred the past few days. She was ready for sex. I need it bad, she told herself, as she lit yet another cigarette to calm herself. She further hoped tonight's score would be good at it and get her involved to the point where her desires were quenched as well as his.

Back aboard *Morozov,* michman Riavin decided to sneak off the sub for an hour or two. For security reasons, he had been directed to remain on board, but he knew his pal Alexei Plavinsky had the gangway watch on deck, and figured he could slip off the sterm of the boat and ask his friend to turn his back when he did so. This ploy would allow the sentry to say with honesty that "I did not see Michman Riavin leave the boat," if any trouble occurred later.

Alexei Plavinsky was Riavin's best friend and the only other known Jew on board. He had been recruited by Ivanov and brought aboard because he had been near the top of his class at submarine training and he also had considerable athletic prowess. He was into the second year of his three-year conscription and couldn't wait to get out, for with the exception of the athletics when *Morozov* was in port, he was not happy in the navy, for instead of visiting foreign ports as he was led to believe, his submarine just went back and forth between the big Pacific Ocean and her home port in Siberia. The zhid thing was also troublesome, and he sensed bias from many in the crew. He now feared what would happen after Ivanov was relieved. At six-foot-two and a muscular 200 pounds, he was big for soccer, but he had exceptional speed for his size, and his leg strength allowed him to propel the ball at a tremendous velocity and with uncanny accuracy. Assigned to the forward torpedo room, the 21-year-old Plavinsky's strength was put to good use moving heavy explosives, torpedo skids (cradles) and other equipment. His brawn was also utilized when he unceremoniously dragged the KGB Agent Tarobrin when he was ordered "removed from the boat" off the gangway with one arm and dumped him on the pier like a sack of flour.

On this particular evening standing the frigid four-hour sentry watch topside, he was glad to see his friend Riavin come up through the forward torpedo access hatch and hand him a hot cup of coffee. As fraternizing between michmen and conscripts was not encouraged in the Soviet Navy, Riavin and Plavinsky were careful to hold any conversations they had on board in privacy such as they had now. "Listen friend, I've got to go ashore for a few hours, and I need you not to see me," Riavin flatly stated.

"I will see nothing," his friend replied.

Plavinsky felt sorry for his friend, and even though he sensed trouble with this "short visit to town," he watched him disappear into the shadows at the head of the pier where the submarine was moored. Having heard some of the crew snickering about Riavin's wife and also once having himself seen her pick up a man in town, he couldn't understand why the michman stayed married to her. With a wife like that and a sister under arrest for subversion, Yevgeny must be at the end of his ropes, he accurately concluded.

Clad in winter blues, Riavin showed his ID and a fake off-base pass to the submarine base security guard, saluted and walked to a nearby bus stop where he would wait for the scheduled city shuttle that would drop him near his apartment. He had no idea what he would find when he got there, for he was not expected. Feeling a helpless, gut-wrenching anguish that comes with a love-hate relationship, Riavin didn't know whether he'd "kiss her or kill her," but resolved to "see her one more time."

Following the steward's directions, Stepakov drove to the club, and as he parked the car he saw her standing nearby watching him. He opened the window and asked if she had a light. When she approached the car he smiled and inquired if she'd "like to come inside where it was warm?" Attracted by his good looks and warm smile, she got in the car, and noticing his rank insignia when she lit his cigarette with her lighter, she said, "My name is Yelena, and what can I do for you tonight Captain?"

Stepakov drove slowly down the deserted street where they quickly agreed upon the price for her services. He then asked if she would mind just staying in the car with him rather than go to a hotel. "I must get back to the base by nine," he explained. Yelena took a long swig from her vodka bottle and snuggling close to him, placed her hand on his thigh and said passionately, "You are in charge Captain, and I want what you want!"

Then following Yelena's directions, Stepakov parked the car in a desolate, unlit spot behind and old deserted apartment building, which had been damaged and vacated because of a recent earthquake. "The rumblings from quakes bring considerably more fear to the local citizenry than threats from the surrounding volcanoes," Yelena remarked as he parked the car, locked the doors and turned the headlights off. "Nobody comes here except rats and seagulls," she laughed.

Then with few preliminaries, they went at each other with a wild passion that surprised them both. "Whores aren't supposed to be like this," Stepakov thought, as he took her for the second time within a half hour. Now fully into what was happening, Yelena met his male thrusts with more than equal desire and moaned hotly into his ear that, "This one is for free Captain!"

After the tryst, which lasted less than an hour, Stepakov told Yelena he must go back to the base. Being careful not to reveal that he was sailing the next day, or even that he was a submarine Captain, he simply told her he wanted to see her again and that, "It's a pity we can't spend the rest of the night together." A breathless and fully satiated Yelena squeezed his hand and asked, "When will I see you again Captain?"

"Soon," he lied, as they drove off.

Now very tired, a disheveled and intoxicated Yelena Riavin asked that Stepakov drop her off near her apartment, where she determined to put herself to sleep with yet another glass of vodka.

Michman Riavin was approaching the apartment building from a darkened side street when he saw the car pull up under a streetlight. Stopping to see who it was, he plainly saw the Navy Captain help the staggering Yelena to the door. He shuddered as he saw her grope at the man, and he was near enough to hear her say to him in a drunken voice, "We must do that again soon, Captain."

Feeling an intense rage building through his body, Riavin stood frozen up against the building as the Captain returned to his car and Yelena could be heard stumbling and cursing as she fumbled for the keys to the flat. He was just about ready to charge into the building after her, swearing to himself to "kill the drunken bitch," when he saw another car, with lights out, pull up to an adjacent intersection. Instantly realizing that this was a KGB tail, and that he would be seen, Riavin instinctively turned and ran back down the dark street, boarded a bus and snuck back aboard *Morozov* without being observed by anyone except his pal Alexei, who was surprised but relieved to see him back aboard so soon.

Apparently not aware that Yelena Riavin was someone already under investigation by a separate branch of the KGB, and considering her "just another whore," the two men who were tailing Stepakov calmly followed him back to the base and routinely made the following entries in their logbook:

"...Captain 2nd Rank Stepakov picked up a prostitute at 7:32 pm in front of the Sofia Club drove her to a vacant lot at

the south end of Provolia Way. They left the lot at 8:07 pm and proceeded to 2722 Knoplasi, where they arrived at 8:33 pm. Stepakov dropped off the woman then went directly to the base, arriving at 9:03 pm. At no time was there any indication that the Captain was aware he was being followed..."

The KGB snoops merely filed this report without informing anyone in higher authority that anything suspicious or unusual went on, as they considered what they had witnessed as a "routine" man/woman liaison. Their job was merely to follow at random several officers a night who leave the base and go into the city. The reports of where, what, when occurred did not get passed on to the local KGB supervisor unless the officers got involved with something more surreptitious than Stepakov's sexual pursuits.

CHAPTER 5

THE VOYAGE

The officers, michmani and crew of the *Morozov* mustered on deck in dress uniform at 7:45 am on an unusually warm and pleasant April morning. With all hands accounted for, the executive officer, Captain 3rd rank Vasili Khudenko, told the men that the new Captain and flotilla commander, Rear Admiral Gomulka, would be aboard shortly, that Captain Stepakov would take command at 8 sharp, and then "inspect the ranks" with the Admiral.

Having slept little the previous night, an exhausted and emotionally drained Riavin stood at attention in ranks with the 12 other michmen assigned to *Morozov.* He saw the group of naval dignitaries coming down the pier with the new captain for the change of command ceremony, but when the Admiral and new Captain were "piped" over the gangway and he got a closer look, Yevgeny Riavin did a double-take when he saw the face of Captain Stepakov. With a pounding in his head and chest, the thunderstruck michman became dizzy with outrage and disbelief as he clearly recognized his new commanding officer as the man he saw with Yelena the night before.

After the ceremony Stepakov told the crew that *Morozov* was important to the Navy and to the Soviet Union.

"The mission ahead of us will be a challenge and an opportunity to gather valuable intelligence that would be vital to our country in time of war."

He next told them that he would demand high standards of military behavior and attention to duty throughout the voyage.

"I am also interested in the cleanliness of *Morozov* and expect this boat to shine from stem to stern when we return from this patrol," he concluded.

Stepakov and Gomulka then inspected the ranks, pausing in front of each sailor, scrutinizing them from head to toe, both front and back. If the Captain or Admiral said nothing after looking a man over, he had passed their scrutiny; but if he was told that his shoes, hat or any part of his uniform was unsatisfactory, his name was taken down the executive officer who would scowl at the unfortunates as he passed by them behind Stepakov and the Admiral. During this inspection, several men were also called to task for need of a haircut or a shave.

Those with discrepancies would be reprimanded after the inspection and put on a list to perform "extra duties" during the voyage. Alexei Plavinsky was one of those on the list.

"This crew must be cleaned up," Stepakov would later tell a chagrined executive officer.

When Stepakov inspected the michmen, he talked to each but made no critical comments about their appearance, as he did not want to embarrass them in front of the crew. In strict and proper naval fashion, he wanted to enhance their authority and show the 65 conscripts aboard that he was solidly behind these michmen and would back whatever discipline or orders they decided to mete out.

"You *michmani* are vital to this boat," he told them.

When Stepakov stood in front of Riavin, he said, "Ahh… michman Riavin…I have heard good things about you and I will be counting heavily on your abilities during this patrol."

Making no response, a rigid Riavin stared icily right through Stepakov without seeing him. A startled Stepakov hesitated a moment, but then moved on to the next michman, attributing Riavin's tenseness to the situation with his sister.

When the inspection ended and the crew dismissed, many talked to one another as they went below decks to change into working uniforms.

One seaman remarked to another that, "The new Captain is a prick! This is going to be like basic training all over again!"

But the feeling among some of the michmen was quite different:

"Now we have a tough Captain…no more bullshit…and that's the way it should be!" was the general feeling in the michman quarters. But there was one michman whose feelings went beyond any of the others.

It was with a burning, nearly delirious surge of determination, that Riavin made a silent oath to himself:

"I will more than get even with you (Stepakov), the Navy and all the rest of you bastards," he solemnly resolved.

* * *

After a day of training sessions, checking equipment and loading supplies, the *Morozov* backed slowly from the pier precisely on time. Despite the balmy weather, melting snow and April slush, the harbor ice was still a month away from break-up and the naval icebreaker *Georgi Sedov* was methodically clearing a channel toward the open North Pacific Ocean.

Commanding from the tiny, open bridge on the *Morozov*, Stepakov was curious as to the maneuverability and "feel" of the 4700-ton vessel. Equipped with three propeller shafts (two for normal propulsion, and a third used only for "quiet" submerged operations) Stepakov slowly backed the submersible from the pier, and when well clear of the dock with room to maneuver, he "twisted" her by backing the port shaft while going ahead on the starboard. In this way he skillfully turned the bow of the boat toward the channel by stopping one shaft and then the other until *Morozov* was aligned exactly to the course that would take her on the first leg of the surface transit to the deep, open North Pacific Ocean. With the stern light of the Icebreaker now visible several kilometers dead ahead, Stepakov ordered "all stop" then "all ahead one third steer course one three seven." He then turned over the conn of the boat to the "officer of the deck" who had been standing behind him, silently watching and admiring the new Captain's ship handling skills.

"Adjust the speed as necessary to remain this same radar distance from the Icebreaker and get all the line handlers below as soon as everything is stowed," Stepakov ordered.

"Slushayus (aye, aye) comrade Captain."

Now with only the four-man "anchor detail" standing at attention on the foredeck of *Morozov*, Stepakov remained on the bridge with the deck officer and two lookouts and watched the huge, black, rounded bow begin to plow its way seaward as the boat slowly picked up speed.

As soon as they reached the end of the channel the Icebreaker was released to return to port and the amazingly calm, open sea lay ahead, glassy under a half-moon and a starlit sky. Astern, the loom of lights from Petropavlovsk could still be seen dimly flickering under the dramatic and surrealistic flashes of the *Aurora Borealis* that rolled across the northern sky like a gigantic, multi-colored, velvet curtain.

The deck officer ordered "the anchor secured for sea" and the detail to lay below. Once this was done, and he was informed that his order had been carried out and that "topside was secured for sea, and all men were below," he received a recommendation from the navigator on the bridge phone to "come to course one nine one and increase speed to 18 knots." Still on the bridge, the captain nodded agreement to the deck officer, who gave the orders over the speaker system to the helmsman, who was two decks below in the control room. The helmsman repeated the order back to the bridge then rang up "ahead full" on both the port and starboard engine order telegraphs. This order was immediately answered from the maneuvering space just aft of the reactor compartment where the *Inzhener* (Engineer) and nuclear propulsion michmani operated the controls for the huge steam turbines that turned each shaft at a speed proportional to the amount of nuclear-heated steam applied to each.

"Answers all ahead full, steady on course one nine one," the helmsman informed the bridge.

"Adjust speed for 18 knots," the deck officer ordered.

"18 knots, *slushayus,"* maneuvering answered, as they adjusted the shaft turns slightly down from the full bell, which would have given them 21 knots. Much faster underwater, the *Morozov* was capable of obtaining speeds of up to 32 knots with an "all ahead flank" bell, an all out speed order used only in an emergency or combat situation. "All ahead full" while submerged provided for a speed through the water of 29 knots.

Before leaving the bridge to go below, Stepakov ordered the deck officer to "Keep a close watch for fishing boats, and inform me of any ship contact that will come within 3,000 meters of us. The boat should be rigged for submerged operations shortly, and we will dive in about an hour," he advised as he disappeared down the long trunk that went from the bridge to the control room below.

Stepakov stood next to the executive officer, who was also the navigator, and informed him of what was in store for the rest of the night.

"I want to dive the boat after we are in more than 100 fathoms of water. We will then obtain a good 'dead-slow trim' before maneuvers."

"What kind of maneuvers, comrade Captain?" Khudenko inquired.

"I want to go to test depth at high speed, and then make steep angle, full speed and full rudder maneuvers up and down several times to get the cobwebs out of the ship and out of the crew! I also want to exercise at missile stations and torpedo (battle) stations," Stepakov said.

"The officers and men are tired, I recommend we do the action stations tomorrow comrade captain," Khudenko replied.

Using the friendly middle name for the first time, and realizing that he was probably rushing things, Stepakov agreed.

"That sounds good comrade Malevich, let's do it that way."

Riavin was busy supervising the final stowage of special armaments in the forward magazine, located just below the forward missile compartment. That afternoon, he and three junior seamen had gone by truck to the submarine base armory to requisition detonator and booster charges for the various torpedoes and missiles on board. These devices would be inserted in cavities on the weapons warheads once the *Morozov* reached the area of operations. When this was done, the missiles and torpedoes would be in an advanced status of readiness, and only electrical settings and interlock authentication security releases, requiring codes help by the captain and executive officer would be necessary prior to an actual launch of a nuclear weapon.

While in the armory, Riavin had also requisitioned small arms ammunition, grenades and plastic explosives -

armaments that were carried aboard all Soviet warships for any "contingencies" that may occur.

After the explosive materials and ammunition had been securely placed in the magazine, Riavin locked the space and reported by phone to the officer of the deck, who was also his direct supervisor as missile and torpedo (weapons) officer.

"Sir, all devices and ammunition have been secured in the forward magazine."

The officer of the deck, Captain Lieutenant Demichev, then informed the captain by phone of this, knowing he wouldn't dive the boat and conduct any underwater maneuvers until everything aboard was "secured for sea."

It was nearly midnight when Stepakov ordered the crew to diving stations.

As the boat had been in port for more than a month, the diving trim of the vessel would have to be adjusted due to calculations involving the actual weights of all supplies, weapons, liquids and personal gear that had come on board or been off-loaded while *Morozov* was in port. Although all such items and their exact weights are supposed to be recorded during the in-port period, errors are easy to make, particularly when weights are estimated. The whole compensation process is based upon figures taken when *Morozov* was last at sea, when a good trim was attained at slow submerged speed. At this time, precise liquid readings in kilograms were taken from all trim, fuel, water, lube and auxiliary tanks. The number of personnel aboard and the location and weights of the various weapons aboard were also logged.

Prior to making this first dive after a long period of time in port, *Morozov's* diving officer was responsible for seeing that all in-port weight changes were recorded. He then factored these in with the figures from the last trim dive, thus determining new tank levels that hopefully would allow for reasonable fore and aft submerged trim as well as taking care of the overall weight of the boat, which should allow for a close to "neutral buoyancy" when submerged. Other factors that affect the trim of a submarine are oceanographic conditions such as seawater temperature, gradient (salt water temperature layers) locations and salinity.

Having been through this "trim dive after a long in-port period" many times, Stepakov was expecting the worst, as he still had no feel for the competency of his officers and crew. His plan was to see how this first dive went, and if the compensation was way off, he would take over the dive himself, trim up the boat, and thus demonstrate that he knew what he was doing. He would then order the diving officer and executive officer (who checked the diving offficer's figures) to meet with him in his stateroom, where he would chew both of their asses out. "I will not tolerate such incompetency," they would be told.

Anticipating exactly what the new captain was thinking, and that this first dive would make a lasting impression upon Stepakov, the executive officer and diving officer had gotten together and meticulously calculated the trim figures again and again until both were satisfied with the result. These figures had been passed to the control room, where the michman in charge of the pumping and trimming manifolds adjusted the trimming tanks accordingly. Once this was done, he reported by phone to the officer of the deck, "The compensation has been entered comrade."

The control room of *Morozov* was bathed in a pale red light, and despite himself, Stepakov was impressed with what he had seen so far. Leaning up against the handles of the raised periscope from the elevated attack station, he could hear and see everything taking place in the control space spread around him. Reports from the sonar room, located below control, came to him from a special speaker system that was within arm's reach of the periscope stand. Communications with the reactor compartment, the bridge, maneuvering, torpedo and missile compartments were also convenient to him on a "captain's order console." What impressed him so far was the quiet, calm manner in which the officers and crew did things. There were no raised or excited voices as orders were given and received. He liked things quiet with no yelling. Having experienced several hair-raising situations during his submarine career, Stepakov always prided himself in "keeping his cool," and he expected others to do the same.

"Ivanov wasn't all that bad," he said to himself.

Captain 3rd Rank Dimitri Litvak was *Morozov's* diving officer as well as her political officer. Now ready to dive the boat, Litvak reported to Stepakov, "Comrade captain, the boat is manned and rigged to submerge on your order. The compensation has been entered."

Stepakov acknowledged with a "Very well," then ordered the radar operator to give him a rundown on all ship or aircraft contacts in the area.

"No contacts within ten thousand meters (6.2 miles) comrade captain."

"Very well radar," then to Litvak, "What is the sounding?"

"Two hundred twenty-one meters (726 feet), depth increasing sir."

Then to the officer of the deck he calmly ordered, "Bridge this is the captain, dive the boat."

The officer of the deck sounded the high-pitched diving alarm, sent the two lookouts down the hatch, then lowered himself down the trunk, pulling the hatch shut over his head and then dogging it shut with seven rapid turns of the closing wheel.

"All below, upper hatch secured," he reported when he descended the trunk ladder the rest of the way to the control room. He then moved to the ballast control station adjacent to the diving control positions in the control room, where he would oversee the michman who operated the ballast control mechanisms.

As the deck tilted downward and the roar of air escaping from the ballast tanks reverberated through control, Stepakov ordered the diving officer to "Come to depth of 21 meters."

Litvak answered, "21 meters, *slushayus* comrade captain," then to the bow and stern plane operators, who sat at their control stations right in front of him, "Come to depth 21 meters, 5 degree down angle."

At a speed of 10 knots, the *Morozov* went swiftly to the ordered depth of 21 meters, which was the deepest depth at which the periscope could be utilized.

"Now we'll see what kind of a trim we have," Stepakov said as he ordered speed reduced to three knots. With reports coming in from all stations and compartments that "conditions were normal," the *Morozov* glided at the ordered depth with a zero angle (up or down). Once three knots were reached, the diving officer had to apply a small down angle to maintain the ordered depth, which was an indication the boat was still light overall. He compensated for this by ordering seawater to flood gradually into the amidships trim tanks until the down angle was no longer necessary. Observing the routine trimming procedure from the periscope stand, Stepakov ordered the boat slowed to one knot. After a few minutes at the low speed, the diving officer observed that he was still able to maintain the ordered depth with a zero angle on the boat. He then proudly reported to the captain, "The trim is satisfactory, comrade captain."

An astonished Stepakov replied with a *"molodets* (well done), comrade," then ordered him to take the boat down to a depth of 60 meters, and to the helmsman, "all ahead full."

After the *Morozov* was up to full speed at a depth of 60 meters and entered deep ocean waters with depths in excess of 2000 meters, Stepakov spoke to the crew over the boat's MC system:

"This is the captain. We are now going to maneuver at steep angles, tight turns and various depths while the boat is at full speed. All hands are reminded to make sure all equipment is secured in your compartment and that you hold onto something to prevent injury. When we get to test depth, all compartments are to check for leaks which are to be reported immediately to control."

The test depth of *Morozov* was 375 meters (1,230 feet), which was the deepest depth that the design engineers could guarantee hull, valves, hatches and seawater systems to withstand the sea pressure at that depth…542 psi.

In addition to testing the crew, Stepakov wanted to test all the systems for watertightness and proper operation. He also wanted to get the feel of the boat by observing how fast or slow she reacted to rudder and diving plane orders while submerged.

"Make your depth 375 meters, 30 degrees down angle," he ordered.

As soon as the diving officer gave these orders to the bow and stern planesmen, they pushed their controls slightly forward, and like an aircraft, *Morozov* reached the large down angle within ten seconds of the order.

With the numbers on the small, digital depth indicator whirring in a blur, the diving officer instead concentrated on the large, clock-like deep depth gauge where the indicating needle moved at a slower, more readable pace toward the red, test depth marker. The stern planesman was virtually standing on the forward bulkhead of the control room as he held the down angle at exactly 30 degrees. When *Morozov* passed 360 meters, the diving officer ordered the down angle eased to 5 down, and then zero, as he leveled the boat precisely at test depth.

* * *

While captain Stepakov put *Morozov* through her paces, he was unaware that they had company. Another submerged vessel - the American nuclear attack submarine *Piranha* was listening from three miles astern.

Having been on submerged patrol off the Kamchatka coast for more than a month, *Piranha* had been tracking, reporting and making passive sonar tapes of all Soviet naval vessels, but particularly submarines, coming and going from Petropavlovsk. Just three days previously she had succeeded in tailing a large, newly built YANKEE class ballistic missile submarine (SSBN) that was returning to Petro on the surface. Moving in from dead astern of the "Russian boomer," the *Piranha* skipper, Commander Raymond Dodge, USN, skillfully maneuvered his boat to a point under the stern of the Soviet vessel. And by carefully controlling speed and depth, he was able to take submerged photographs through *Piranha's* periscope of the propellers, rudder and stern planes of the huge, unsuspecting submersible.

Realizing that this was the first contact by the U.S. Navy with this new class Soviet submersible and that it was the Russian's first known SSBN, Dodge knew that such photos, combined with sonar recordings of the big boomer at different speeds, both submerged and surfaced, would be of extreme value to the U.S. Navy Office of Naval Intelligence (ONI). Now he had another interesting contact, and although there would probably be little opportunity for trail photos, he was maneuvering to obtain high quality sonar tapes of the speedy, but loud, Russian nuke, that *Piranha* designated as "contact HOTEL."

"Christ that boat is loud," remarked sonarman first class Tom Sinclair to the other sonarmen on duty as he adjusted the maze of listening and recording equipment in the *Piranha's* sonar room. In the control room, Dodge, like Stepakov, stood in a raised attack center/periscope stand overlooking everything that went on in the operational spaces around and below him. He ordered the underwater telephone receiver (UQC) turned down, as the highpitched propeller noise from HOTEL reverberated throughout the compartment, then called the sonar room on the sonar/conn MC circuit, "Can you identify HOTEL by class?"

Trained to memorize Soviet submarine noise profiles, U.S. Navy sonarmen, particularly submariners, not only had to have good ears, they were also highly skilled and extremely capable technicians, a fact that made it difficult for the navy to keep them, as such technicians were in high demand in the civilian electronics industries.

Sinclair listened for a few more moments, then replied, "Affirmative captain, it's a three screw CHARLIE class."

"What is your estimate of HOTEL's speed?"

"Turn count indicates close to 30 knots captain."

Leaning over his stand, Dodge asked the same question of the executive officer, Lieutenant Commander Robert Calligan, who was plotting *Piranha* and HOTEL on the attack plotting console.

"I concur, captain, somewhere between 28 and 31 knots."

Dodge now wondered if HOTEL was operating locally for just a few days of training, or heading elsewhere on a more serious mission, similar to *Piranha's.* It made a difference, for if HOTEL continued on a steady course, depth and speed out of the immediate area, such data would have to be sent by immediate message to the fleet intelligence headquarters, who kept track of all known communist warships worldwide.

Speaking quietly to his exec, Dodge asked his opinion. "What do you think Bob, is this one heading south, or just exercising out here off Petro?"

"It's too early to tell captain, but I recommend we report HOTEL now, then send a followup if she leaves the area."

"Concur, have ops (the operations officer) draft the contact message," Dodge ordered.

Sonar then reported, "HOTEL is making a high speed turn to the right."

"Very well sonar, what is the range to HOTEL?"

"Seven thousand three hundred yards, sir…Now he's turning back to the left."

"Very well, sonar, can you tell what depth HOTEL is operating at?"

"Various depths, captain. They're going up and down like a yoyo! Right now they are at about 500 feet and the range is increasing."

"Very well, sonar, let me know when the range to HOTEL gets to 12,000 yards." Then to the helm, "All ahead one third, make turns for five knots. Back to sonar, "I'm clearing our baffles (turn ship to listen on sonar astern, where passive sonar cannot pick up quiet contacts due to propeller turbulence), take a good listen all around, and report any new contacts."

Keeping a good distance astern of *Morozov,* Dodge kept his vessel at slow speed, allowing the fastmoving Russian nuke to rapidly increase the range between them.

Aboard *Morozov,* Stepakov was satisfied with the rigorous trials he had just put his boat and crew through and called his executive officer to control for further orders.

"I want you to set the regular watch now, and go to the course and speed for our long transit south. We will go at 16 knots at a depth of 100 meters. I will write night orders now and have them delivered to you shortly."

"Slushayus, comrade captain."

Aboard *Piranha*, Dodge ordered the boat to periscope depth.

"Six eight feet, sir," the diving officer reported.

Dodge then ordered a small transmitting antenna raised, and then pressed a button to call the radio room.

"Send the contact message and report to control when it has been receipted for."

"Radio, aye."

* * *

In addition to ONI in Washington, D.C., *Piranha's* contact message, which was classified secret, was also sent to the U.S. Submarine Flotilla Headquarters in Yokosuka, Japan (SUBFLOT SEVEN) and the Submarine Force Pacific Headquarters (SUBPAC) in Pearl Harbor, Hawaii. The Commander in Chief of the Pacific Fleet (CINCPACFLT) was also on the list of addressees for this message.

In Pearl Harbor, Captain Art Mobley, the SUBPAC operations and intelligence officer, was enjoying a cigarette with his morning coffee while scanning the radio "traffic" that had been received overnight. Most of the morning's messages were of a routine or logistics nature and were of little interest to him. Mobley swiftly flipped through page after page of a one inch stack on the hinged, aluminum message board, looking mainly for traffic to and from the various SUBPAC nuclear attack submarines (SSN's) deployed to the western Pacific (WESTPAC), which at present numbered seven. He knew that two, the *Piranha* and the *Mako,* were in the northern zone on intelligence gathering missions, while another, the *Mullet*, was in the central Pacific en route to relieve the *Sea Bass*, moored at the U.S. Naval Station in Subic Bay, Republic of the Philippines. Two other U.S. "fast attacks", the *USS Guppy* and the *USS Orca* were on patrol off the coast of North Vietnam, tracking and reporting all vessels going in and out of enemy seaports. The seventh deployed SSN was the *USS Moray,* moored in Hong Kong Harbor alongside the U.S. Navy submarine rescue vessel (ASR) USS *Whistler*, while both crews enjoyed four days of shore leave.

Mobley rose from his chair when he read *Piranha's* latest contact report and moved to the large wall chart where red tacks marked the exact positions of recent Soviet naval contacts. These included *Piranha's* detection of the Soviet CHARLIE class nuke, which had already been placed on the chart during the early morning hours by the SUBPAC operations duty officer.

"Dime to doughnuts this one is heading for Nam," he said to his assistant while pointing to the contact marked just south of the Kamchatka Peninsula.

"Well soon find out sir," responded Lieutenant Commander Al "Stubby" Fusina. "There's another message further down on the board from SUBFLOT 7 directing *Piranha* to track her for another 12 hours, make a final report then return north again to the Petro area."

"That sounds like the way to go, and now let's get all the contacts plotted on the op-boards so I can brief the admiral at 0900."

* * *

Aboard the *Morozov*, michman Riavin's depression worsened, and although he doggedly went at his duties in a robotic, trance-like manner, he had now resolved to take his own life, and had only to decide when and how. Plavinsky, his only real friend on board, offered little solace, for he was also in ill humor of late.

"I don't know if I can handle 60 days of this shit!", he complained to Riavin as they whispered to each other in the upper section of the forward torpedo room, where Riavin was checking torpedo fire control electronic circuits while Plavinsky labored nearby cleaning and scrubbing a remote section of bulkhead splotched with hydraulic fluid, lube oil and heavy grease.

Riavin knew what Alexei meant, for unobserved, he had overheard a few of his fellow michmen in the quarters discussing Plavinsky, and what was in store for him.

"Now that we have this new captain, I don't have to coddle that zhid Plavinsky anymore," said the michman who was Alexei's immediate supervisor to another michman while the two of them sipped coffee.

"You should work his zhid ass off on this cruise and make it one he'll never forget. As far as I'm concerned, we have two zhids too many on this boat!" the pal chipped in.

"After he finishes the upper compartment bulkheads, I'm putting him in the escape trunk for a few days for a complete scouring and then a fresh paint job. And after that, I'll find another way to bust his ass!"

Not letting on the exact words he had overheard, Riavin told Alexei that he knew they were going after him on this trip, and warned him, "Not to be surprised if the bastards put you up in the trunk for a few days."

"Christ Yevgeny, I can't wait to get off this son of a bitch. These next weeks will seem like forever. I've worked hard on this boat, and being a Jew or an athlete should have nothing to do with how they treat a man. It's tough to figure out what motivates these michmani."

"The best thing to do is not to let them know they're getting to you. Work with a smile or a whistle, it'll drive them crazy. If they see that you won't crack, they'll give up on it."

"Easier said than done," Alexei grumbled.

* * *

Back in Pearl Harbor, Captain Mobley briefed Rear Admiral Calvin "Cal" Carpenter, Commander Submarines Pacific (COMSUBPAC), on the latest submarine movements in the Western Pacific theater of operations.

"Admiral, I recommend we follow up on this CHARLIE boat that *Piranha* has been trailing, for they may be headed to do some snooping off Yoko (U.S. Naval Station, Yokosuka, Japan), and not transit south to Nam. Also, they may work off Yoko for a few days and then head south again. The spooks (naval intelligence analysts) over at Fleet have now officially determined this one to be a positive Soviet SSN and have designated her as CHARLIE FOUR."

"I agree with what you say about follow-up Art, and I understand from Fleet Intelligence that PATRON 6 (U.S. Navy anti-submarine aircraft) out of Atsugi (U.S. Naval Air Station, Atsugi, Japan) will pick up the trailing with sonobuoys, and our sosus system (permanent sonars on the bottom of the ocean) off the Ryukyu Trench (between Okinawa and Japan) should detect this boat soon if she's at high speed and cavitating (high frequency sound generated by high speed propeller rotation). In any case, keep your eye on this one, for if CHARLIE FOUR moves toward Nam, make sure FLOT 7 notifies our boats there that this ruski is on the way."

Within 24 hours it was confirmed by PATRON 6 that CHARLIE FOUR was still heading southwest at high speed, and as Admiral Carpenter predicted, the sosus system had also picked up the Russian nuke.

* * *

Still unaware he had been detected and now almost four days out of Petro, Stepakov called a meeting of all off-watch officers in the wardroom to explain his strategy and what would be expected of the officers and crew now that they were nearing their assigned area of operations. Senior Lieutenant Nesenkin, the officer in charge of the *Riga One* intelligence gatherers was also present at this meeting.

Stepakov began by telling the nine *Morozov* officers and Nesenkin that the mission was about to begin.

"We will soon pass between Luzon and Taiwan into the South China Sea, and we can expect to encounter American naval forces at any time. I plan to slow after dark tonight, come up to periscope depth, check our position, send off our location report and let comrade Nesenkin here spend four hours monitoring whatever he can pick up from units of the American seventh fleet." He then placed a chart of the area on the wardroom table, and referring to a stack of messages, pointed to places where the Soviet naval intelligence system placed American naval units and where they were believed to be headed.

"Right now there are two destroyers and an oiler coming down the Formosa Straits from their base in Sasebo (southern Japan) and they're probably headed for the Vietnam area." Moving his finger down the East China Sea to the Formosa Strait and then to where it opened into the South China Sea, he explained further.

"These ships should pass to our west tonight and may present an opportunity for *Riga One.* Also, they send their ships in and out of Kaohsiung (port in southern Taiwan) and Hong Kong on a regular basis for crew recreational leave. There is also considerable traffic between Cam Ranh Bay (South Vietnam) and the big U.S. Navy repair base in Subic Bay."

Senior Lieutenant Nesenkin spoke next.

"Comrades, the most important part of our mission is to gather intelligence from the American carrier task forces of their seventh fleet. They keep at least one of these groups continually at an area they call "*Yankee Station*" just off North Vietnam. Even though we cannot attack these forces that are wreaking tremendous damage on our comrades the VietCong, we will be sending messages directly to them warning of impending bombing raids whenever we can determine the enemy is launching aircraft for just such a purpose. We will also detect, record and observe many things that could be of vital importance to our country in the future. These ships and aircraft are utilizing the latest electronics, communications, fire control, radar, sonar and other equipment available in the west. It is the task of *Riga One* to monitor and record as much of this as possible, and then let our experts at home decipher and analyze it all when we return."

Stepakov nodded in agreement with Nesenkin's remarks and went on:

"American naval ships that are observed and identified by us will be reported promptly to our Fleet headquarters in Vladivostok. The flotilla in Petro will also be informed. As some of these contacts will be more important than others, I will decide which will be reported and at what priority these reports will be made. But, I must emphasize, that all contacts, regardless of how they are detected, will be reported immediately to both comrade Nesenkin and myself."

The *Morozov's* communications officer then handed Stepakov a message that had been received the last time the boat was at periscope depth, and had just been decrypted.

"Aha," said Stepakov, as he quickly scanned the message. "This is exactly what I mean. Fleet is telling us that an American nuclear carrier, a cruiser and six destroyers are preparing to leave Subic Bay in two or three days for the Vietnam area, where they will probably relieve a similar force now at *Yankee Station*, which most certainly will depart that area soon, either individually or as a group. Fleet wants data on both groups, which means we will track the Task Force coming out of Subic, then report the ships that are leaving the Vietnam area and what direction they are heading."

Looking first at the chart and then at Nesenkin, Stepakov took a long drag on his cigarette and then made his plan as he spoke it.

"Once we round Luzon, we will head south right down the eastern boundary of our assigned area to a point about 60 kilometers west of Subic Bay, in the southeastern corner of our assigned operation area."

Pointing to the spot he just described, and then tracing his forefinger around the boundaries of the area in which

Morozov was ordered to remain within - an area which generally covered all of the South China Sea north of the 13th parallel (latitude 13 degrees north) and included the Gulf of Tonkin, Stepakov held the rapt attention of *Morozov's* officers as he coolly described the situation and the role they would play:

"This way we will be in an optimum position to pick up the carrier group when they leave Subic Bay and it should provide an excellent surveillance opportunity for both *Morozov* and *Riga One.* Comrade Nesenkin is in charge of all technical aspects of this surveillance, and he will coordinate his team's efforts with the officer of the deck in control, who will keep me informed. We will put this boat wherever comrade Nesenkin desires as long as it is safe to go there and is within our assigned operation area."

Then to the Navigator, "After the four hours at periscope depth tonight, lay out the track I just described. I want to reach the point off Subic Bay at midnight the day after tomorrow and figure in no more speed than is necessary to get us there at that time. We will also come to dead slow speed once an hour, make a 360-degree turn to listen astern, and then come to periscope depth for observations, communications and electronic listening. That is all comrades, now get your men and equipment ready for the task ahead."

* * *

The next morning in Pearl Harbor, Stubby Fusina was again thumbing through the previous night's operational message traffic when he came across one from FLOT 7 advising that sonar contact with CHARLIE FOUR had been lost. "Christ, the Ops boss won't be happy about that one," he said to himself.

When Captain Mobley arrived, Fusina showed him the message and pointed to the last known position on the wall chart...just north of the Philippine Island of Luzon.

"Well it doesn't surprise me they lost him. The sosus system is lousy between Luzon and Taiwan, but at least we now have a good idea where he's going, and I'm sure that either *Guppy* or *Orca* will pick this guy up once he gets near Nam. I'm glad FLOT 7 notified everybody of the situation, and who knows, maybe the tin cans (destroyers) or airdales (navy air) will be the next to detect him. From what *Piranha* reported, this baby is as loud as a freight train."

Fusina then proceeded to show Mobley several new Soviet submarine contacts that were picked up overnight.

"It looks like another boomer coming out of Petro, another nuke off Guam and CHARLIE TWO just west of DaNang that appears to be heading northeast at speed. It's probably the boat that CHARLIE FOUR is relieving down there."

"That's good work Stubby, and I concur. Now for the 0900 briefing, let's get the quartermasters to bring the wall charts up to date to include all our units local and deployed, all our FBMs (polaris missile submarines), all the ruskis, and a complete rundown and listing of exactly where all SUBPAC units are located this morning. Include yard overhaul, upkeep, transit and new construction ops on the west coast. You never know when the Admiral is going to ask what a particular boat is doing right now, so we must include everything, not just those deployed to WestPac."

"Aye, aye, sir."

CHAPTER 6

DISASTER

Morozov passed down the western coast of the Island of Luzon without incident; neither observing or detecting anything but small merchant ships and fishing boats. Reaching the planned position just west of Subic Bay precisely on time, Stepakov ordered the boat to periscope depth and to raise the various masts as required by *Riga One* for their electronic eavesdropping. He also told the navigator to prepare the seventy-two hour position and check report that would inform the flotilla in Petro they had arrived "on-station as ordered." This check report was a simple coded message that was sent three times in ten minutes, in the blind, that is, the message went out with the assumption that the Soviet communication system would pick it up, for no receipt was required. This type of communication consisted of about 30 coded words that went out in what could be described as a "compressed electronics shot" that lasted no more than a tenth of a second. These "shots" could be picked up by sensitive Soviet receivers up to 3,000 miles away. The purpose of this message was simply to inform the Soviet Naval High Commands in Vlad and Petro at least every three days where *Morozov* was and that they were operating normally.

Unlike many Soviet submarine captains, Stepakov, despite his degree in engineering, had little interest in nuclear power. He considered himself more of a hands-on deck officer and tactician who preferred to leave all details of the safe operation of *Morozov's* propulsion system to the *Inzhener,* who in turn, was quite happy to have a captain who "stayed up forward" and spent little time back aft nosing around the engineering spaces and asking a million questions. Although given three months training in nuclear physics and propulsion at the Soviet Navy F.E. *Dzerzhinsky* higher naval engineering school in Leningrad, Stepakov was more interested in overall reliability and safety than highly technical submarine engineering details, of which his knowledge was adequate but basic. But now, after nearly a week at sea, he was pleasantly amazed that the boat had yet to incur even a minor engineering casualty, for in addition to the pressurized nuclear reactor and dual steam turbines, the *Inzhener* was responsible for the operation and maintenance of the myriad pumps, motors, compressors, oxygen generators, and the maze of all hydraulic, water, electrical and air systems aboard. Thus, Stepakov was more than satisfied so far with the efficiency and reliability of all this equipment, knowing from past experience that breakdowns were commonplace in the Soviet submarine force. In fact, it was normal and constant routine on a submarine cruise for one thing or another to be under repair or beyond repair. In addition to equipment breakdowns, dealing with fire, flooding, smoke and other emergencies are disciplines ingrained in submariners the world over, and Stepakov was more than satisfied with the crew's performance during the emergency drills that the executive officer had held on a daily basis. Now that they were in the patrol area, he would order these drills discontinued until *Morozov* headed back toward Petro. Stepakov again felt respect for the previous commanding officer and sent him a mental message:

"I am sorry, comrade, you screwed up with the bastards from the KGB, but I thank you for leaving me one damn good submarine. You did a better job here than anyone gave you credit for. The crew shows good training, and the machinery is in good shape."

Now resting on his bunk, he mulled over the operational, engineering and crew situation; and then in further thought concluded that despite the "smooth sailing" so far, he should stay on his toes, for he knew that one serious engineering casualty, or a series of small ones could ruin what looked to be a bountiful, if not glorious first patrol for him as a commanding officer. This brought to mind some advise he once received from his father. "It's when things are going smoothly that you must worry," he had warned.

Before dozing off for the night he recalled a conversation with his father that took place less than a year previous, shortly after the Soviet nuclear submarine *Kolinsk* was lost in the north Atlantic with 104 men on board, including a close friend, who was the boat's executive officer. His father blamed new construction priorities. The "numbers game" as he called it.

"We are building these boats far too fast Petrovich. They are trying to keep up with the west and this is now the fourth nuclear boat we have lost in the past five years. And as you know, another three had serious nuclear casualties at sea and had to be either towed to port or scuttled in the ocean where they foundered. Others have had explosions or bad fires in port, and Christ only knows what other catastrophes have occurred that I haven't heard about! They don't exactly broadcast it when we have an accident…the goddamn KGB doesn't want anybody to know we're having these problems. What's going on is insanity! They must slow down, build these boats with care, and forget the numbers game."

Stepakov agreed with his father but knew what he said was only half of the problem, and told him how he saw it. "They're also building them faster than the men can be trained. We're sending these boats to sea with only a fraction of the crewmen technically competent. It's not like the old days when every man aboard knew what he was doing. Also, they didn't have nuclear power, nuclear weapons, high-tech electronics and computers on the boats back when you served, and right now we do not have enough good technical people available to man half the boats we have in service."

It seemed as if he had just shut his eyes, but after six good uninterrupted hours of sleep as the boat listened and waited, Stepakov was awakened by the buzzing of his phone which he answered with a simple, *"Dobroye Utro"* (good morning).

"Dobroye Utro" comrade captain, this is the officer of the deck. *Riga One* has detected signals from the east which they believe came from the convoy leaving Subic Bay."

"Very well, control, I will call comrade Nesenkin and get back to you with orders."

Conferring with Nesenkin, Stepakov said he was concerned they could be spotted by aircraft while up near the surface and that he wanted to go to a good sonar listening depth to await passive sonar contact. Nesenkin agreed, and believed they would have little trouble picking up the ships on sonar. "I will secure electronic intercept operations at this time and head for the sonar room where the michmani are setting things up for the listening phase."

After lighting his first cigarette of the day, Stepakov called the officer of the deck, who was conning the boat from the raised periscope stand in the control room and ordered him to "Lower all masts and antennas, rig the boat for combat quiet, go to the third propeller for dead slow speed and make your depth 50 meters. Call me immediately when sonar contact is made with the task force. I will be in the wardroom having breakfast."

It was nearly noon before sonar contact was made with the American naval task force that had departed Subic Bay that morning.

Now in the control room, Stepakov received a call from Nesenkin who calmly reported the news.

"Well comrade Captain, the Amerikanski's are right on schedule. We now hold a distinct sound level indicating a small Flotilla of ships about 40 kilometers away, bearing 170. They are moving westward at about 22 knots and are about 4 hours out of Subic Bay."

Chuckling to himself at Nesenkin's "right on schedule" comment, Stepakov remembered his early training at the *Frunze* academy, where it was drummed into the cadet's heads that, "The American navy nearly always sails its ships at 0800!"

Conferring with Stepakov in the control room, Nesenkin said he would like to get closer to the convoy in order to get in a position to make sonar recordings from astern. Measuring the distance from *Morozov* to the carrier force with 40-year-old brass dividers given to him by his father when he graduated from *Frunze,* Stepakov did some rapid calculations on the chart to determine the course and speed required to place the boat where *Riga One* could get into position to optimize their sonar listening effort.

"We will need 25 knots, and since there is a sharp layer at 60 meters, we will go to 67 meters to stay under it and minimize detection. But before we begin I want to send out the convoy's position to fleet along with our own position, which will also cover us for another three days before we have to send another check report."

Within 20 minutes, *Morozov* had come to periscope depth, transmitted the message, and then gone down to a depth of 67 meters (220 feet) to close the task force.

Hearing the announcement over the all-compartment speaker system to "secure from combat quiet," members of *Morozov's* crew who were not on watch, reluctantly rolled out of their bunks to resume the daily work routine. One of these was a disgruntled Alexei Plavinsky, who found himself ordered to the forward escape compartment (trunk) for cleaning, scrubbing, polishing and eventual painting.

A small, 6 ft. x 4 ft. tube-shaped space located in the upper section of the forward missile/torpedo compartment, the escape trunk is like a miniature separate pressure tube within the pressure hull. Once flooded and pressurized, it allows for the escape of surviving personnel if the submarine was bottomed and unable to surface. It can also be used by frogmen to go in and out of the submarine while submerged. The Trunk can accommodate six men at a time and is fitted with a floatation buoy tethered to a large reel of extra-strength nylon line. When an escape takes place, this buoy is released up through the open upper hatch. Then as the buoy soars upward to the surface, it drags the line behind it, which is used to guide escapees to the surface. A small, inflatable life raft is also stored in the space. This small but efficiently packaged raft also contains some emergency rations, water and a few first aid supplies.

The escape trunk is not connected to the submarine's ventilation system, but has its own air, oxygen and carbon dioxide absorbent capability. It has a communication box that allows men in the tube to talk on a speaker to the missile/torpedo compartment directly below and the control room. There is also a sound-powered phone installed to the boat's handphone system that can ring-up any compartment. The trunk has an upper hatch that is used for access to and from the forward section of the submarine from topside, when it is in port. Under this hatch is a heavy steel extension which is the same diameter as the hatch and extends two feet down into the trunk. The lower hatch allows access to and from the missile/torpedo compartment and is fitted with a small deadlight of three-inch thick, pressure-resistant clear glass. This deadlight allows observations from the trunk to the compartment below when the lower hatch is shut or from the compartment up into the trunk to view the status of flooding or whether escaping personnel or frogmen have vacated the space. The view from below up through the deadlight also provides a final check of the trunk condition prior to opening the lower hatch.

Feeling the deck below him gently vibrate as the submarine picked up speed, Plavinsky crawled up into the trunk while carrying rags and a bucket of water and squeezed through the small, lower hatch opening in to the damp, foul-smelling space that had been sealed since the boat left port. After turning on the compartment light, he opened two valves allowing oxygen mixed with compressed air to ventilate the space. After he was satisfied with the aeration, he shut the valves, opened a carbon dioxide absorbent can then closed and dogged the lower hatch, as he had to stand on it to accomplish the scrub down. He also wanted it dogged and shut to prevent anyone from below lifting the hatch and spilling his cleaning water which he had placed on it.

As Plavinsky toiled in the escape trunk, his shipmate Riavin put his deadly plan into motion. His head reeling from recent comments about his wife and sister he overheard in the michman's quarters, he now convinced himself to do the unthinkable…he was going to destroy himself, the *Morozov* and everyone in it!

Riavin went to the forward magazine, to which only he and two officers held keys, presumably for a routine inspection, temperature and humidity checks. Instead, he went straight to boxes marked "DESTROY SHIP EMERGENCY EXPLOSIVES." These containers held plastic explosives that were to be used to destroy highly classified equipment, papers and anything they wanted to prevent from falling into enemy hands in the event *Morozov* had to be scuttled and abandoned in waters where an enemy could either capture or salvage the boat. Opening the box, he removed a thick, heavy sheet of wrapped plastic explosive and slid it up under his shirt. He also took an explosive device no bigger than a stubby pencil and an electrical switch and wires, small enough to fit in his trouser pockets. He then left the space, shut and locked the magazine hatch and headed aft. The rest of his plan was easy. He was required to make weekly checks of two "special missiles" that had been loaded aboard *Morozov* in Petro. After assembling the usual tools and electronic meters for the checks, he called Captain Lieutenant Demichev in the officer's wardroom to request permission to conduct the weekly maintenance procedures on the missiles aft.

"Permission is granted Riavin. Check with control before you start and report to me when you are finished and the missile tubes are secured."

Unlike other Soviet submarines of the CHARLIE class, *Morozov* carried two nuclear-tipped SS-N-6 ballistic missiles aft in addition to the eight SS-N-7 conventional warhead missiles housed in tubes outside the forward missile/torpedo compartment. The two aft nuclear missile tubes were astern of the control room and they extended all the way from the keel of the submarine up through three decks. Each of the spaces around the decks held special missile firing and monitoring equipments, but the only access to the missile itself was through tube doors on the upper deck. These doors allow certain self-guidance and firing system circuits within the missile to be checked. The bottom portion of the huge nuclear warhead is also within easy reach of whoever is conducting the checks on the upper deck.

Having overheard Riavin's request and short conversation with Demichev, other michmani, who were playing cards in the mess room, paid little attention as he gathered additional gear from his locker and left the quarters en route to the starboard, upper missile tube space.

With *Morozov* now up to a speed of 25 knots and cruising at a depth of 67 meters, Stepakov decided to try the boat's automatic depth and course system. Speaking calmly from the raised periscope stand in the control room, he ordered the diving officer to energize the system.

"Go to autopilot course and depth control."

"Slushayus, sir."

The diving officer then ordered the bow and stern planesmen and the helmsman to put their planes in the automatic control position.

"Go to autopilot course 170 and set depth at 67 meters."

After the control had been switched, the diving officer closely observed the depth gauge and the gyrocompass course heading display panel on the forward bulkhead directly in front of the helmsman. After several minutes, he appeared satisfied and reported same to Stepakov.

"Comrade captain, depth and course are holding exactly as set, 67 meters and 170. Request permission for the planesmen and the helmsman to smoke."

"Very well, I want to stay in automatic for another ten minutes to give the system a good test. You may allow the men to smoke, but be ready to go back to normal operation if either system fails."

Like an aircraft in auto flight control, but in the ocean instead of the air, *Morozov* was now plying 220 feet under the South China Sea at a speed of 25 knots and precisely on a course of 170, without a human hand in use.

Riavin was now alone in the upper level of the special ballistic missile compartment. He called control on the compartment phone and advised them that he "was ready to open the access hatch, had permission to do so from Demichev and that his tests would take no more than 20 minutes." This call was necessary, as the opening to the missile access hatch would cause a light on the hull panel in the control room to turn from green to red, which in turn would cause immediate concern and alarm from the michman in control who watched the panel to monitor valve and hatch positions throughout the boat.

Picking up the phone from the bulkhead, the diving officer heard Riavin's request and told him to wait.

"Captain, michman Riavin requests permission to access the starboard aft missile tube for weekly checks. Comrade Demichev has approved."

"Very well. How long will it take him?"

"Twenty minutes, comrade Captain."

"Tell him that permission is granted, but he must take no more than that, for we will shortly be going to combat quiet again."

Remarkably calm and at peace with himself, michman Riavin felt neither fear nor remorse for the horrendous act he was about to commit. Opening the watertight door, he swiftly entered the upper missile compartment, removed the plastic explosive from under his shirt and laid out the other items he required for the job ahead. After unlocking and freeing the dogs on the missile access door, he pulled it open, and looking inside, viewed the monstrous weapon within. Not concerned with opening the small cover plate on the missile itself, which gave access to the guidance circuitry, he instead took a small spray can of adhesive. Reaching up into the tube to the lower part of the warhead he liberally covered the area where it would hold the plastic in place until detonation.

After packing the heavy plastic over the sticky adhesive on the lower side of the warhead, he connected the charge wire in the small, pencil-like detonator, which he immediately plunged into the dark gray, powerful, plastic explosive. He had now merely to throw a small switch to end the torturous paranoia and hatred that raged within him. Holding the tiny firing switch in one hand and staring at the hideous creation in front of him, Yevgeny Riavin's pent-up emotions suddenly roared out of his body with a final burst as he screamed his final words to his sister: "WE ARE ABOUT TO BE TOGETHER AGAIN EMMA. THESE BASTARDS WILL NOW PAY FOR WHAT THEY DID TO THE BOTH OF US!"…

The explosion ripped into the nuclear warhead of the missile and sent an enormous shock blast and an immediate release of deadly radiation that within seconds whooshed through *Morozov's* wide-open inter-compartment hatches and the boat's ventilation system, instantly killing nearly every man aboard. The blast was so catastrophic that men died even before they could yell or move toward a switch or valve handle. Boris Petrovich Stepakov died while lighting a cigarette, his hand frozen in mid-air and the unlit cigarette still tight between his lips. It was over as swiftly as an electrocution. The charge created by Riavin was powerful enough to obliterate his body instantly, destroy the missile warhead, blow apart both ends of the missile compartment, starting fires at both places and rupturing internal water, air and fuel pipes. But it did not create a nuclear explosion. Such a mega-ton chain reaction is designed to occur only when the precision internal detonation system activates upon completion of the missile's flight to target.

Miraculously, and despite the velocity and power of the blast, it did not rupture the pressure hull, nor did it blow open to sea the thick, double launching hatches over the tip of the missile, although it did create a sizeable upward bulge of the outer hatch. The most potent direction of the blast was downward into the guts of the *Morozov,* which, despite the carnage, still barreled along at 25 knots, course 170 at a depth of 67 meters. This, while small fires raged in various parts of the boat, electric circuits sparked, alarms blared and lethal wafts of smoke drifted throughout the grisly scenario. Another miracle was the fact that one crewmember was still breathing…Seaman Alexei Plavinsky.

Knocked unconscious by the shock of the explosion, Alexei lay crumpled at the bottom of the escape trunk on top of the tightly dogged lower hatch that saved his life. He was bleeding slowly from a wound on the back of his head, which struck a bracket when the concussion of the explosion violently shook the hull of the submarine from stern to stern. Protected from the deadly release of radiation by the air tightness of the trunk, he had survived, but his ordeal was just beginning.

The westward bound US task force was steaming 25 miles ahead of *Morozov.* Its escorting destroyers and frigates were all actively pinging with their sonars as a means of detecting any nearby submarines. Due to the speed of the convoy and accompanying noise in the ocean from the many turning propellers, none of the escorting vessels were in a passive (listening) sonar mode. Thus, none of them detected the blast from the trailing submersible.

But way back in Hawaii, the U.S. Navy intelligence operated sosus system recorded a sharp underwater disturbance simultaneously from two of their detecting units to the west of Luzon. The officer observing the readout knew of the carrier task force in the area and determined the big blip on the recording sheet was probably attributable to their training activities. However, he dutifully reported the "disturbance" to his superior who informed him that his estimation of the disturbance was correct.

"They were scheduled to hold some depth charge exercises en route to the Gulf of Tonkin, and this is probably what caused the underwater explosion trace," he was told.

* * *

Morozov, although now severely damaged, continued on a course of 170 that soon took her out of the assigned operating area and headed her directly toward a cluster of islands northeast of the Philippine Island of Palawan. Broken cooling water pipes and small electrical fires in the reactor compartment had caused the reactor to malfunction, resulting in a gradual reduction of the submarine's speed. Now, after seven hours, the speed was down to 6 knots, and the reactor was about to reach a point where safety systems would automatically cause a complete shutdown. The boat was also slowly taking on seawater from ruptured circulating salt water piping near the reactor. When the propellers finally ceased to turn, *Morozov* continued to drift in the same direction it had been headed until it slowly and gently came to a complete halt, grounding softly upon a sand covered reef at a depth of 220 feet.

CHAPTER 7

ESCAPE

After spending many hours in an unconscious state, a severely concussed and groggy Alexei Plavinsky stirred in the forward escape trunk. Passing in and out of consciousness, he kept trying to open his eyes, not yet realizing that they were functioning, as the space where he lay was in darkness. Throughout this delirium he could hear the "urp, urp, urp" of distant radiation alarms, the significance of which took time for him to comprehend.

At some point Alexei sat up, put his hand to the throbbing lump on the back of his head which was now covered with coagulated blood and blurted, "What happened? Did we get torpedoed or depth charged?" And as the fog eventually lifted from his brain, a panic started to sink in which he instinctively tried to check by remembering his basic submarine training and other disciplines learned in athletics.

"A submarine is no place for panic," he was told. "Yelling, screaming and temper tantrums are never tolerated, regardless of the situation. One must think, and in order to think clearly, one must remain calm."

Submariners are also trained to find valves and switches while blindfolded in order to function in the dark when power is lost. Many of these switches and valves that are vital have uniquely configured handles, so they can be identified by feel. Most important are the emergency lights, of which there were two in the escape trunk. These lights draw electricity directly from the submarine's huge battery cells, which are used for propulsion when the nuclear plant is shut down. Plavinsky found the grooved switch and was relieved when both lights functioned and brilliantly illuminated the trunk space. Still sitting on the lower hatch, he could not figure out what happened. All he remembered was a slam of his head, and he had no idea as to how long he had been unconscious …and he could not even recall what he was doing in the trunk in the first place, and "What the hell were those alarms going off?"

Despite a swimming head and a slow-to-recover thought process, Plavinsky determined that he should try to stand up and pull himself together. He then slowly got to his feet and felt the dizziness gradually subside. Still trying to collect his thoughts to assess the situation, he instinctively opened the oxygen and compressed air valves to ventilate the trunk and clear his head. He also glimpsed the depth gauge, which read 65 meters, the same as before the catastrophe. His next urge was to open the hatch to the compartment below and find out what had happened there and to the boat. Despite a sharp pain that ripped down the back of his neck when he moved, he gingerly bent over to open the lower hatch, but first looked through the deadlight and glimpsed a sight that froze his senses…two very dead shipmates at the foot of the ladder, their eyes bulging from faces shaded a ghastly purple and mouths gaping wide as if frozen in a scream. He could hear the radiation alarms continue to blare with blue warning lights flashing in the dim glow of emergency lighting that came on automatically when the nuclear power plant and generators shut down. This vivid and grotesque scene removed all thoughts of opening the hatch to the deadly scenario below him.

Plavinsky sat very still in the cramped escape compartment for a good 15 minutes contemplating what he had just seen and despite the obvious possibility of his own death, forced himself to "think, think, think." Finally organizing his options, he mentally put them in order and then repeated them back to himself.

"First I will call the other compartments on the phone and find out what has happened. Then if no response, I have no option but try to escape to sea." With a shaking hand, he cranked the phone set mounted in the trunk. Aware that this phone circuit was self-powered, he knew that if there was no response from any compartment, that the entire crew was dead. He cranked and dialed each compartment twice…no response. He then turned on the MC system that could be used between the trunk, control and the compartment below. In a loud voice he spoke into the mounted speaker, "Control, this is the escape compartment." Still no answer.

As the dreadful realization that he was the only one aboard still alive sunk in, Plavinsky now knew that the only way he could survive would be to attempt an escape.

As a first step, he again checked the pressure and depth gauges in the trunk, making sure that the stop valve to each was fully open to sea pressure. The depth gauge read 58 meters (190 feet) which was the depth of the sea from the surface to the deck of *Morozov.* The pressure gauge confirmed the depth. After considering the depth and pressure, he concluded that his chances were 50/50 of reaching the surface without suffering an embolism or the bends. In submarine school he had made such an escape in a training tank, but that had been from 50 meters…58 was risky…but staying where he was and doing nothing meant a slow sure death.

Plavinsky continued to find a way of fighting off claustrophobic panic and somehow forced himself to think with logic. By carefully watching the depth and pressure gauges, he theorized that the boat must be grounded, as neither reading fluctuated even a fraction. He confirmed this by determining that the boat was not moving, as he could not feel any vibration or hear water noises from above. He thought about time of day, but as he did not own a watch and there was no clock in the trunk, he had no idea what time it was. It would make no difference in his plans to make the escape as soon as he was ready, but daytime would be preferred, as he could see upward as he rose from the submarine.

Next he inspected the equipment he would need. The large reel with 100 meters of line and attached buoy was in place and ready to be released once the upper hatch was opened. The escape device, (there were six in the trunk) was laid out and looked over. It was simply a kapok life vest fitted with special straps to keep it around a man's chest, preventing it from rising faster than a swimmer. A set of goggles was also provided with each vest. Alexei remembered the training he received in the use of the device when the instructor told him, "The most important thing to remember is to keep blowing out air from your lungs as you go up. For if you hold your breath, which is a human instinct underwater, you are dead! You will embolize."

He then examined the packaged life raft and noted that it was marked on the outside with instructions for use. Inside the package he found a small can of drinking water, of which he was in dire need, first-aid supplies, a fold-up paddle, inflation cylinder and some emergency flares. "I'll drink when I get to the top," he decided.

Like most submarines worldwide, *Morozov* was fitted with an emergency buoy that was countersunk in the superstructure deck above the forward torpedo/missile compartment. This large, steel buoy was also equipped with a reel that held 400 meters of cable. Once found, this buoy and cable, which leads downward to a bottomed submarine's forward escape trunk hatch, could be used by a submarine rescue ship to bring up surviving crewmembers. Plavinsky knew the use of this buoy was impossible, as the release mechanism was in the compartment below him. He was on his own and would have to make a "free ascent."

The 21-year-old Russian submarine sailor now sat back and made the final plan for his escape. "Everything must be done in the proper order and I must be ready to handle unforeseen problems," he said to himself. Then aloud he went over the escape procedure step by step, and then checked his plan with the "Escape Instructions" engraved on a steel plate mounted in the trunk, a plate he had polished many, many times in the past. His final thought was that he would cut loose the light, wooden, cylindrical buoy when he reached the surface and place it in the raft…just in case the raft didn't stay inflated; he'd have something to hang onto. He checked to make sure his knife was sheathed to his belt for this purpose.

Plavinsky donned the escape jacket, looped the straps under his crotch and attached them to the bottom rear of the life jacket. He then ducked up under the steel tube that protruded downward from the upper access hatch and turned the wheel to completely undo it. Seated firmly with sea pressure, this hatch could now be easily opened with a push once the pressure in the flooded escape trunk equaled the sea pressure outside.

"Here we go," he said with remarkable calmness as he slowly opened a valve to flood the escape trunk, and then another to pressurize the space. Having no idea where in the Pacific the submarine was, he was pleasantly surprised at the warmth of the water now rising above his ankles.

The escape procedure involves flooding the escape trunk from sea until the water reaches a level just above the hatch extension. The seawater is held there by increasing air pressure until it is equal to sea pressure. Once this is achieved, the undogged upper hatch will either spring open by itself or it can be pushed open by hand, and the escape tube is now open to the sea. No place for those with claustrophobia, the men in the trunk preparing to make the ascent stand shoulder to shoulder around the hatch extension with their heads just above water and pressing against the curved upper part of the trunk. Everything below their chins is underwater. They hold their noses and "pop" their ears to equalize with the pressure. Their lungs also compress with the pressure, and this compression is what allows them to make the ascent without breathing inward. As the escapee leaves the submarine and rises to the surface, the lungs expand as sea pressure decreases and this requires the swimmer to constantly blow out air as he rises toward the surface. The speed of the ascent is also important. An uncontrolled, rapid rise to the surface will cause the infamous divers' malady called "the bends," which can only be treated in a recompression chamber, without which the escapee probably would not survive. Even worse would occur to a diver who held his breath, not allowing the air from his expanding lungs to be expelled. This would result in pressurized air bursting into the bloodstream and to the brain, causing a usually fatal embolism. Personnel making an escape do so freely, that is, without any breathing apparatus, but they must have a taut line leading to the surface to hold onto as a means of controlling ascent speed. This is done by the vertically positioned escapee locking his feet loosely to the line and grasping it with both hands in front of the crotch. Once the rise to the surface of the sea begins, he keeps blowing out air and adjusting the speed of ascent by changing the grip on the line with his hands so as not to pass his own exhale bubbles.

Not too fast…not too slow…no panic…keep exhaling… never try to breathe in…

Plavinsky balanced the air and flood valves in a fashion that allowed the water to rise slowly as the pressure increased. After it reached his waist and the pressure increased by several atmospheres, he was able to remove one hand from his nose and equalize the pressure within and outside his body by breathing through his nose and swallowing every few seconds. Now with both hands free he let the water rise to his shoulders, then shut the flood valve and increased the air pressure until the trunk pressure gauge matched the outside (sea) pressure gauge. He then heard a welcome "thunk" as the upper hatch opened by itself. He pushed the ascent buoy up through the hatch, controlling the spin of the line reel with his hand as the buoy soared to the surface. Watching the reel closely, he waited until it stopped spinning and the line went slack, indicating the buoy had reached the surface. He then tied off the ascent line so he would have a taut, straight guideline to the surface. Lastly, he placed a ring tied to the buoyant, plastic life raft package around the upward leading ascent line and pushed the raft up through the hatch so it would rise up the line and be at hand when he arrived on the ocean surface.

Now ready for the final and most dangerous phase of the escape, Plavinsky donned the goggles, took a last deep breath of the steamy, compressed air from the trunk and ducked under the hatch tube while grasping the ascent line with one hand. The first thing he felt was a huge pull on the escape jacket to go up. He fought for control by grabbing the line with both hands while trying to lock the line under him with his feet. Once he was so aligned, he found it took all his strength to hold onto the line to prevent an uncontrollable rise. His chest ached and he had the sensation of being completely out of breath, but his experience in the training tank taught him that breath would surely come out as he went up the line.

"I've got to hold on, keep myself vertical, blow out hard and follow bubbles," he kept repeating to himself. Looking straight up as he rose, he could see the bright surface of the ocean above and at that moment he knew he was going to make it. The last few meters were the easiest, and he popped to the surface of the warm South China Sea on a bright April morning not far from the Calamian Island Group, just north of the Philippine Island of Palawan.

Once on the surface, Alexei inflated the raft, unfolded the paddle and then cut the buoy from the escape line, that sank slowly back to the ocean floor. He placed the buoy in the raft before sliding into the bright orange rig himself. Once inside, he quickly found the attached emergency fresh water can, popped the top and gulped greedily while squinting at the high, searing, tropical sun. Never having been in a warm climate, he was amazed at the high air temperature and the lack of wind resulting in a flat, calm sea. Now completely exhausted, he lay back in the raft, which felt like a softly undulating, luxurious mattress, the effect of which put him immediately to sleep.

It was nearly three in the afternoon when Alfredo Gabizon pulled in the last of his long fishing lines baited for tuna, marlin and many other species that inhabited the waters around the Philippine Island of Palawan. Satisfied with the day's catch, he was just ready to start the huge 150-horse outboard motor on the stern of his fishing craft and head for home when he spotted the bright orange raft a good five miles to the west of him. Curious what the strange colored object could be, the 45-year-old Filipino moved in for a closer look. Then he could make good speed in order to return ashore before darkness set in. As the loud boat neared the raft, Alexei was awakened by the roar of the outboard, and still wearing the ugly, black goggles, suddenly sat up, causing a badly startled Alfredo to veer away until sure of what he saw. Alexei waved at him and he slowed down and approached the raft until he was within ten feet. He stopped his boat dead in the water to study the man in the orange raft and decide if there was any danger or if this was some kind of trick. Unable to communicate at first, Plavinsky smiled at the fisherman, took off the goggles and paddled toward him. Alfredo now thought the safest thing to do would be to tow the raft and the large, Caucasian passenger behind him. Then he realized that with the raft in tow he wouldn't be able to make enough speed to reach port before nightfall. Now looking closer at Alexei, Alfredo noticed the wound on the head of the stranger and thought to himself, "He's probably an American flyer who bailed out of his plane coming from Vietnam," and his instincts told him there was nothing to fear and that he should take the man into his boat and bring him ashore and get a doctor.

Motioning with both arms to come aboard, a suddenly grinning Alfredo said words of greeting in his native tongue as Alexei came alongside, slipped on board, and with a sudden strong impulse to keep the items that saved his life and not wanting them to be found at sea brought the raft and buoy over the gunwale of the fishing boat. He deflated the raft as Alfredo once again roared the engine and headed for port at full speed.

* * *

It was now the 13th of April, and at the Soviet Pacific fleet headquarters in Vladivostok, a puzzled Captain First Rank Ivan Kursky scanned the morning fleet operational traffic expecting a follow-up report from *Morozov*. Speaking to his aide, he indicated that perhaps there could be a communications problem.

"Stepakov reported visual and sonar contact with the Amerikanski Flotilla two days ago, but we have yet to receive the follow-up as how many and what kind of ships and aircraft are involved. Our comrades in Vietnam are also interested, and will be after us very soon for information."

"They may have been detected and kept deep…unable to get up shallow enough to send the message," the aide responded.

"Perhaps, but I want you to get the submarine flotilla operations office in Petro on the secure phone. I will talk to Captain Semenov and find out if they have heard anything."

Not particularly fond of Captain Anatoli Semenov, or submariners in general, when Kursky contacted him on the phone, he offered a brisk *"dubroye utro"* then proceeded to coldly tell him there was a problem.

"Have you heard anything from *Morozov* since the check report 48 hours ago?"

"Nyet comrade, but we should hear something shortly. They may be in a tactical situation that has prevented them from sending a follow-up message."

"The Admiral (Pacific fleet commander – Admiral Gusev) will want answers to this sometime today. I want you to send a top priority message to *Morozov* telling them we need immediate information with follow-ups every eight hours."

Later that morning, Kursky explained the situation to Admiral Gusev, who called him to his office after seeing the message from the flotilla to *Morozov.*

"If we don't hear something back from them by midnight tonight, we will have to take further action. If they then miss their 72-hour check report tomorrow we will have to notify Moscow, Leningrad and get some additional units into that area to look for *Morozov* and to get more data on the Amerikanski flotilla…keep me informed on this one."

"Slushayus, comrade Admiral."

* * *

In Pearl Harbor, it was still the 12th of April, being to the east of the International Dateline, and Captain Art Mobley was also curious about the whereabouts of the same Soviet submarine and asked Lieutenant Commander Fusina to make some phone calls.

"Stubby, I want you to call Yoko, Pacfleet ops and the fleet intelligence office to see if anyone has word of contact with CHARLIE FOUR."

After nearly an hour on the phone, Fusina reported to Mobley that nobody had re-detected CHARLIE FOUR.

"Maybe they left the area, or riding under a merchie… (running submerged under a merchant ship, matching speed and course and thus masking their detection), but there IS one thing I think we ought to check on," Fusina offered.

"What's that, Stubby?"

"Fleet Intelligence recorded a sharp underwater explosion two days ago from the *Sosus* system west of Luzon, that they attributed to our task force which was en route from Subic to the *Yankee Station.* They say one of the escorting tin cans had permission to drop a few live depth charges while en route as some sort of test, but they never verified if any charges were actually dropped. I think we should find out."

"You're damn right we should find out, but the way to do it is for PacFleet to find out from 7th Fleet, since we are not in their chain of command. Let me call Ruby (Captain Rubin Martinez, Pacific Fleet intelligence officer) and see what he can find out for us."

A few hours after the conversation with Martinez a message went out to the 7th Fleet Commander.

SECRET
P – 122135Z APR 72
FM: CINCPACFLT
TO: COMSEVENTH FLEET

1. REQ INFO ANY DEPTH CHARGES OR OTHER ORDNANCE DROPPED BY ANY UNIT TF 72 DURING RECENT TRANSIT SUBIC TO OP AREA. SEND DATE, TIME AND POSITION OF ALL LIVE DROPS TO THIS COMMAND ASAP.

Upon receipt of the message, Vice Admiral Marc Langlois, USN, commander of the 7th Fleet, sent a nearly duplicate message to the commander of task force 72. The response was immediate and to the point!

NEGATIVE DEPTH CHARGES OR ANY EXPLOSIVES DROPPED BY ANY TF 72 UNIT DURING TRANSIT SUBIC TO OP AREA…

When he read this message, Martinez at Fleet Headquarters called Mobley at the nearby SUBPAC compound.

"Art, I think we're onto something here, and the admiral wants a meeting in an hour in his office with you and I and

Admiral Carpenter (Rear Admiral Calvin "Cal" Carpenter, Commander Submarine Force Pacific").

"Sounds good Ruby, we'll be there, and if possible, I think we need more detailed analysis of the *Sosus* explosion report…can you have someone from the *Sosus* group attend?"

"That's a good idea Art, but I'll have to let the Admiral decide if he wants them there. This whole thing may turn out to be nothing…we'll just have to wait and see."

Admiral Dexter Collins rose from behind his desk to greet the two submarine officers, whom he knew well. He then introduced them to a civilian intelligence specialist, a Mister Edward O'Brien. A neatly attired Filipino steward's mate offered coffee to all, and after each declined, the Admiral said, "Thank you, Sorocco," and the steward left the office.

Admiral Collins got right to the point. "Gentlemen, Ruby here tells me there's a possibility an underwater explosion detected west of Luzon by *Sosus* may have something to do with a Soviet submarine that was tracked into the vicinity, and then lost. I want to do whatever is necessary to find out the source of the underwater explosion and to prove or disprove any connection to the Russian nuke. Maybe we should send one of our submarines into the area to see what they can sniff out. We could also try some flyovers and perhaps send a surface ship or two into the area to search." He then went to a large chart of the area in question brought to the meeting by Mr. O'Brien. Pointing to the estimated position of the explosion, Admiral Collins asked O'Brien to explain his determination of the spot of the blast.

"Admiral, the explosion was actually picked up at exactly the same time by two separate detection units on the ocean floor. The cross bearings of the large disturbance combined with the estimated range of it from each listening unit gives us an excellent estimate of the position of the blast that we feel is accurate within three nautical miles." Then holding up two large sheets of graph paper marked TOP SECRET, O'Brien pointed out the huge blips on each recording sheet and explained further, "We apologize and feel badly about not bringing this immediately to your attention, but we thought the disturbance was from the task force…"

"That's under the dam, O'Brien, and in this case, no harm has been done, but in the future, all disturbances such as this one will be reported immediately to fleet headquarters. It's nice for ONI (Office of Naval Intelligence, Washington, D.C.) to hear about this, but we must also be cut in. Is that clear?

"Yes, sir, Admiral."

"Now, Cal, what do you think of all this?"

"Well, Admiral, I certainly concur with your assessment of the situation, but I think we should use caution in searching the area with surface ships and aircraft because if CHARLIE FOUR did indeed have some sort of accident, the Soviets will start a search and rescue operation within a few days if CHARLIE FOUR fails to send in check reports. If they see us milling around a certain spot in the South China Sea, they'll know real fast we're looking for the same thing, and that maybe we know something that they don't."

Admiral Collins lit his pipe then turned to his intelligence officer and asked, "What do you think Ruby?"

"Admiral, I concur with Admiral Carpenter. If the Russians find us searching a specific area, they will know we probably have better data than they have, and in fact we'd actually be helping them find CHARLIE FOUR. They may even suspect one of our boats had a collision with CHARLIE FOUR while playing cat and mouse. If they operate their submarines similarly to us, and we believe they do, then they will have to search a huge ocean area, as they allow the boat a big, free space to operate in and rarely know the exact position of the submarine at a given time. It may also be unwise to send one of our submarines in there right now, for if CHARLIE FOUR did in fact have some sort of disaster, the Ruskis will have their own boats in there pronto looking for something. I think we should wait and see what happens over the next few days and not show our hand at this time."

Admiral Collins nodded slowly in apparent agreement with Martinez's assessment and then spoke to Mobley.

"Art, do you think the Soviets also heard the explosion, and do you agree with Ruby that they probably wouldn't have an exact position on CHARLIE FOUR?"

"There's no way of knowing for sure whether or not they detected the disturbance, Admiral. We don't believe they have anything out there like our *Sosus*, but there is always a chance one of their submarine units picked it up, but we have no evidence of any other submarines in the area except CHARLIE FOUR. In response to your other question, sir, what Ruby said about exact positions is correct. However, if one of their boats had a casualty and was able to get off a message they would certainly send their position. So if CHARLIE FOUR did indeed have a casualty and reported it, the Soviets would already be at the scene. So either the blast is not related to CHARLIE FOUR, or CHARLIE FOUR is on the bottom somewhere. We'll just have to be patient and vigilant in anticipation of the ruskis showing their hand in the next few days."

Admiral Collins then spoke to Admiral Carpenter, "What about sending one of our boats in there, Cal? Could they snoop around and still remain undetected?"

"I think we could get away with it, and we should do it right now, for if a large Soviet search force shows up in a few days, we could then pull the boat out of there to prevent detection."

The Commander in Chief of the Pacific Fleet glanced at his watch, an indication the meeting was about to end. "Gentlemen, I want to emphasize that if in fact CHARLIE FOUR and the explosion are one and the same, we have a very sensitive situation on our hands. Everyone who has been involved so far in this situation must be sworn to secrecy. I will call the CNO (Chief of Naval Operations), and let him decide who should be informed about this, and who shouldn't. You Cal, will have to inform FLOT 7 in Yoko and tell him also that mum's the word. I also agree that we could get away with putting one of our boats in there right now, but the crew must not know what they are looking for. Limit the mission knowledge to the captain and one or two other necessary people. When I talk with CNO I'll explain the situation and our plan to scout the area with one of our nuclear boats. I'm confident he'll agree to the decision, but I'll let you know right away if he feels otherwise."

Glancing at Carpenter and then Mobley, the Admiral asked, "How soon could they have a unit in the area?"

Mobley had already anticipated this one, and with a nod from his boss responded. "Admiral, the *Sea Bass* is in Subic right now and is RFS (ready for sea). She's just waiting for the *Mullet* to arrive next week and then she's scheduled to return to Pearl. We can get her underway for this operation within hours, and she's only six hours from the blast point."

Admiral Collins wrapped things up. "Unless CNO disapproves, which I highly doubt, *Sea Bass* it is, and I want to be kept abreast of any new development. Art and Ruby will stay in constant touch on this one, but minimize anything in writing, such as message traffic that pertains to this situation. Use the secure phone whenever possible. Thank you, gentlemen."

While leaving the fleet headquarters, Admiral Carpenter commended Mobley. "You did a good job in there Art, and I'm glad it's us that put Fleet onto this situation rather than vice-versa."

"Stubby deserves the credit on this one Admiral, he's the one who put two and two together with the *Sosus* report."

Within a half hour, Mobley received a phone call from Captain Martinez at Fleet Headquarters. "It's a go on *Sea Bass* Art. Once you get organized, let us know verbally what their ETA (estimated time of arrival) on station will be."

Mobley notified his Admiral that the operation was a go, and then placed a call to Captain Frank Kelly, Commander Submarine Flotilla Seven, in Yokosuka, Japan, who is the direct commander under which *Sea Bass* operates while in the western Pacific. Explaining the situation to Kelly, Mobley reiterated the need for minimizing the "need to know" aspect of the operation and to tell Mac (Cdr Warren MacDonald, USN, CO, USS *Sea Bass*) that "This operation should only delay their return to Pearl for a few days, but we need to know something ASAP. Have him search with active and passive sonar out to a circular distance of 25 miles from the position I just gave you. Tell them to use the special wreck charts, that show exact locations of known steel-hulled vessels sunk on the bottom of the ocean, to determine if they detect anything new."

* * *

Alex Plavinski thought he had died and gone to heaven. Even the odor of the fresh fish in the boat seemed pleasant, and everything he observed around him was like something he had once seen in a movie when he was a boy. As the boat approached land, he was treated to the sight of his first palm and coconut trees, a sparkling white beach and the spectacular scene behind the boat where a very red sun slowly set into an almost unreal glass-like sea. The fishing boat was also like something he had never seen before. It looked like some sort of ancient native sailing craft, but it had a huge, modern outboard motor on the stern that looked like it didn't belong there.

Despite the roar of the engine, they finally got to communicate, in rough English. After yelling their first names, Alfredo had asked Alexei how he ended up in the raft.

"Where you come from…you come from ship or airplane?"

As his mind and body had been completely involved in the primary goal of escaping alive from the submarine, Alfredo had given little thought to what he would say if rescued. Should he tell the truth or fabricate a story and try to find a new life somewhere? He knew there was no way he could help his shipmates now entombed in *Morozov*, so as he tried to unscramble his brain to present a logical explanation of how he ended up in the life raft, he decided first to find out where he was, what Alfredo's nationality was and where he was taking him. If his country's ally, the North Vietnamese found him, he would have to tell the truth, but what if the South Vietnamese or Americans picked him up…then what would he say? His own country could not blame him for not telling the Americans that he escaped from a Soviet submarine, and that his rescuer knew about where it was located, as it would give them the opportunity to salvage it. As the crew of *Morozov* had been told nothing about their mission except that they were headed south to operate off the coast of Vietnam and to conduct surveillance of American naval units in the area, he had no idea where he was or who the small, dark-skinned man was who rescued him. Pretending he couldn't understand what Alfredo was asking, he asked some questions of his own.

"Where we go, Alfredo?"

"Busuanga Island," he replied while gesturing ahead toward the eastern horizon with his finger. "We will be there soon."

"What nation?" Alexei asked.

"The Philippines."

Alexei knew some geography and remembered that the Philippines were friendly with the Americans, who had military bases there. Realizing he had yet to regain full mental sharpness since his ordeal, he decided to work out a story about his origin later, and right now tell Alfredo a phony nationality, but one that spoke with a similar tongue, and thus cover his Russian accent.

"I am Polski…from Poland," he blurted.

They entered a small bay just before darkness, and Alfredo told Alexei they were almost home as he pointed to distant lights flickering from a modest house above the beach with a small dock nearby.

"I will take you to house where you can rest while I take fish to town. My daughter Maria will feed you while I'm gone. If doctor in town I will bring him back with me."

Not wanting to bring attention to himself until he could work out a good story, Alexei asked Alfredo not to mention him in town.

"Thank you, but I am better now and don't need a doctor. Also, I ask you please, at least tonight, not to tell anyone you found me, I will explain fully tomorrow."

After making the boat fast to the dock, a shaky Alexei held on Alfredo's shoulder as they made their way a short distance up a narrow path to a house with a grass roof, a wide veranda and fishnets sprawled everywhere. Sounds of strange, but pleasant music wafted from the house as Alfredo called his daughter.

"Maria, come see what I caught today!"

As they slowly went up the wide stairway to the veranda, 19-year-old Maria Gabizon strode out the open front door and gasped as she saw her father helping the big, muscular Alexei up the stairs.

"Magandang gabi po," (good evening) she stammered in her native (Tagalog) tongue.

"Kumusta po sila?" (how are you?) Alfredo replied, then in his rough English, "Use English…Maria, this is Alexei. I found him way offshore, adrift in a life raft."

They both stared at each other and exchanged smiling "hello's" as they entered a large, airy living room as Alfredo motioned for Alexei to sit on a cushioned bamboo couch and then spoke to his daughter in Tagalog.

"I am going to take the fish to Coron (town on Busuanga), and I believe this young man could use a bandage, a beer and some food. I will return in about two hours and will eat in town. My instincts tell me we can trust this man." Then he said to Alexei, "I will say nothing until we talk tomorrow. Please be comfortable here and get a good night's rest."

Alexei tried not to stare, but he had never before seen such a beautiful woman. Well over five feet and taller than her father, she had raven black hair, full red lips and dark flashing eyes. Her skin was a light tan, and she had a magnificent figure. In plain sailor's talk, "she was well put together from stem to stern."

"What happened to you, Alexei?" she asked while looking at the gash on the back of his head. But before he could answer she told him softly, "I will get some iodine and bandage for that, but first you will have a *SanMiguel* (beer)." And as is the custom in the Philippines when hosting guests from far away, Maria treated him like royalty. "You will be our special guest tonight Alexei."

Now fully relaxed after two bottles of beer and a delicious meal that Maria called *"chicken adobo,"* Alexei asked her all about herself, and was relieved when she told him she was not married, nor did she have a boyfriend.

"And what about you, Alexei? Where are you from? How did you end up in the life raft? Do you have a wife? What about a girlfriend? Where is your family? How did you learn to speak in English so well?"

Alexei smiled and replied.

"I am from Poland…I am single…I have no girlfriend… my parents are dead and I have no family whatsoever…I am alone in this world. I learned English from step-parents who immigrated to Poland from Britain."

Ignoring for the moment Alexei's obvious reluctance to talk about how he ended up in the raft, Maria went to a bookcase across the room and pulled out an Atlas of the World. Thumbing through the book until she found the large red map of Poland, she brought the book to Alexei, and asked about his town.

"Show me where you from."

Alexei picked up the book and pointed to Warsaw.

"Oh Warsaw…the capital," she nodded.

"Yes, a big city, but please show me a map of the Philippines so I can see where we are now."

Maria retrieved another book that contained a large, foldout detailed map of the Philippine Islands. Spreading it out on the table, she pointed out Busuanga Island to the northeast of Palawan. She then put her finger on the big island of Mindanao.

"We live most of the year down here in Zamboanga," she explained. "Papa comes up here to Busuanga twice a year just to fish. In Zamboanga he runs an automobile repair garage."

"What do you do there, and is your mother in Zamboanga?"

"I do commercial art work, and I also create paintings of my own," she said while gesturing to several watercolors just behind them on the wall…and my mother died when I was a baby. I don't remember her. That's a picture of her next to the watercolors."

"They are beautiful, and so is she. You are very talented, and I see where you got your beauty."

Alexei thumbed through the atlas and found the map of the South Pacific Ocean. Finding Busuanga and Palawan, he figured that Alfredo took him no more than 30 miles in the boat to shore, and he couldn't have drifted very far in the raft before he was picked up. He was puzzled as to what the *Morozov* was doing in the remote area of these islands, but as a lowly seaman who labored in the torpedo and missile spaces, he had no knowledge of anything of an operational or navigational nature. "Only Alfredo and I know the approximate location of the *Morozov*," he thought as he made a mental picture of the blue sea just west of Busuanga Island. The map also gave him an idea about the story we would fabricate and how he ended up in the raft. But first he would ask Maria some questions about politics, and as it turned out, the gist of the conversation pleased him greatly.

Realizing that Poland was a communist country, Maria explained that she and her father did not support communism, but they were not exactly delighted with their own government either. "My mother was of Australian blood and her mother, my grandmother, still lives there. That's how *I* learned English. My Filipino grandfather fought in the mountains of Mindanao as a guerrilla against the Japanese in World War II. My Australian grandfather fought with the Americans in the war, and we are pro-American, but we do not necessarily agree with the war in Vietnam. What about you Alexei, are you a strong communista?"

"No, I'm not. I'm non-politico in any way," he answered as he continued to piece together the life raft story.

She wanted to know more: "What about religion? Are you a churchman?" Alexei thought a few moments then, with a shrug of his shoulders answered nonchalantly:

"I'm probably part Jewish, but I've never been in a synagogue – so I guess you could say that I'm not a churchman. What about you?"

"I am a Catholic, but Papa and I rarely go to church. I'm a believer, but I just don't go for all the ceremonial stuff. How one lives and behaves is more important than going to church...but you should remember Alexei, that here in the Islands there are those who hate Christians and Jews, so if you are going to be here for awhile, you should keep quiet on the subject and in any case don't tell someone you are a Jew. It's not fair, but as you probably know, there are many anti-Jews all over the world. I am not one of them."

Nearly having a slip of the tongue and blurting out...*back in Rostov*...Alexei caught himself, cleared his throat and responded..."Back in *Warsaw* I saw just what you're talking about, so here in the Philippines I will be non-politico and non-religion as I don't know or care that much about either subject."

Putting on a serious expression, and fully convinced he should not tell these people he was from a sunken Soviet submarine, Alexei decided to tell Maria a story now, rather than wait until morning. He told her he was a sailor on a Polish freighter that was en route from Hong Kong to New Guinea, and that while the ship was in Hong Kong, he had decided to defect to the west but the captain found out about his plans and had him locked up until the ship left port.

"After dark on the first night out of Hong Kong, I slipped undetected over the side with the life raft. They wouldn't have found I was missing until the next morning, and hopefully, they think I am dead. They won't discover the raft missing either, because I had it stashed away for several weeks."

"What will you do now?" she asked.

"I must lay low for awhile in case my government starts looking for me and asks your country and others if I ended up on their shores."

"Why don't you ask for political asylum?" she suggested.

"Maybe we can talk about that tomorrow, but right now, despite your delightful company, my eyes are trying to shut."

Despite his protestations that he should sleep on the couch, Maria insisted he use the large bedroom, and after they said good night to one another, Alexei laid back and had some final thoughts buzzing through his head before drifting into a long, deserved sleep. He found himself quite smitten with Maria, and thought back to when she applied the bandage to the back of his head and how the fragrance of her perfume and the flowers in her hair had him wondering if what was happening was real or some kind of delusion. How could he go from what he just experienced at the bottom of the sea…to this? But the powerful, mesmerizing effect of this most interesting woman he had known for less than two hours was further cementing his decision to reveal to no one that he was in fact a Soviet submarine sailor.

CHAPTER 8

WHERE IS CHARLIE FOUR?

Within four hours of being notified of their newly assigned mission, the USS *Sea Bass* was backed slowly from her berth at the U.S. Navy Base, Subic Bay, Republic of the Philippines, by a squat U.S. Navy harbor tug. The bullet-shaped American nuclear submarine was finishing up a six-month deployment to the western Pacific from her homeport in Pearl Harbor. During the deployment, *Sea Bass* had worked tracking Soviet and Chinese submarines in the South China Sea and the shallow East China Sea. She had also done some surveillance off North Korea and the Soviet Kamchatka Peninsula. From a mission standpoint, the deployment had been entirely successful, and in addition to Subic Bay, the crew had enjoyed port calls in Hong Kong, Yokosuka, Japan and Pusan, South Korea.

After hearing of their latest orders, the boat's executive officer had ordered stores and fresh water to be topped off, for they did not anticipate returning to port after the mission was completed. They would go directly from the search area back to Pearl Harbor. At quarters that morning he told the crew that they had to conduct a brief survey on the way home, but that it "probably wouldn't delay their scheduled arrival time back in Pearl."

Prior to leaving Subic Bay, the captain met in his small cabin with the executive officer, the sonar officer and the boat's leading sonar man, Chief petty officer Ray Shorey. The Captain explained what they were about to do and warned them about the security aspect.

"This is a highly classified mission, and no one on board besides the four of us are to be told what I'm about to tell you. There is a possibility that the Russians have lost a nuclear boat not too far from here, and we are being ordered to carefully search an area just to the west of Subic where the spooks believe the boat may be. This is hush-hush because if we locate the boat, it is imperative that neither the Russians, nor anyone else, find out we have done so. The exact position will be classified Cosmic Top Secret. When we get there this afternoon, I want only Chief Shorey or one of us to be in the sonar room with the chart the exec is about to show you."

Lieutenant Commander Bernard "Bernie" Hall, who was both Executive Officer and navigator, laid out a special chart of the South China Sea marked Top Secret.

"Gentlemen, this is a *WRECK* CHART; that is, a chart that shows magnetic anomalies on the ocean floor." Pointing to such a spot that was marked with an "X" and a corresponding number, Hall explained further. "These are sunken steel-hulled ships, or in some cases aircraft, most of which were put on the bottom during World War II. There are Japanese, American, British and Australian ships down there and many others that were never identified as to who they belonged to and when they went down. What we must do is make a complete active sonar search of the area I have circled here around the data position out to a radial distance of 25 miles. You will notice that there are five known wrecks within this area which we should be able to pick up and plot accordingly. What we're looking for is a trace that isn't on this chart…and even if we find one it may not be what we're looking for, it could be yet another sunken vessel that was not detected by the survey ships that made this chart.

But if we find a stranger, we will make an immediate, coded message report."

After sailing westward from Subic Bay into deep water, *Sea Bass* submerged and proceeded at full speed at a depth of 300 feet straight to the position of the suspected detonation. After arriving there, the boat slowed and used active (pinging) sonar to try and pick up something stationary on the bottom. This went on for nearly 24 hours without success, although they did find the previously charted wrecks in the exact positions they were plotted on the special chart.

"At least we know our sonar is working okay and if there's anything else down there we'll pick it up," predicted Chief Shorey to the sonar officer. Having surveyed all the way out to 25 miles with negative results, the captain ordered the boat up to periscope depth to raise the "whip" antenna and send the "negative" message. After this was sent, the *Sea Bass* remained at the shallow depth in order to receive incoming messages. There were three such messages on the "sked", the first of which had an IMMEDIATE precedence and was short and to the point!

IMMEDIATE – SECRET
160912Z APR 72
FM COMSUBFLOT SEVEN
TO USS SEA BASS

1. DEPART AREA IMMEDIATELY AT BEST SPEED.
2. COMMENCE TRANSIT AS PER PREV. SKED.

* * *

In Vladivostok, captain Kursky's phone rang at three in the morning, alerting him to get to headquarters right away and to call Captain Semenov in Petro on the secure phone.

Having thrown down a few too many vodkas the previous evening, Kursky rubbed his aching head, and cursed loudly while looking for where he left his shoes. "I'll bet this is about *Morozov*," he said to himself as he rushed to the car that was waiting to take him to the headquarters. Once he got on the phone, his fears were confirmed. An obviously distressed Semenov told him they had lost contact with *Morozov*.

"They are many hours overdue with their check report, and have not responded to any of the messages we have sent out over the past 36 hours. I recommend we get a search underway."

A clearly irritated Kursky told Semenov to keep trying to send contact messages to *Morozov* and that he would notify his Admiral and Moscow of the situation.

"Remain at your headquarters. We will contact you shortly with a plan of action," he told him before hanging up the phone.

After a conference with his boss, Admiral Gusev, the Russian Pacific Fleet Commander, made several calls to the Soviet Naval High Commands in Moscow and Leningrad and a plan was formulated to search for *Morozov*. Gusev also decided that the search should be coordinated from his headquarters in Vladivostok, and ordered Rear Admiral Gomulka (Submarine Flotilla Commander in Petro) and Captain Semenov to immediately fly there. "We will work on this together from here. It will simplify the communications by coordinating everything from one headquarters," Gusev ordered. As a first step, he ordered the Soviet nuclear attack submarine *Komsomol* to reverse course and proceed at high speed to the last known position of *Morozov*. *Komsomol* had left the South China Sea area three days previous, when *Morozov* arrived and she was now just east of the Ryukyu Island chain, south of Japan, heading back to Petropavlovsk after being at sea for three months. He then ordered two TU 95 turboprop long range naval reconnaissance aircraft from the Kamchatka military aerodrome to depart immediately for the wide search area to the south.

Gusev also contacted the Soviet survey ship *Lebedev,* which was operating from a position just west of the Island of Guam, and ordered her to proceed immediately to the search area. Equipped with advanced underwater survey equipment, *Lebedev* had been assigned to the area off Guam to keep tabs on the American fleet ballistic missile submarines that transited to and from their Island base. Gusev directed Kursky to find another spy ship to take *Lebedev's* place off Guam, and to "Get her there at best speed."

Back in Moscow, Fleet Admiral Matelov had the grim task of calling his old friend in Leningrad, Petr Stepakov, and telling him what he knew of the fate of *Morozov* and his son.

"This is not an easy call to make, Nikalaich, but I must inform you that *Morovoz* is missing somewhere in the South China Sea. We haven't heard from her in three days, and we've started an all-out search effort. There is still hope, comrade, but I wanted to tell you where we stand."

There was a short silence on the line as the elder Stepakov gathered his composure. "I appreciate you calling me, comrade," he stammered, "and I must admit to having bad luck feeling about *Morozov* in the back of my mind. They're just building these boats too fast these days, and Petrovich and I talked about this. Can you have someone on your staff keep me informed?"

"I will do better than that Nikalaich. We have saved a seat for you on the senior officer's shuttle plane from Leningrad to Moscow at two this afternoon. You can stay at my quarters until the situation is resolved or for as long as you want. My car will pick you up at the aerodrome when you land."

"I thank you, comrade. That plan is sure better than wandering around here all day and night driving myself crazy wondering what's going on and waiting for the next phone call...and don't worry about security. I will tell no one what has happened."

* * *

The first sign for the U.S. Navy that lent credence to the theory that Russians had a missing submarine in the South China Sea was when the intelligence system reported that the northbound submarine contact, designated as CHARLIE TWO, had reversed course, and was "making in excess of 25 knots heading southward." The second sign was when the U.S. Air Force radar detected "two Soviet aircraft proceeding south from the Kamchatka Peninsula at an altitude of 26,000 feet". U.S. jet fighters were scrambled from their base in Alaska, homed in on the big turboprops, shadowed and radioed in their course, speed and altitude. The big, silver planes with bright red stars on their wings and tails were positively identified as Russian "BEARS", long range naval recon aircraft. After initial contact and tracking by the air force, U.S. forces in Japan and navy fighters from the 7th fleet took over the surveillance of the BEARs, which included close-in photography for the spooks to study.

At fleet headquarters at the Makalapa Gate in Pearl Harbor, the word was sent out to all commands in southeast Asia to *"Keep track of Soviet search efforts by careful reconnaissance, but not to interfere in any way with what they're doing."*

Captain Ruby Martinez was compiling all reports coming in from the far east and kept his Admiral informed of any new developments, a few of which just appeared on the message board.

"Admiral, we just received a message from Submarine Squadron Eleven in Guam…the Ruski snoop ship has just left the area at high speed toward the west. Also sir, 7th fleet reports the two BEARS are now circling at low altitude over a wide area, probably for a visual search for CHARLIE FOUR and to try and raise the boat on low power radio frequencies in case she's on the surface with some kind of casualty that wiped out their ability to communicate at long range."

"Everything seems to fit in except the fact that *Sea Bass* came up with a zero…by the way, have they departed the area yet?" the Admiral queried.

"Yes sir, they're already through the straights en route to Pearl."

After three days, the Russians ceased all aircraft flights over the South China Sea, but the *Lebedev* and the submarine *Komosmol* continued a random, disorganized crisscrossing of a broad ocean area.

In Vladivostok, Captain Kursky was conducting a briefing for both Admirals, Captain Semenov and 12 other high-ranking staff officers. Standing before a large wall chart of the South China Sea, where he had plotted the last known position of *Morozov*, the boundary lines of her assigned operation area and the track of the U.S. Navy forces that *Morozov* had been trailing, Kursky announced he had come to a conclusion:

"Whatever happened to *Morozov* must have occurred to the west of her position when she reported the Amerikanski Flotilla, as *Morozov* would have followed them toward

Vietnam from astern. We know the exact track of the Amerikanskis, and where they are now. Therefore, we should search close to the track I have plotted rather than the random search pattern our two units are presently conducting."

"How deep is the ocean along that track?" Admiral Gusev asked.

"Over six thousand meters, comrade Admiral."

"And how many sunken ships lie at the bottom near the search area?"

"There must be over a hundred, comrade Admiral."

"And how can our forces determine if any of these wrecks is *Morozov*?"

"It will be most difficult, comrade Admiral. They will have to plot every contact they detect and see if it matches the known wrecks that are on the special charts. Those contacts that are uncharted will have to be carefully plotted, and then investigated one by one."

"And how will we investigate them Comrade Captain?"

"Since we as yet do not have a bathyscape that can go that deep, we would have to lower special cameras to take pictures of the wrecks. *Lebedev* has two such cameras on board, and she is also equipped with a submersible radiation detector that can pick up emissions from a crushed reactor or damaged nuclear weapons from the ocean floor. We used such a detector with good results just last October to locate the nuclear attack submarine *Skoru*, which had an explosion and went down in the Norwegian sea."

Admiral Gusev then rose from his chair and turned to face the other officers in the briefing room.

"Comrades it must be understood that we have looked into every possibility that the Amerikanskis had something to do with *Morozov's* disappearance, but reliable intelligence sources tell us that they had nothing to do with it. Although both our navies chase each other around, never has either used live weapons on one another. Also, if we considered an accidental collision, where one of their destroyers or carriers, or even one of their submarines, caused the destruction of *Morozov*, we would have known from an increase in the Amerikanski's message traffic, damage to ships and other signs. They are not as good at keeping secrets as we are!"

The Admiral did let on something that among those in room, only he and Rear Admiral Gomulka were aware of: That the Soviets were able to break the teletype codes of certain U.S. Navy operational messages due to an intelligence leak from within the U.S. Navy itself…

Submarine flotilla commander, Admiral Gomulka, spoke next. "Comrades, it is most important for us to find out where *Morozov* is located. As most of you know, she has newly designed missiles and torpedoes on board, as well as highly classified communications and detection equipment brought on board by *Riga One.* We must make absolutely sure none of this could fall into the Amerikanski's hands. Therefore, although it's a tragedy if *Morozov* is on the bottom, it would be far better if she is sunk in 4,000 meters versus being on the bottom in shallow, salvageable waters where our enemies may find her before we do. Admiral, I recommend we send more vessels for an all-out search effort."

"Thank you, comrade Gomulka, and I fully agree with your assessment. Therefore, I want *Lebedev* to begin her survey along the track recommended by comrade Kursky, and I also believe we need to deploy a cruiser, an oiler and a re-supply ship as soon as possible. Now I ask Admiral Gomulka…how long will *Komsomol* be able to stay with the search?"

"Comrade admiral, she can remain in the area for another week, but we are ready to sail another boat to the search area tomorrow morning to relieve *Komsomol*, which has been at sea now for about 90 days."

Admiral Gusev finished the briefing with another order to Kursky.

"Comrade Captain, I want you to get a cruiser, an oiler and a re-supply ship ready to deploy to the search area within 24 hours. If by then we have not detected *Morozov* we will sail them, and place the Captain of the cruiser in on-the-scene operational control, but the overall command of the search operation will remain here in Vlad…that is all comrades, but I ask Admiral Gomulka, Captain Kursky and Captain Semenov to remain for further discussions."

While the meeting adjourned and officers left the briefing room, Kursky called over a subordinate and told him to "start drafting the operational order immediately." Gusev picked up the phone and called the Soviet Pacific Fleet Political Officer, Rear Admiral Vladmir Ivanovich Panov, who was in the same building, and told him to "come right away to the briefing room for a conference."

Panov arrived within five minutes and Gusev greeted him, "Ah, comrade Ivanovich, I know you are busy, but we have a difficult situation here, which may, or may not, involve your expertise. We have a missing nuclear submarine, the *Morozov*, and considering there were some problems of a political nature on board which required a change of command just before we sailed her, I want your office and the KGB to investigate if there could be any connection, regardless of how remote, between those problems and the boat's disappearance."

With the search for *Morozov* now well under way and the political arm of the Pacific Fleet and the KGB now involved,

Admiral Gusev knew he had done all he could up to the present, and now felt he should make a follow-up phone call to the Commander in Chief of the Soviet Navy, Fleet Admiral Viktor Matevlov, on the secure telephone line to Moscow. It was now three in the afternoon in Vladivostok, and as it was eight in the morning in Moscow, it would be a convenient time to call. Classifying the call as "urgent," Gusev had to wait only a short time before his phone rang back.

Quite used to the eleven time zones that span the Soviet Union, Matevlov didn't have to glance at the "Siberia Time" clock to know it was about 1500 hours in Vladivostok. Anticipating the purpose of Gusev's call, it was with a feeling of dread and foreboding that he greeted Gusev with a "Good afternoon, comrade, and what is happening in your part of the world? Is there good or bad news today?"

"I'm afraid it is bad sir. We still have not heard from *Morozov*, and we must now assume the worst. Also sir, our intelligence system tells us we can rule out the possibility that *Morozov* is missing due to a collision with any Amerikanski navy units." Then after explaining what was being done in organizing the search and investigating the cause of the tragedy, Gusev told Matevlov.

"I know that you and the senior Stepakov are close friends and go way back to the Great Patriotic War, and although all hope is not completely lost, please convey my sincere sympathies to the Admiral and tell him we are doing all we can."

"Thank you, comrade, and I will also inform the chairman, the minister of defense and Gurenko (KGB head) of the situation. Keep me informed of the progress of the search, and particularly if they find any flotsam. Also keep me informed of the actions of the Amerikanskis while all this is taking place, and are you convinced they had nothing to do with this?"

"I fully agree with the intelligence report. We had no knowledge of any of their subs in the area, and as you know sir, with what we glean from their communications systems, they would have let on something by now had there been an accident. But speaking of the Amerikanskis, and just to make sure, I would like to request that you have the code people closely analyze all the traffic they intercepted from the southeast Asia area from three days before *Morozov* was last heard from up until now. Maybe the Yankees know more than we think they do!"

"It will be done, comrade. You will remain in overall charge of this search mission. I will see to it that any and all information from this end that has anything to do with this will be sent to your fleet headquarters. Keep me informed with daily situation reports, but send me immediate notification if anything new or unusual occurs. Your reports will go only to me, and I will decide what gets disseminated here in Moscow. In that regard, I realize that the KGB will be doing their own thing, and that their reps in your office will be talking to their counterparts in Moscow…but that is the way it always is, and they will do what they have to. Goodbye for now."

* * *

As the Americans watched and waited, the Soviets intensified the search for *Morozov,* with a small group of four ships and a submarine now methodically looking and listening for any sort of clue. While this was taking place, some disturbing reports were brought to the attention of Admiral Gusev in Vladivostok. The first came from Admiral

Panov, following up on Gusev's order to investigate any "remote connection" between the *Morozov's* disappearance and the personnel and political problems that existed onboard before she sailed. Working with KGB senior agent Tarobrin, Panov uncovered some startling and unusual bits of intelligence, which he immediately carried to his fleet commander's office.

"Comrade Admiral, I am embarrassed and angry to report that there were some things that we should have known before the *Morozov* sailed, but the local KGB in Petro screwed up, and did not put two and two together…the left hand didn't know what the right hand was doing! There also were some screwups on the *Morozov* and at the submarine base armory."

"Get to it, Ivanovich. What should we have known?"

"There is a zhid michman aboard *Morozov* by the name of Riavin, who is the boat's leading and most experienced nuclear armament technician. It seems that he was scheduled for officer training upon the recommendation of the previous captain Ivanov, but the michman's sister was arrested by the KGB for subversive activities involving the publication of an underground, anti-government newspaper that got distributed in some of our big cities. Our plan was to arrest the michman and cancel his orders to officer training. But after the incident, of which you were informed, where Ivanov attacked Tarobrin who wanted to arrest Riavin, the flotilla agreed to have Ivanov relieved, but insisted that michman Riavin remain on board and make this patrol, as they had no replacement for him. Their argument was that since there was no evidence that the michman was involved with his sister's activities, he was not a security risk and was needed on board. While all this was going on, the KGB in Petro also interrogated Riavin's wife, who lives there and is not a zhid.

They reported that she also had nothing to do with her sister-in-law's activities, but they did determine that she is a prostitute and that she is an alcoholic…both security risks. Now the next thing we dug up is a real shocker! We found out that Stepakov went to Petro to get laid the night before *Morozov* sailed and ended up with this Riavin whore. A low-level arm of our Petro KGB that tails certain officers and officials, followed them to a vacant lot where they parked for awhile. Then Stepakov dropped her home, and then he went directly to the base, arriving around 9 pm. It wasn't until agent Tarobrin and I started asking questions that this connection was made. The idiots knew who Stepakov was, and they knew who she was, but they failed to put the two together! But even if they had, I don't know what we would have done about it."

"Was michman Riavin ashore that night or aboard *Morozov*?"

"As far as we can determine, comrade Admiral, he was aboard. The flotilla commander says he was restricted to the boat until they sailed. Also, if he was at the apartment, and she knew he was there, she probably wouldn't have had Stepakov drive her up to the door."

"So where does this leave us, Ivanovich?"

"Well, there is something else that bothers me, comrade. We checked out everything that was loaded on board the *Morozov* at the submarine base this past month, and in addition to the usual stores, spare parts, missiles and torpedoes, they took aboard plastic explosives and demolition gear, these last two on the day they sailed."

"And what bothered you about that, comrade?"

"The explosives and demolition equipment were all picked up and signed for by michman Riavin. We also checked as to the need for a large sheet of plastic explosive, and the records show that *Morozov* shouldn't have needed any more plastics because there was no record of them having expended any. Also, the plastics they carry on board are in small squares for equipment demolition and not in large sheets. These discrepancies should have been picked up by the armory, but they weren't. The officer in charge of the armory operation should be held responsible for this transaction that never should have been made!"

"Who signed the requisition for this big plastic sheet?"

"The signature says Capt. Lt. Demichev, but we believe it was forged. The bottom line is that michman Riavin was obviously distressed and perhaps deranged enough to have caused a disaster. He also knew how to use plastic explosives and had access to them on the *Morozov.* Regardless of whether he knew about Stepakov and his wife, the business with his sister and the cancellation of his orders to officer school could have been enough to put him over the edge…Comrade Admiral, I believe there is a good possibility that this man is responsible for the loss of *Morozov.* This Riavin should have never been allowed to stay on board…he should have been institutionalized!"

"Well, Ivanovich, I hate to say it, but I tend to agree with you. About an hour ago I received a call from Moscow regarding some Amerikanski messages that were recently decoded by some of our specialists. I had asked Admiral Matelov to have them study everything they had and to look at the time frame around when *Morozov* disappeared to see if they could find any clues as to her fate. Although there are only certain messages they can decode, and these only on certain days, they did come across something quite interesting. My counterpart, the Amerikanski Pacific Fleet Commander, sent a message to their 7th fleet asking if the task force, which was en route from Subic Bay to the

Vietnam area about the time *Morozov* was last heard from, had dropped any depth charges or other explosives during their transit. The answer came back negative…and that means to me that somebody or something reported an underwater explosion to them. Unfortunately, there was no position given for any detonation, and the specialists haven't decoded anything else about it. But I think it fits in. Why else would a fleet commander want to know if any ships dropped charges unless he knew something? I believe he was looking for what caused an explosion in the water near the task force. It was also determined from the message that the task force heard nothing."

"What can be done now, comrade admiral?"

"I will continue the search effort for another week, and if we have not had any success by that time, I will call it off. But then we will watch the ocean area where we believe *Morozov* lies and see if the Amerikanskis come up with anything. Perhaps they will detect her for us. They've been watching our search efforts, and they must know by now what we're looking for. From studying the charts, and assuming *Morozov* was in her assigned operation area when she foundered, the odds are she was in unsalvageable waters of over a thousand meters, and will probably never be found. But we will keep track of the Amerikanskis just to make sure. I thank you for your efforts in this matter Ivanovich, but I want you to keep working with the KGB on this and perhaps have them alert agents in the Philippines and East Malaysia to see if any flotsam or bodies have washed up anywhere. The islands of Mindoro and Palawan in the Philippines are the nearest to the operation area. I will see Gomulka next to hear out his conclusions before sending him and comrade Semenov back to Petro."

"The KGB is now going to say the Navy went against their recommendation to take this man Riavin off the boat before it sailed. Do you think there will be repercussions?"

"They may relieve comrade Gomulka for this. After all, *Morozov* was in his flotilla, and if heads are to roll, his will be first, and Semenov may go with him. Our boss (Fleet Admiral Matelov) and Stepakov's father are close friends, and in fact, he is presently the guest at the Admiral's quarters awaiting word of the fate of his son and the boat. And as you know, the Premier and other high-up political bigwigs also know and admire the retired Admiral Stepakov, and will push for swift retribution against those deemed responsible for the loss of his son and the *Morozov*."

After Panov left his office, Admiral Gusev summoned his chief of staff and related to him the results of the investigation to date, his conclusions and other details pertaining to the missing submarine.

"Prepare a complete report of this matter and have it ready for my signature by tomorrow morning so we can get it on the courier flight to Moscow by noontime."

"It will be done, comrade Admiral."

"Gusev next called Admiral Matelov in Moscow and told him there was no progress with the search effort, but they were uncovering some evidence that indicated "there's a definite possibility that *Morozov* was sabotaged by a crewmember."

A stunned Commander in Chief responded in disbelief!... "*Eb Troyu Mat* (Jesus Christ) comrade, how could such a thing happen? Do you know who this sonofabitch is, and does the KGB concur with your findings?"

"So far, everything points to a zhid michman by the name of Riavin. The KGB and Panov uncovered enough to show this man was probably deranged, had a motive, had access to explosives and he also serviced the missiles on board. Also, comrade, your code specialists intercepted an Amerikanski message that indicated an underwater detonation had taken place near the area where *Morozov* should have been…it looks bad, comrade Admiral."

"Keep up the search and continue the investigation and send me what you have gathered so far on the next courier flight. I can assure you, comrade, that some asses are going to swing for this one! But swinging asses aside, right now our biggest concern is that *Morozov* is definitely in unsalvageable waters, and we must not rest until that is positively determined…and this comes straight from the top. The Premier himself knows our latest weapons and other technology are on board, and he told me in no uncertain terms that "none of this must ever get into the wrong hands."

Repercussions from Moscow were swift. The commander in chief initiated the immediate relief of both Gomulka and Semenov. He also demanded that formal court-martial charge be brought against the officer responsible for the operation of the armory, and the michman in charge of the operation when Riavin requisitioned the plastic explosives. Despite the lack of proof-positive that Riavin destroyed the *Morozov*, Admiral's Matelov and Gusev concurred that the irregularities already uncovered during the on-going investigation warranted the disciplinary actions. The pot was further stirred by KGB Chief Gurenko who complained to many in the highest levels of the Politburo, "The Navy did not take our advice, this Riavin character should have been removed from the submarine when we recommended it. We should have done the same with him as we did with his zhid sister," he lamented.

Other than those at the upper echelons of the Soviet Navy and the Politburo, no one was told of the missing submarine.

Like past Soviet submarine disasters, plane crashes and several serious nuclear reactor accidents, there were no notices in the government controlled newspapers, television or radio. Mum was the word, and although there were rumors at the submarine base in Petropavlovsk that "something must have happened on the *Morozov*," it would be many weeks before the loss of the boat would be acknowledged and reported to selected naval commands and finally to the family members of the missing men. Even then, notice of the loss was never officially acknowledged or revealed to the general public.

After reading the details of the "Preliminary *Morozov* Report," the senior Stepakov came closest to summing up the debacle when he expressed his point of view to his friend and host, Admiral Matelov:

"Demichev should have known his leading nuclear weapons michman was unbalanced and dangerous to have on board. Officers are supposed to know their men! And this business about having no replacement for Riavin is unexcuseable. Whoever runs the personnel training branch of your Navy should be called to task. We should not be building and sailing these boats faster than we can man them. We'll never know if my son's indiscretions with Riavin's wife had anything to do with this, and he certainly didn't know who she was, but it doesn't matter, Riavin never should have been aboard the boat when it left port."

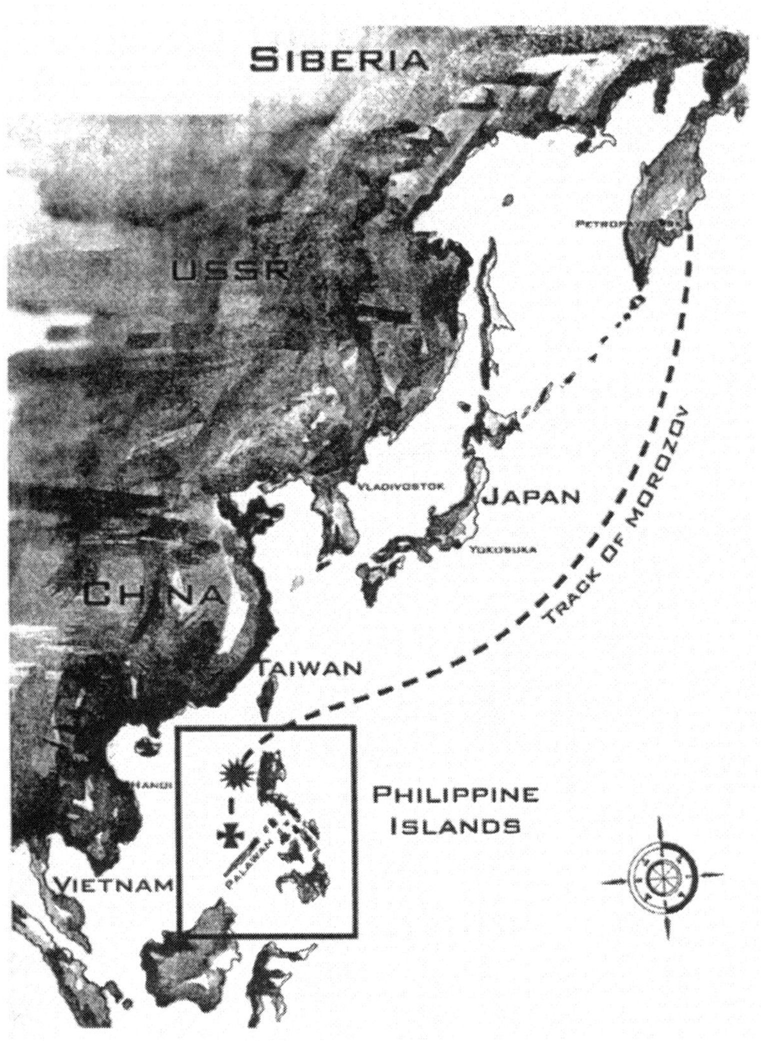
SIBERIA
USSR
CHINA
VLADIVOSTOK
JAPAN
YOKOSUKA
TAIWAN
TRACK OF MOROZOV
PHILIPPINE
ISLANDS
HANOI
PALAWAN
VIETNAM

CHAPTER 9

ZAMBOANGA

May arrived in the Philippine Islands with extremely warm, humid weather and light breezes. With the southwest monsoon season still a month or two away, those who could work or play near the ocean found the climate more bearable than those less fortunate who lived and worked in the steaming, jungle-infested inland areas. Here on the remote, exotic sands of Busuanga Island, a young man from the slums of the bleak, Russian city of Rostov found himself in paradise. Far at sea, a search was still in progress for the missing Soviet submarine, with one Russian and one American nuclear boat continuing the search effort with zero results. Leaders of both navies had now determined that the submarine probably exploded while submerged and broke up as it sank somewhere in the South China Sea, which resulted in parts of the vessel being strewn over a wide area in over 2,000 feet of water. By the end of the first week of May, both navies called off the search, and the fate of CHARLIE FOUR and *Morozov* was soon put on the back shelf at Fleet Headquarters in Siberia, Japan and Hawaii. The U.S. navy was more perplexed than the Soviets, as they could not figure out a logical reason why nothing was ever found near the position where SOSUS supposedly detected an explosion. "CHARLIE FOUR may have survived the initial blast, managed to maneuver elsewhere, where she eventually sank," was the "official" U.S. Navy intelligence determination. They didn't know at the time how right they were.

After his escape ordeal, rescue at sea and the warm welcome he received from a beautiful woman on a dream-like tropical island, Alexei Plavinsky slept as never before. Despite a throbbing head and ears still ringing from the extreme sea pressures he endured, he slept straight through the night and the next day, awakening in the late afternoon as the lovely Maria appeared at the foot of the bed and spoke to him softly in English.

"Good afternoon Alexei, you sure slept a long time. I was worried about your head wound, but Papa said that as long as you were sleeping as sound as you were that you would be okay. And how would you like something to eat and a nice cold beer, Alexei?"

Sitting up in bed and staring at the smiling Maria, Alexei blinked a few times and realized that he hadn't been dreaming after all, for here was the queen of his dreams standing right in front of him.

"Is your father here?" he asked.

"Yes, he has just returned from fishing, and he wants to talk and have a beer with you. I told him about your escape from the ship."

"Oh Maria, what is that engine noise I hear down below?"

"It's a generator," she replied. "There is no electricity on the Island. We keep it running all the time and I refuel it every day."

Putting on the freshly washed and dried trousers and still wearing the Navy-issue undershirt he had worn throughout his ordeal, Alexei shuffled barefooted out of the bedroom into the pleasantly cool living/dining area where a grinning Alfredo greeted him with a cold beer and a warm handshake as Maria busied herself in the kitchen. The two then sat facing each other across the small table where Alexei had studied the maps the night before. Alfredo explained that the doctor was out of town but that it didn't look like he'd be needed anyway, as Alexei looked quite well. He then asked of his future plans.

"What will you do now, Alexei? Where will you go? How can we help you?"

Turning down the offer of a cigarette from the chain-smoking Alfredo, a grateful and humbled Alexei looked him straight in the eyes and spoke with his strangely accented English.

"Thank you, but I have never smoked...and sir, I am very grateful you found me at sea and brought me to this wonderful home. Now here I am, with only the clothes on my back. I would like to repay you for what you have done for me, and I'm willing to do any labor you desire, and maybe I can be of help on your fishing boat. I want you to believe me that I am not a criminal or someone in any kind of trouble or a person with any kind of ulterior motives. And I don't believe that anyone is looking for me. If I could spend a few more days here in this isolated area to get my thoughts together, it would be most welcome and I promise to earn my keep."

Something had convinced Alfredo that the finding of this tall, muscular young man floating alone in a desolate part of the South China Sea was no mistake. He believed it was a divine act of God that was meant to be. He also connected it to Maria, and maybe this fellow who appeared from nowhere would become her mate. In fact, he had been worried about Maria for some time now, and the main reason he brought her with him to the "fishing house" this time was to have an opportunity to talk to her about her future. In particular, he was worried why she showed no interest in the slew of young men who sought to date her. A beautiful, talented and intelligent young woman like her should have boyfriends, and yet she spent a lot of time with a girl pal of hers…was she just interested in women or was she only waiting for the right man to come along?

Taking a long swig on his beer straight from the bottle, Alfredo laid out the whole situation.

"We will be up here for another two weeks before we return to Zamboanga City. You are welcome to stay here with us during that time. I will take you fishing with me, and that will take care of your keep. I should explain to you that this house is owned by a man named Quintal, who lives most of the time in Zamboanga, and owns the auto repair shop I run down there. He lets me use this house a couple of times a year for fishing, and he uses it occasionally for business purposes. Now if you want to be with us for awhile, and you desire to remain temporarily in the Philippines, I will raise him on the radio, as there are few phones on the island, and he will send us a passport you can use for at least six months. He can also arrange such things as visas and working papers. Let us just say, he is "connected." If you decide to go to Zamboanga City with us you will at least need the passport. You will also need some clothing, which we can get in Coron with some of the fishing money. By the way, Maria said you have experience repairing and servicing automobiles. Maybe you could work in my shop…what do you say to all that?"

A flabbergasted Alexei let it all sink in and agreed to everything that Alfredo proposed, including the work in Zamboanga. "But what will we tell people who see us, people you know, and others, who I am, and what am I doing here. I don't want to get pegged as some kind of foreign agent or be followed around by the police."

"We will simply say you are a tourist, and when we get to Zamboanga City, Quintal can arrange for citizenship papers, for this he will ask a fee, and that will cover you for everything. But I see no problem in Zamboanga, because it is an international port with people of all colors from all over the world visiting or working there. You would not stand out down there like you do up here. Now if we get the passport, you should come up with a new name, and maybe change your nationality. What do you think?"

"I will stay with Poland because of the language, and as long as my passport or other papers are good fakes and not checked out with the Polish Embassy, I guess it will be all right. However, I should change my name…at least my last name. Let me think about it."

Maria had overhead the entire conversation, and when she brought the food to the table she asked Alexei what would be his new name.

Remembering the names of some Polish sailors who attended submarine school with him several years ago, he came up with an alias.

"I will be Alexei Walewski from Warsaw," he declared.

After the evening meal, Alexei and Maria left for a barefoot stroll on the beach as Alfredo got through to Quintal in Zamboanga on the radio set and within five minutes made all of the arrangements to obtain the passport. The only thing they had to do was have a photo made of Alexei in Coron and send it to Quintal on the next boat. As soon as this was received, the passport would be sent special delivery back to Coron, where it could be picked up by Alfredo within four days time. When Quintal asked where the big European stranger came from, Alfredo told him that he was a survivor of a small cargo vessel that sank two weeks ago and that he found him drifting at sea in a rubber raft.

"He's not a spy, if that's what you're thinking, and he's fully qualified to work for me in the shop. He's also big enough and strong enough to be a bouncer in one of your clubs. I think you'll like this man," Alfredo said. "He just doesn't want anything to do with his country, and he claims he is not in trouble there, nor does he have any relatives anywhere."

Alfredo was not far off the mark in his worries about Maria. As beautiful and as desirable as she was, she had a very dark secret, and this secret involved the very man her father owed his livelihood to - Emilio Quintal, a man she detested from the bottom of her soul. Unbeknownst to Alfredo, Quintal had sexually assaulted his daughter at the age of 13 and continued to pursue her to this day whenever he got the urge. He got what he wanted from Maria by reminding her that he held all the strings to her father's livelihood and happiness.

"Your papa wants to keep his house and his auto shop and he also likes to use the fishing house up north from time to time doesn't he?" was the line he used to coerce and threaten her into having sex with him. Maria thought of him as a fat monster with an ugly, sweaty body and foul-smelling breath, and over a period of time her revulsion of this vulture soured her toward normal male/female relationships. She tried to date some of the young men who pursued her, but she never became comfortable and gradually rejected all of them, and in the process, became unsure of her own sexuality. Her disgust for the odorous, groping Quintal had affected her deeply.

Although Maria never had any kind of a physical relationship with her girlfriend, who had once told her she "liked both men and women," she thought about it from time to time and wondered if she was destined to become one of "them." But now at the fishing house on the remote Busuanga Island, no such ideas came to her head as she quite miraculously felt drawn like a magnet to this intriguing stranger from the sea who appeared on her doorstep just 48 hours ago. And now in the late afternoon as they walked together in the warm, soft sand, she knew it was more than just the friendly, person-to-person pleasure of his conversation that she wanted. She had now become attracted to him physically. His looks and his body put thoughts in her head she never dreamed possible.

"Two days, and I'm falling for this man?" She asked herself, and then on impulse took his hand in hers and laid her head on his shoulder as they both took in the setting sun while the terns and gulls soared just above the dark blue waters between them and the western horizon.

On his part, Alexei could not believe what was happening. The horror of his experience aboard *Morozov* was still fresh in his thoughts and working against the powerful urges he felt for this lovely lady of the Philippines walking next to him in this movie-like tropical scenario. Pangs of guilt came into his mind as he thought of his shipmates buried forever under the sea. Perhaps he should turn himself in and report what happened to the local authorities…maybe they would send me back to Russia, and our navy would come and find the boat…but then again, the locals would probably turn me over to their friends, the Amerikanskis, and I would probably never be heard from again. Are they out there looking for the *Morozov* now, and what do I do if somebody discovers it? Divers would find the open escape hatch with the escape lanyard still attached, and conclude some men may have gotten out. If there were Navy ships out there searching right now, the fishermen pals of Alfredo in Coron would be talking about it, and he would find out where I really came from…and if the searchers do show up, they'll be looking for survivors and information right here. I must keep my eyes and ears open while fishing offshore with Alfredo these next two weeks. I must also try to convince Maria and Alfredo to tell no one I am here. The passport photo in Coron may be a problem. I shouldn't be seen there. The move to Zamboanga is a smart one, but I must not leave a trail behind me.

And what about this woman? Should I trust her and her papa? Why should they trust me? Is Maria one of those oversexed girls who will do it with anyone? Should I make a move for her tonight, or is it too soon? Should I tell her who I really am and where I came from? Why do I care so much for her?...we just met!...is it only because I have been without a woman since the trip to the whorehouse in Petro just over a month ago? No, it can't be, this Maria is more than raw sex for a man, I just have a feeling...

Maria interrupted his brainstorming with a puzzled smile and some questions of her own.

"Why are you so deep in thought Alexei? Is something wrong? Are there other things you want to tell me?"

"No, I think it's just the shock of being here. It's like something from a movie." Then motioning to a nice spot nearby, they sat just a few feet from the water's edge and watched the sun disappear below the cloudless horizon. Making small talk, Alexei said he felt refreshed, and thanked her for the use of one of Mister Quintal's tropical shirts, some shaving gear and the new toothbrush she found for him.

"What kind of a man is Mister Quintal?" he asked.

"To tell the truth, I don't like him at all, but he helps papa in business, lets him use this place once or twice a year for fishing, and he owns our house in Zamboanga. He's been a necessary evil to us. Quintal is connected with all sorts of politicians and criminals and even some of the rebellious Muslim tribes in Mindanao. He has no loyalties whatsoever.

He just goes where the money is, and he doesn't care where it comes from. He has his filthy hands into all kinds of businesses, including liquor, drugs and prostitution. Papa doesn't realize how dangerous this man is, or maybe he just doesn't want to know. He's blind to it all, and I wish with all my heart we didn't have to deal with him. I don't know what he will ask you to do in Zamboanga City as payment for his providing you with a passport, but I ask you to be most careful in any dealings you may have with him. Never trust him."

Alexei thanked her for warning him about Quintal, and then they talked about going to Coron for the passport picture, and he asked again that his presence on the island be kept a secret. She agreed with what he said, and then told him something that made his heart pound.

"I know we just met Alexei, but I like you very much and find myself strongly attracted to you. Somehow I think you feel the same for me, but don't interpret this to mean I'm a loose woman…I am not, and have only been with one man, and that one person was a very bad experience. I am telling you these things because I believe we should be up front with each other. I would be dishonest if I said I didn't want you. What do you say to that Alexei?"

"You are correct about my attraction to you, Maria, and for me, it is far more than physical. I have never had a serious relationship with any woman, for as a seaman, I've never been in one place long enough for anything lasting, but regardless, you are the most beautiful woman I have ever laid my eyes upon." They then kissed and embraced in a manner that was gentle and tentative at first, but soon built to the point where they were crushing themselves to one another. Maria whispered in his ear that as much as she wanted him right now, "Tomorrow night would be better, as papa will be spending the night in Coron."

The next morning, the three embarked in the old car that Quintal kept at the fishing house as a means of getting back and forth to Coron. Alfredo agreed to keep Alexei's existence a secret, and they suggested he stay in the car while in the town except for when he got out for the passport snapshot. Knowing that one of his drinking buddies in Coron owned a Polaroid camera, Alfredo drove the couple to the house, went to the door and gave the pal a few pesos to keep quiet, then motioned for the two to enter the house where the snapshot was taken and placed in their hands in less than two minutes.

"Perfect!" she declared as they returned to the car. She let the photo dry and placed it in a preaddressed envelope marked for immediate delivery to Quintal. Alfredo delivered the envelope to the ferry landing, where it was posted to arrive in Zamboanga the next morning. Next they went to a local store where Maria an Alfredo picked out a few items of clothing and a pair of sandals for Alexei, and it took some time, for few people in the Philippines wore clothing or shoes his size. They did the best they could, and Maria told Alexei that, "These will have to do until we get to Zamboanga City. They had no trousers long enough for you, but I can let out the cuffs of this pair when we get back to the house."

After they returned to the fishing house, Alfredo packed a few things and told the two he was going back to Coron to play cards with some friends, but he would be back bright and early in the morning for breakfast and then he and Alexei would go fishing for the day. "Make us a good lunch to bring with us tomorrow," he told Maria as he went out the front door.

The two spent a quiet afternoon at the fishing house talking about Zamboanga and listening to music on the radio. Avoiding all talk about the subject that was very much on both of their minds, they instead feasted their eyes on one another while relishing within what both knew was going to take place that night. A musical duo named *Simon & Garfunkel* were tuned in on the radio, and the sounds fascinated Alexei, who had never heard anything like it.

"They are fantastic. Where do they come from?"

"They're from the states, but they're popular all over the western world right now."

Late in the afternoon they went for a swim in the ocean, and Maria warned Alexei of sharks. "There are occasionally great white sharks in these parts, and it is not wise to go out too far." "You should also be careful out in the boat with Papa, for when you pull in fish it attracts them," she warned. Heeding her words, Alexei stayed close to shore and cringed at what could have happened to him while at sea after leaving *Morozov*. After a light supper on the beach, they again viewed the setting sun now low in the western sky, and when Alexei asked more about the sharks, Maria told him a chilling story that took place two years previous in Coron. It involved a young woman who was grabbed by a great white shark while washing clothes in shallow water near the shore.

"Witnesses saw the shark coming, but their warnings were too late. It got the woman by the legs, dragged her under and took her out to deep water. Two days later, a fishing boat came into Coron with a huge shark aboard which they had just caught. They had this big white hauled up the mast by the tail so all could see it when they entered the harbor, and because Filipino's love fresh shark meat, the sight of it coming in on the boat attracted a crowd. Papa was at a nearby café having a beer when the boat came in. He said over a hundred people were waiting on the pier to buy some of the shark meat as soon as the boat was tied up. But you can't believe what happened next."

"It must have been the same one that got the woman," Alexei said.

"Well, Papa says that after they made fast to the pier, hauled down the shark and started to cut it up, there was a silence for about five minutes. Then those in the café heard yelling and screaming from the direction of the pier, and then people in a complete panic ran from the pier and down the streets of the town as if the devil was on their tail. It seems that when they sliced into the stomach of the shark, the woman's head tumbled out on the pier, driving the crowd berserk. Needless to say, they didn't sell any shark steaks that day!"

When the tropical twilight turned swiftly to darkness, only the occasional crash of the surf on a nearby reef punctuated the peace and quiet they enjoyed on the deserted beach. And soon after the first stars appeared, as if on signal, they just looked at each other, and without a word, strolled hand in hand to the fishing house, entered the large bedroom, disrobed, and began a night of lovemaking that left them both breathless and in awe of one another. Theirs turned out to be a unique physical match-up that found each body with a craving for the other that went far beyond the imaginations of both man and woman. Completely honest and uninhibited, their unbridled passion went on for most of the night, and when Maria arose before dawn to prepare breakfast and pack a lunch for the men, she incredulously wanted Alexei again, but let him sleep, knowing he would have to work with Papa on the boat all day. She was astounded at the physical surge of passion that now possessed her and dominated her thoughts.

"My God," she declared to herself, "he and I did all those things on and off for the whole night, and already I want him again!…Is this the devil, or is this the way it's supposed to be?"

* * *

The sojourn at the fishing house on Busuanga Island went on blissfully for Alexei and Maria until they and Alfredo said farewell to the comfortable abode and left for Zamboanga. During the last ten days, Alexei became an adept and eager fisherman and Maria seemed to take on a glow from the love she had found with this unusual young man from far, far away. Papa Alfredo also seemed happy. Now fully convinced that his discovery of Alexei was a predestined will of the Lord and that the rescue also seemed to solve the questions he had about his daughter's lifestyle, he felt contentment and was comfortable with the situation that he knew from early on would end up with the pair in bed with one another. "Now I will have Alexei as a son, and Maria will have him as a husband," he predicted. Far from being a prude, Alfredo had long scoffed at the old-timers contention that a "physical" marriage was not realistic and that economic status was far more important than "love/sex American style" as depicted in the movies. To most Asians, a young woman marrying a financially secure, older man was an ideal match-up, but Alfredo thought differently. His marriage to the gorgeous Australian, that began in 1951 and ended with Colleen's tragic death in a plane crash three years later, was a time he would never forget. They both enjoyed making love whenever and wherever they felt like it and each believed it was actually unhealthy to abstain. "Enjoy me to the fullest," she used to say…"just as I enjoy you." She made him a very happy man, and he had carefully raised their daughter in her memory.

Alexei talked with Alfredo about his feelings for Maria while they fished.

"I'm afraid your daughter has cast a spell over me, sir. We want to stay together."

"I would have to be blind not to have noticed what's going on between you two. I saw it right from the start, and I can tell you she's not a run-around. As beautiful as she is, she's never had a real boyfriend, but I have a good feeling about you two and have no objection to you and Maria sharing the big bedroom in the fishing house, and you're both welcome to share a room at our house in Zamboanga when we get there." Then laughing, he turned to Alexei and quipped, "Just don't keep me awake making noises in there!"

Alexei, who never had a real father and never held Roland Salisbury in that image, told Alfredo that he had the deepest respect for both him and his daughter, and that from now on he would like to call him *papa* just like Maria does.

"I never had a papa, and don't even know who he was or what his name was…and believe me, I'm not trying to butter up to you…but I just feel more comfortable calling you that."

Several times while fishing they came near the spot where Alfredo found Alexei in the life raft, and although Alexei didn't know where they were, Alfredo did, and he'd mention it to him. Each time Alexei expected to see naval ships or aircraft milling about, and was somewhat surprised when none were seen. Nor was anything reported on the local radio stations or on the English language American Armed Forces network about the loss of a Soviet submarine near the Philippines. And apparently there was nothing in the old, out-of-town newspapers that Alfredo picked up at the ferry pier, for he certainly would have mentioned it. Alexei contemplated his situation over and over, and was still looking for answers…"What if it was all a mistake? Maybe the only dead men on the boat were those I saw in the torpedo room. Maybe the phones in the trunk didn't work, and there were enough men alive onboard to have gotten the boat underway again…Maybe they're back in Petro now… this whole thing is crazy. Will I ever know what happened? What is in store for me in Zamboanga? Will there be any problems with the fake passport that arrived right on schedule from Mister Quintal?"

It was with a feeling of dread and foreboding that Maria packed their belongings for the two-day trip south, and like Alexei, she also had many questions on her mind. The days and wonderful nights at the fishing house had passed far too swiftly for her, and now it was back to where she would have to deal with Quintal. Determined never to let him touch her again, she thought about the repercussions. Would he kick us out of the house? Will he accept Alexei? What will the bastard do if I tell him that Alexei and I want to get married and that there would be no more fooling around? Would he tell Alexei or papa bad things about me? Perhaps I may have to string him along for awhile until I can come up with a good plan for a way to handle this. Maybe Alexei and I could emigrate to Australia, to where grandmother lives in Brisbane.

The three left Busuanga Island by ferry from Coron on a steamy day in the middle of the month of May. The ferry took them to Puerto Princesa, the capital of Palawan. Arriving in the evening, they had a one-hour stopover before boarding a larger ferry for the overnight trip to Zamboanga City, located on the tip of the long peninsula that extends westward from Mindanao, where the ferry docked just before noon the next day.

With hardly a glance, a surprised and relieved Alexei was swiftly waived through customs at the bustling, crowded pier at Zamboanga City. Accustomed to the strict checking of papers and passes in the Soviet Union, Alexei shrugged with a sheepish grin when he and Maria left the ferry and waited on the pier for Alfredo. "They didn't even look at me to see if I was the same man in the picture," he said.

"They're only interested in catching people with drugs, arms or contraband. There are problems here between the Moros and the Christians, and they look for smugglers and agents they've been forewarned about. Apparently you didn't fit either category of what they're looking for today so they zipped you right through."

After Papa Alfredo joined them, they carried their baggage through the throngs of people milling about the extensive marketplace that took up most of the dockside area. Papa flagged down a brightly decorated vehicle driven by a pal that would take them to the house where they lived. Alexei stared at the car and many roofed and painted bicycles that were beeping their horns and seemed to be moving in all different directions at once.

"What do they call these?" Alexei wanted to know.

"The cars are *jeepneys,"* Maria explained. "It's just a cultural thing, they're like taxis in other countries, but everyone who owns one here in the Philippines decorates their *jeepney* to the fullest."

As they entered the vehicle, Alexei noticed the outside of the car fitted with a myriad of mirrors, horns, religious artifacts, tassels and strange signs in several languages. "Papa, what is the company name that makes these things?"

"They were originally made in the U.S. as army jeeps used here during the war against the Japanese. When the Americans left, they let us keep the jeeps, and we converted them into taxis, buses and private cars. Now they're made from new in Manila."

Maria put her hand in Alexei's and pointing to the shining front hood asked him, "Do you like the paint work and designs on this one Alexei?" Scratching his head, Alexei said he'd never seen anything like it. "Where do they get them painted like this?"

"Most of them here in the city are done right at papa's garage, and I do the painting and design work. Papa and I will show you the whole setup over there this afternoon."

The house was built right on the shore, and had a large porch that extended out over the waterway. Bigger than others in the vicinity, it had a spacious, screened living room, two bedrooms, a kitchen and a bathroom. In a bragging way, Maria told Alexei the house was modern by Philippine standards.

"Unlike most homes here, this one actually has a toilet and a shower. But most dwellings here, and throughout the islands, have no plumbing whatsoever."

Still haunted with second thoughts and constant curiosity as to the true fate of *Morozov* and his shipmates, a troubled Alexei nonetheless settled nicely into the house and the domestic lifestyle. Papa went right back to his routine at the auto repair shop across the street from the house, and a rejuvenated Maria busied herself with painting jeepneys and redecorating the house and the bedroom she shared with Alexei. The two had become inseparable, and they established a physical and emotional bond far beyond anything either one had ever experienced or expected. Maria was virtually aglow with her love and whistled and hummed as she went about housework and painting jeepneys at the shop.

On the night of their arrival Quintal paid a visit, and as was his habit, he walked right in the front door without knocking an entered the kitchen where the three were eating. He immediately took an interest in Alexei, and between puffs on his cigar proceeded to talk to him and feel him out.

"So you come from the sea to live in Zamboanga. I hear from Alfredo here that you are a good auto mechanic, and that you also are an experienced fighter. These are two talents I can use. We just lost a mechanic at the shop, and if Alfredo wants you, you have a job there, and you will work directly for him. Also, I can use a bouncer at one of my clubs two or three nights a week, and from the size of you, I think you'll fill the bill. It is good you speak English, for most here can use it, but you will also have to learn some of the local dialects. In addition to *Tagalog,* you will hear *Cebuano* and *Chabacano*. If things work out we will talk about permanent resident papers sometime in the near future, but the passport you have is good for another five and a half months."

Maria was relieved that Quintal seemed to take little notice of the obvious attraction between her and Alexei, and did not voice any objection to him living in the house. "Perhaps he will now leave me alone," she concluded.

Before leaving, Quintal told the three that he would be out of town for at least two weeks. "I've got to check on things in Subic and Manila," he said. As he went out the door, he motioned for Alexei to follow. Once outside he questioned him about the *ship that sank* and if he was wanted by police anywhere. "You must tell me the truth about yourself, for if you don't I will find out anyway. In my business I have contacts of many nationalities, including Poles."

Alexei told Quintal the same story he told Papa and Maria and explained that Alfredo must have misunderstood him when he spoke of a sunken cargo ship. “My country thinks I am dead, and that is exactly what I want them to think. I ask you not to let on to anyone that I am here or what my real name is. I am not wanted by police anywhere, and just want to start a new life for myself.”

“And is Maria part of that new life? Are you and she sharing the bed? What does Alfredo think of this?”

“Yes, Maria is a part of my new life, and Papa and I have an understanding. But whether or not we share a bed is our business. My aim is to marry her when I can establish a citizenship somewhere. I don’t want to ask for political asylum, as my name would become public and my government may make trouble. I appreciate what you have done so far to help me, and I will work hard at both of the jobs you offered in return. We just want to be left alone.”

Quintal simply grunted in response, told him what his wages would be and then promptly entered the back seat of his chauffeured sedan, slammed the door and sped away. Lighting another cigar while the sedan weaved along the crowded, dusty roadway, Quintal considered what Alexei told him and rightfully sensed that he was not telling the truth about where he came from. He put it in the back of his mind that he would eventually find out who *Mister Walewski* really was, and when this was known he would find a way to sell or barter the information to whoever may be looking for him. Quintal also resented Alexei’s relationship with Maria, and now asked himself why he went along with the passport scheme. But he reasoned that he would wait to see if he could sell off information on Walewski, and then when he was out of the way he could get back to having more sex with Maria. Quintal also knew that if he turned Walewski in to local government authorities that Maria would know who did it, and he didn't want that! What he had always wanted was to make a prostitute out of Maria. Over and over he had said to himself that "A beautiful *Mestiza* (offspring of Filipino and Caucasian) like her with the light skin, big breasts and perfect body could make a fortune for the both of us in Manila. The rich Jap businessmen would stand in line for her!" He also knew that *Mestizas* are admired throughout the islands, and a beauty such as Maria could name her price wherever she worked. He saw it as a waste of talent for such a woman to take up with the Pole Walewski.

Maria was frantic while Quintal talked privately with Alexei, and prayed he wasn't telling him evil things about her. After Alexei returned to the house they went to the bedroom and she asked him about the conversation.

"What did Mister Quintal have to say?"

"He wanted to know about a cargo ship that sank, and I told him about my jumping ship with the raft, and asked him to keep quiet about it. He also asked about us, and I told him we would marry when I get permanent papers somewhere…I tell you, Maria, I don't like this man, but a job is a job I guess."

"We must never trust him Alexei. He is an evil bastard that would sell either one of us down the street in a second if he could pocket some pesos doing so!"

"What does he do up in Manila, and where is this Subic?"

"I don't know everything he's involved in, but it is said that he deals with smuggled goods and gambling rackets in Manila. It is also mentioned that he owns whorehouses in Subic, which is a big U.S. navy base on the island of Luzon. He recruits girls from all over and sends them there to learn the trade. Then he brings the more desirable ones to Manila.

He hinted to me a few times that he could find employment, as he called it, for me up there."

"Maria, I probably shouldn't ask you this, because what is past is past for both of us, but is Quintal the man you said you had an unpleasant sex relationship with?"

Laying her head on Alexei's chest, Maria started to sob as she told him the truth.

"Yes, the sonofabitch forced me to when I was young. He threatened papa's job and the rental of this house if I refused him. Alexei, I don't like to talk or think about it. The bastard makes me sick to my stomach! We must someday get away from here and away from him, but we must also take care of Papa's well-being when we do so."

Alexei sighed deeply, hugged Maria close to him, and resolved to somehow do something about Mister Quintal, his new employer. Bending down and bringing her face gently toward his, he spoke to her with a determined passion.

"I want you to tell me if he ever tries to lay a hand on you again." Still shaking, Maria clung to Alexei. "Ohh, please hold me, Alexei. I don't want you ever to let me go..."

* * *

Over the next few weeks, Zamboanga City became a most busy and interesting place for the tall, laid-back Russian. The work in the auto shop was hectic, and Alexei jumped back and forth from one repair job to another as priorities were non-existent, creating a helter-skelter atmosphere. Papa was a nice man and a good mechanic who was liked by all who worked for him, but he lacked the ability to organize properly. Spare parts were also a problem. Much of what was used as replacement parts were not new, but taken from wrecks and junks. Alexei was quite popular with the other men who worked with him in the shop, and they were all in awe of his raw strength, which he demonstrated by lifting the front end of vehicles with his bare hands and pushing the jacks under the wheels with his feet before removing tires. Using the American slang for a Polish man, the other mechanics gave him the name "ski," and it wasn't long before other locals began calling him the same thing. Finding the Filipinos extremely friendly, Alexei seemed to fit in nicely with the local lifestyle. The crazy music from America seemed to be everywhere, even in the jeepneys where they played plastic tape cassettes incessantly. The same sounds played all day at the auto shop, and Maria kept the radio blasting away at the house, sometimes to the irritation of Papa Alfredo who would holler at her to "turn it down, it is way too loud." Occasionally he would command her in local *Cebuano* dialect to do something about the noise. *"dili gusto ko"* (I don't like that!).

Alexei was constantly haunted about the true fate of the *Morozov.* Although he was quite positive that it was still laying on the bottom somewhere north of the island of Palawan some 300 miles away, he couldn't figure out why the submarine hadn't yet been discovered. He also considered his options when somebody eventually found it and resolved to swiftly disappear with Maria when and if the *Morozov* became news. The one thing he had made up his mind about was that he did not want to return to Russia - either voluntarily or involuntarily. It was not his fault what happened to *Morozov* and his shipmates. He also realized that keeping low profile in Zamboanga was important…but it wasn't always easy to do, because most of the people there were much smaller than he, and because of his size he stood out. There were, however, some Caucasians and a wide variety of other races in the city, many of whom spoke different languages, so the fact that he wasn't Filipino was not as important as his size. As white Russians were not known to be any bigger than whites from other countries, why should he worry? He reasoned that until the word gets out that a Russian sailor may be loose somewhere in the Philippine Islands, he had nothing to worry about...With that in mind, he took a chance and decided to play soccer for a local team that also had several Caucasian players on the roster. Sure he was a superior player, but he'd only participated in Navy leagues in Russia...no one would know him here in the Philippines.

The game of chess was a different matter, for although it was played just about everywhere in the world, the Russians hold the reputation of being the best. "I'd better be careful what I say and do in a chess match," he told himself, and he was quite surprised to find out that Filipinos were fanatical about the game which he had enjoyed and been fairly good at since his youth. At the *Club Sulu*, where he worked as the bouncer on weekend nights, he was constantly in a chess match with one of the bartenders or locals who found the big man quite difficult to beat. Because of his macho presence there was very little trouble at the club, and when someone did become a problem, Alexei would see them to the door and that would be the end of it. Nobody dared to mess with him. Maria became quite jealous of the girls who worked the bar, and with good reason, for they were curious about the tall, handsome foreigner with the easy smile, and some would ask him to dance when things got slow, but he would always politely refuse. "Bouncer should not dance while on the job," he would answer. Each and every night when he returned to the house Maria was waiting with a cold beer and a warm kiss. The lovemaking seemed endless, and they both now talked of somehow getting married and raising a family.

"I may already be with child," she told him.

Little did they know that their blissful days and nights in Zamboanga City were numbered, and the weeks ahead would severely test the mettle of them both.

CHAPTER 10

DISCOVERY

It was the last week of May at the U.S. Navy Officers Club at Subic Bay, Republic of the Philippines, and the Friday evening happy hour was in fully swing. The long bar was crowded with navy and marine officers and many long tables were filled with carrier pilots who were glad to be alive and relax after two months flying combat missions over Vietnam. Empty chairs and turned over glasses signified a place of honor and represented fellow airmen who were either killed or missing in action. Dice cups were in use everywhere as games of "ship-captain & crew" and "shanghai dice" were taking place with drinks and money on the line. Commander Ron Carmody, the skipper of the destroyer USS Stiles, was in such a game with junior officers from his ship and Lieutenant Commander Sam Gallagher, skipper of the submarine rescue vessel (ASR) USS *Whistler,* in Subic for minor repairs. Carmody and Gallagher were friends who had served aboard the same diesel powered submarine in the mid-sixties. Ron Carmody was a graduate of the US Navy Academy who had spent all of his early naval career exclusively in submarines, but with the advent of nuclear power, and despite an excellent performance record, he was not selected for the necessary training in that field that would have allowed him to continue his submarine career in nuclear boats. Seeing the handwriting on the wall, that without the training, he could never hope to command one of them, and like many officers at that time who were in a similar position, Carmody opted for the destroyer navy, where he had a successful tour as executive officer, and for the past year as commanding officer of the *Stiles*. Gallagher had an entirely different background. For ten years, he was an enlisted man aboard various diesel submarines where he served as quartermaster/signalman, responsible for navigation and visual signaling. After rising to the grade of chief petty officer, Gallagher was selected for officer training in Newport, Rhode Island, and was commissioned an Ensign in 1962. He subsequently served again in submarines, where he qualified as an officer and received the coveted "gold dolphins" in 1964. Two years later he and Carmody served together on a fast attack diesel submarine out of San Diego. He then was trained in deep sea diving and salvage at the Washington, D.C. Navy Yard, before reporting aboard the ASR *Pelican* where he was the executive officer and navigator for two years before assuming command of the Pearl Harbor based *Whistler* in 1971.

During the friendly dice game, Carmody asked Gallagher about ship operations.

"What are you up to next week Sam? What kind of work will the ship be doing?"

"We've got ISE (independent ship exercises – training), and we're going to lay a moor and have a week of hard-hat diving so all our divers an get in their bottom time, and the XO and I will also get some time in the water."

"What will you dive on? Do you have a specific place to go, or do you find an old wreck out there from the war?"

"We don't know yet, the XO is looking at the wreck charts to find something we can dive on that is not too far from here and is in reasonably shallow water."

"What's reasonably shallow?"

"Less than two hundred fifty feet."

"The reason I'm asking you these things is because of something unusual that happened while my ship and another were en route here from Singapore last week. On the way, we were doing some sonar training and vectored each other to real or imagined targets. Just northwest of Palawan in about two hundred feet of water, we picked up a solid, stationary target. We passed right over it several times and got an exact position, because it didn't appear on any of the wreck charts. It's probably a World War II relic that just hadn't been found and charted yet, but it may prove to be something interesting for you to dive on next week."

"That sounds like something to look into, and the water depth is desirable for what we want to do. There will be no problem scheduling this, for when it comes to ISE, they let us go just about anywhere we want to do our thing. But this contact…did you have to report it to anyone?"

"No, we didn't have to report it as it was just another spurious and stationary contact that was not positively identified. This happens all the time, and we're only required to send out messages on *positive* or *probable* submarine contacts that the spooks keep track of worldwide. An uncharted wreck doesn't attract much interest, but we'll probably include the position of this one in a letter to the Navy Hydrographic Office. I'll have the exact position of the wreck sent over to your ship tonight."

The next morning, Gallagher phoned his operational commander in Yokosuka, Japan on the secure line. Speaking to the operations officer, he laid out his plan for *Whistler* to proceed to the wreck and conduct diving operations the following week from Tuesday through Friday and return to Subic Bay Saturday morning. Everything was promptly agreed upon, and no mention was made to Gallagher of the missing Soviet submarine, as the area where the diving operations were going to take place was well over a hundred miles from where they believed the mysterious explosions took place. In fact, the U.S. Navy was now not entirely sure that CHARLIE FOUR was on the bottom somewhere. The Soviets had stopped searching, no debris was ever found or sighted, and a second, careful sonar search by the USS *Mullet* also failed to turn up anything. Several intelligence specialists believed CHARLIE FOUR had an explosion but somehow survived and eventually crawled home to Petropavlovsk or another port. Someplace where the Soviets had friends. "Maybe they snuck into a remote port in North Vietnam," one staff officer in Pearl Harbor theorized. Others thought she had a catastrophic explosion that spread pieces of the boat over a wide area in extremely deep ocean water. That would explain why no large, prominent sonar trace was ever detected. Detractors to this theory noted there was never any flotsam sighted, and asked why the Soviets kept looking for the boat two weeks after the explosion.

Although word of the possible Soviet nuclear submarine disaster had now spread quietly among many in the U.S. Navy, it had yet to appear in newspapers anywhere. CIA and ONI operatives had failed to turn up any new information from their intelligence networks in the Soviet Union or southeast Asia. But this was not unusual and, as one senior U.S. intelligence officer pointed out, "The last time they lost a boat it was two months before we found out about it, and to this day, the Soviets have yet to publicly acknowledge such a loss. In fact, they have never admitted to losing any of their nukes except the one that surfaced in the north Atlantic before it went down for good. Our aircraft got pictures of that one, and we actually offered them assistance before one of their ships showed up and picked up the survivors just before the boat went down. The pictures ended up in newspapers worldwide."

The USS *Whistler* was constructed during World War II, and although modernized, had been in service constantly since that time. Designed basically for submarine rescue operations, the 250-foot vessel was also capable of conducting deep sea salvage evolutions and could tow vessels as large as an aircraft carrier if necessary. The ship had a complement of 6 officers and 100 enlisted men, of which 24 were deep sea divers. Equipped with a submarine rescue bell, *Whistler* was fitted to bring a bottomed submarine's survivors to the surface and she could also connect air hoses to a sunken submarine's ballast tanks or compartments and blow her to the surface if the submarine was in salvageable waters, that is, no deeper than the divers were capable of going - 400 feet, using helium-oxygen. The diving gear used by the *Whistler's* divers were the old mark-5 "hardhats", some rigged for just air, and some for helium-oxygen, which allowed divers to work deeper and longer than the rigs that just utilized compressed air. Double tank scuba gear was also carried aboard, but it was limited for safety reasons for use of only up to 130 feet below the surface. For just-under-the-surface shallow work, such as diving to repair a ship's underwater hull or rudder, a *Jack Brown* facemask fitted with air supply hoses was used by the divers. The ship also carried special tools that enabled the hardhat divers to weld or cut (burn) through metal underwater. Plastic explosives were also stowed aboard to be employed under the sea by the divers to blast apart huge anchor chains or other objects needing removal to facilitate salvage or an undersea repair. Like their cousin the ARS (ocean salvage ship), the ASR is like a 2000-ton seagoing tugboat, a workhorse, with a tough, hard-nosed crew, that played just as hard when ashore as they worked on the ship.

The crew of *Whistler* enjoyed their stay in the port of Subic Bay, a place they visited frequently while their Pearl Harbor based ASR was deployed to the western Pacific. Other ports of call in Japan, Korea, Hong Kong and Taiwan were enjoyable places to visit, but far too expensive for the average sailor. In the town of Olongapo, right outside the main gate to the Subic Base, sailors found the drinks dirt-cheap and the women plentiful and inexpensive. The food, however, was questionable. Men were warned before leaving the base to forego all meals in Olongapo, a town which during the late sixties and early seventies was considered by many to be one of the most immoral places in the far east, and called by some, "the largest brothel in the world."

Before getting underway from Subic Bay on the last Monday in May, the *Whistler* crew mustered under the shelter of the huge white canvas tarp that covered most of the fantail area of the ship's stern. As the rains signaling the beginning of the monsoon season pounded on the tarp above them, the ship's executive officer, Lieutenant Thomas Ramos, USN, told the crew what was in store for them for the forthcoming week.

"We are going to a place just southwest of here where we will lay a two point moor over an old wreck, that should be easy to locate on sonar. Once tight in the moor, we will commence diving operations, first with mark-5 hardhats, then later in the week with helium-oxygen. We will also get in some scuba diving before the week is over. All divers including designated officers and chief petty officers will participate. Also, once we get in the moor tomorrow morning, I want to remind all of you that there will be no fishing allowed at any time. There are many big sharks in this area and fishing brings them around. We don't want to have happen what took place last month off Okinawa when we had to secure all diving operations. The plan is to wrap up the diving ops on Friday morning and return back here to Subic next Saturday morning for a two-week upkeep period."

After an uneventful but wet transit to the position where *Stiles* had the sonar contact, Captain Gallagher ordered the sonar tracking to begin. Equipped with a modern SQS-series sonar system, *Whistler* had both an active and passive capability. The ship's sonar gear was located with the radar consoles in the "combat" compartment just aft of the bridge. There was also a sonar repeater on the bridge where the captain or the officer of the deck could monitor contacts and echoes. Proceeding at slow speed toward the position of the wreck, labeled "initial posit" on the navigational chart, the sonar pings could be heard throughout the ship as the search commenced. Within ten minutes, sonar reported a contact.

"Bridge, sonar, we have a solid contact bearing two one three range seven zero zero yards."

Seated in the captain's chair on the starboard side of the covered bridge, Sam Gallagher leaned forward to view the sonar repeater and saw the solid contact at the same position reported from sonar.

"Very well sonar, this looks like what we're after, but I want to search all around the initial posit out to five miles to make sure it's the only one around here."

"Sonar aye."

After determining that the large blip was in fact the only one in the area, Gallagher ordered the officer of the deck to maneuver the ship directly over the wreck contact, where they would drop a marker buoy prior to anchoring.

"Let sonar coax you to the drop spot, and then release it to windward so we won't drift over it."

After dropping the marker buoy on the wreck, Gallagher let the officer of the deck, Warrant Officer Ben Tolliver, maneuver the ship for the two-point anchoring moor. Like most of the ship's officers, Tolliver was an ex-enlisted man. He was also the ship's diving officer and the first lieutenant responsible for everything topside, including anchor gear, booms, cranes and the ship's boats. Both Gallagher and XO Ramos held him in high regard. He was also respected by the men, who knew that, like the captain and exec, that he was once "one of them." As diving officer, he was responsible to the captain for the maintenance and use of all the ship's diving gear, including the rescue bell and two hyperbaric chambers used to decompress divers on the surface (SUR-D) and to treat diving accidents such as the bends.

Tolliver first moved the ship to a plotted position where the stern anchor would be dropped. Once on the bottom, the stern anchor cable would be paid out as the ship moved ahead of the buoy marking the wreck to another plotted position where the bow anchor would be lowered. Once it was set, the ship would be moved to the desired position by heaving in on the stern wire with the towing engine while the bow anchor chain was let out. The mooring plan was not as simple as it sounded. In addition to ocean depth and chain-to-depth ratio, it had to take into consideration wind and current direction to provide for a lee (shelter) on the port side aft where the diving would take place. If conditions changed, the moor would have to be adjusted. For submarine rescue evolutions, *Whistler* would lay a precise "4-point" moor, which involved the use of four huge, red mooring buoys and four anchors dropped with precise accuracy so the ship could center directly over a sunken submarine. Such a moor requires exacting navigational techniques coordinated with superior deck seamanship.

With little coaching from the captain, Tolliver positioned *Whistler* exactly as planned, ordered both bow and stern chains tightened, and after getting reports that both anchors were holding, turned to the captain and said the ship was positioned.

"We're right there, captain. Request permission to secure both the bow and stern anchor details, secure propulsion and set the regular at-anchor watch rotation."

"Very well, Ben. That was a good job."

Getting the word from Tolliver to set the at-anchor watch, the boatswain mate stepped to the microphone for the ship's MC system and after a shrill blast on the "boatswain pipe" announced:

> *"NOW SECURE THE FORE AND AFT ANCHOR DETAILS, SET THE REGULAR AT-ANCHOR WATCH. ON DECK SECTION THREE."*

It was now late morning, and captain Gallagher called for a meeting in the wardroom of the ship's officers and the *Whistler's* master diver, senior chief machinist mate Anthony (Tony) Drummond. He told them the diving would start after the noon meal, and that he wanted either Drummond, Tolliver or the exec on the fantail directing the undersea training. "I want one of you back there at all times, and you can buzz me either here in the wardroom or in my cabin if you have any problems."

The procedure for the hardhat diving was discussed in great detail. The plan was for divers to be sent down two at a time on the diving "stage" that would be lowered by the ship's port boat boom. If possible, the stage would be let down in a fashion so that it would come down alongside the wreck. Then the divers would inspect what they found, but not enter the wreck or go up on the deck until it was determined what the wreck was, and what condition it was in.

"Under no conditions will the first two divers attempt to enter the wreck or go up on deck," the captain ordered. "Whatever this thing is, it may have been here for many years and could be rotted and falling apart. We don't want anyone falling through a deck or fouling up air hoses down there. We've got all week, and I want to go about exploring this thing slowly and carefully. By tomorrow we should be able to dive off both sides of the fantail simultaneously. It will be good training for all, and I want to use both hyperbaric chambers to surface decompress the last sets of divers each day."

Lieutenant Ramos then asked the diving officer if the rotation had been worked out to include all the divers onboard. Tolliver passed a copy of the rotation list to Ramos who looked it over carefully to ensure that no one man was scheduled for more than one dive a day for decompression considerations. He then asked the engineering officer to report the status of the ship's air banks and compressors.

"All the banks are topped off (full) and all three compressors are in commission. We will charge the banks each night after the diving has been secured. I see no problem as long as the compressors stay on the line. As you know XO, they're over 30 years old, and the last time one of them crapped out, the spare part was nonexistent, we had to have it made on the base."

After the noon meal, the fantail area aboard the USS *Whistler* was a beehive of activity. The rain had stopped, the seas were calm and the air was hot and muggy. The men working with the heavy, cumbersome mark-5 hardhat diving apparatus, umbilical air and communication hoses wore khaki shorts and sneakers and sweated profusely while hoping for a cool ocean breeze to come up. The first two divers were boatswain mate first class Bernard (Buck) Oslowski from

Cleveland and his partner hull technician first class Scott (Scotty) Horvath from Baltimore. In charge on deck for the first dive was the ship's master diver, senior chief Drummond.

The mark-5 hardhat diving gear had been in continuous use in the U.S. Navy since 1914. The only modification was the addition of a speaking transducer on the upper left part of the helmet and the associated cable that is tethered with the air supply hose up to the surface where the diving supervisor can talk to each diver and relay messages between the two. Each helmet and breastplate is marked with either a red or yellow triangle, and when they talked to the surface they would call themselves either "red diver" or "yellow diver". Oslowski and Horvath sat on benches and peeled the heavy canvas diving suits over long underwear. The canvas suits were fitted with rubber cuffs that fit tightly around the wrists, but kept air in the suits while allowing free use of the hands for the necessary underwater work. Assisted by four other divers in the dressing process, enormous lead shoes were slid over the canvas part of the suits that covered the feet. Then the breastplate is bolted to the rubber neck of the suit. A lead belt of more than 50 pounds is fitted around the waist and held in place with large leather straps crossed over the shoulders. The air hose and transducer cables are screwed to the helmet with heavy duty brass nuts and an air control inlet valve is tied to the suit in a way that the diver can reach it to increase or decrease the air coming into the suit. The weight of the breastplate and helmet is 65 pounds and with the lead belt and lead shoes, the whole rig weights more than 150 pounds. It is extremely uncomfortable for the divers while they are on deck waiting to get in the water. Even a big, strong man must use tremendous leg strength to rise from the dressing bench and board the stage. Hardhat divers cannot wait to get underwater where air pressure enters the suit and lifts the weight of the breastplate and helmet from the shoulders. Most hardhat divers wear a "horse-collar" padding over the shoulders as a buffer from the ponderous and angled edges of the breastplate. Some divers considered themselves tougher than others however, refused the optional padding and referred to those who wore it as "candyasses."

The last thing to go on the diver is the helmet, which screws onto the circular ring at the top of the breast plate. The helmet is fitted with three pressure-resistant glass ports and a circular glass faceplate that is hinged and is the last thing to be locked shut before the diver rises to get onto the stage. All four ports are protected by brass guards to prevent breakage of the glass. The helmet also has an exhaust valve mounted on the lower right side. This valve is set before the dive begins, but can be adjusted by the diver either by hand or by a "chin-push" lever inside the helmet. The "chin-push" allows the diver to dump excess air merely by moving his chin against the flat, round lever and pushing outward. Once he releases the pressure, the chin lever returns to its original position, ready to be pushed again when necessary. On the lower left of the helmet there is a brass, toggle-style valve called a "spit-cock." This toggle-valve can be moved by hand and lets a small amount of water into the helmet. This valve is used when the face plate fogs up. The diver turns his head to the left, opens the toggle, sucks in some salt water and then spits it up against the inside of the faceplate to improve visibility. But visibility or not, U.S. Navy hardhat divers are trained to work underwater completely in the blind. All of *Whistler's* divers were at one time or another trained at the old Navy School of Diving and Salvage in Washington, D.C. in the muddy and putrid Potomac River, where they were required to perform mechanical feats on the bottom that, in most cases, was three or four feet under the black, viscous mud. This training involves the use of hand tools, underwater welding/cutting devices and the rigging of hoses, hoisting straps and a variety of other training projects and the eventual raising of a sunken vessel prior to graduation. Those who survived this arduous training regimen were grateful for it, as they found things easier when they got "out to the fleet," where in most cases, they are able to see, even if dimly, what they are working on. The Washington school included grueling physical conditioning, scuba and classroom work and was most effective. Each man had to perform in the most difficult conditions imaginable…under the mud, under the ice and inside wrecks where one could not see an inch in front of the faceplate. But such was not the case this day in May, just northwest of the Island of Palawan in the warm and reasonably clear waters of the South China Sea.

Oslowski and Horvath had made hundreds of dives such as they were about to embark upon and both were anxious to get under the water where they could "hit the air" and get the weight off their shoulders and back. Not a profession for a frail man, hardhat divers must be strong enough to stand on deck and walk to the stage or ladder to the water. Big men have a definite advantage and Oslowski and Horvath were well over six feet tall, and physically strong. For the first dive of the day, Horvath was designated "red diver" and Oslowski "yellow diver". Before their faceplates were shut, chief Drummond spoke to each through the five-inch diameter opening.

"I want you to keep an eye below the stage on the way down. Sonar says the wreck is off to the side, and not right under us, but to make sure, watch below. I don't want the stage to come down on top of it. You're going to 215 feet and the bottom time will be about 15 minutes. Okay, let's get up now and get on the stage." Both divers *klunked* to the stage, took their positions and held on as the stage was swung over the side and, without pausing, commenced being lowered into the sea. As the descent started, both divers were required to report "okay red" or "okay yellow" almost continuously on the way down to Chief Drummond, who manned the communications from *Whistler's* diving station on the fantail. This is done to ensure that neither diver is having problems equalizing pressure in the eardrums, which could rupture if not cleared. Unlike other diving where a man can hold his nose and blow to equalize, or use a nose plug, a hardhat diver, whose hands are isolated outside the suit, must lay one side of his nose at a time up against a piece of canvas "nose rag" that extends up into the lower helmet from top of the suit and can be pushed with the nose up against the lower inside rim of the faceplate as a means of closing one nostril at a time to keep up with the increase in sea pressure as the stage proceeds to the bottom of the ocean. Occasionally a mere sniffle or minor cold can hinder a diver's ability to equalize, and when this happens, the stage is stopped until the diver can clear. If a man is having a problem clearing he says, "hold red" (or yellow), at which time the diving supervisor stops the stage wherever it is. Back in the "old days" many of the original Navy hardhat divers had their eardrums pierced to alleviate the equalization of sea pressure problem. Although the piercing worked, many eventually suffered deafness or other maladies, and the Navy banned the piercing in the 1930s. As the sinuses, eardrums and passages in between are not the same for everyone, some divers can equalize by merely swallowing rapidly on the way down. Oslowski and Horvath fit into this category. Prior to the implementation of the speaker system between the diver and topside, all communications were done by using "tug signals" on a rope. Such signals are still taught to divers, for if the communications wire failed for some reason, the tug signals could be used through the umbilical hoses between the ship and the diver. The signals are also used for shallow mask diving and also for some scuba dives where a tending line is used.

The diving stage with both men standing to each side went straight down without either man requiring a hold to equalize. As the stage passed 170 feet, a shocked Horvath glimpsed a sight through the clear water that he couldn't believe. "Hold red," he hollered into the helmet, and as the stage came to a halt, he heard the voice of Chief Drummond, "What's the problem, red diver?"

Pointing over the rail of the stage while grabbing the arm of Oslowski to show him what he saw, Horvath spoke with a loud and surprised voice into his helmet.

"Topside, this is red diver. We are even with the top of the wreck, which is about 30 feet way, and it is a goddamn submarine, and it's not an old one…it looks like a fuckin' nuke!"

A flabbergasted Chief Drummond responded, "Very well, red diver. Now I want you to calm down, look again at what you see and send up more details." Then to Oslowski, "Yellow diver, how do you identify the wreck?"

"Topside, this is yellow diver. I see a submarine painted black with no numbers. It looks like it hasn't been here very long. It has a round hull, rounded bow and the bow planes are at deck level just forward of the sail. This ain't no wreck…it's a big, new-lookin' nuke submarine."

Then from red diver…"Chief, the forward escape hatch is open, and there is a line leading from it that's hanging over the side." Chief Drummond told both divers that the stage would remain where it is for now and that they should continue to study what they were observing. He picked up the intercom phone and buzzed the captain's cabin.

"Captain, you're not gonna believe this, but I've stopped the stage at 170 feet. Both divers say we've got a nuke submarine down there. It doesn't look very old and the forward escape hatch is open."

"Jesus Christ, Chief. Hold them where they are, I'll be right back there."

Arriving on the fantail with the executive officer in tow, Gallagher picked up the mike and spoke simultaneously to both divers.

"Red and yellow divers, this is the Captain. It is very important for you to pass up to us everything you see, no matter how minor or insignificant you may think something may look, it could be important. You will go to the bottom next, and we will direct you from there." He told the XO to get a recorder to document everything the divers report. To Drummond he ordered, "Chief, I want you to put them on the bottom and get an estimate of the length and beam of the sub. Also the number of screws (propellers), the shape of the sail and any other details they may see. I'm going to want each of them to make me a sketch of what they have observed when we bring them up. In that regard, after their bottom time is up, bring them straight up for surface decompression. I want to get another set of divers down there, and then I've got a feeling we'll be getting the hell out of here!"

"Aye, aye, Captain."

Captain Gallagher told the XO he wanted the diving officer (warrant officer Tolliver) and chief Mitchell to get dressed for the next dive.

"Both Ben and Mitchell have served on nukes, so they may be able to see some things that Oslowski and Horvath wouldn't notice. Also, have the engineer bring the radiation detector back here. You never can tell, if this is a nuke, and it's had some sort of casualty, it may be hot. Have both divers checked as they get off the stage and prepare to have them hosed down if anything is detected."

"Aye, aye, Captain, and whose boat do you think this is?"

"I don't know, Tom. It could be a *Chicom* (Chinese Communist), but I don't think they have any nukes yet. It could also be a boat from an Arab country. Intelligence reports say they've been supplying the rebels in the Philippines with arms…but they aren't supposed to have any nukes either. If this were actually a nuke it would have to be a Russian. We would have been informed if one of ours or a Brit was on the bottom."

Once on the bottom, both divers left the stage, and with one slow step at a time, Oslowski proceeded toward the stern of the wreck while Horvath went forward. Chief Tolliver directed each diver to stop when each was exactly abreast of the bow and stern respectively. He would then measure the distance between their bubbles and make an estimate of the length of the vessel. When Oslowski reached the area right under the stern he made a report.

"Topside, yellow diver. I saw bubbles coming from the after part of the vessel about halfway between amidships and the stern. This is definitely a sub. I am standing right under the stern planes and rudder, and it has three screws. I repeat THREE screws!"

Horvath told Chief Drummond what he saw near the bow.

"Topside, red diver, I am abreast the bow. It is bullet-shaped like a nuke. There is a line hanging over the starboard side with nothing on the end of it. The line is half-inch and looks about 200 feet long. Also, I can see what looks like eight outer doors to torpedo tubes. This is a big sonofabitch and I see no weed or barnacles. It looks new!"

From Chief Drummond on the fantail, "Good job, red and yellow divers. Now proceed back to the stage. Let me know when you're both aboard with hoses clear. We're going to bring you straight up and do the decompression in the chamber."

"Red diver, aye."

"Yellow diver, aye."

The normal procedure in bringing divers up on a stage from such a depth would be to bring them up slowly in steps to prevent the bends or an embolism. The diving tables are used to do this and depth and bottom time are used to compute the decompression procedure. For the bottom depth that Oslowski and Horvath were exposed to for approximately 15 minutes, they would have spent nearly an hour decompressing at several depths before they could be brought on deck. With surface decompression (Sur D), the divers are brought straight up and rapidly undressed by tenders, then rushed into a decompression chamber (*Whistler* had two) where they were pressurized then "brought up slowly in the pot." A diving qualified hospital corpsman and another diver control the decompression.

When Horvath and Oslowski emerged alongside the fantail, they were checked over with a radiation detecting device. Oslowski's suit showed traces.

The order was given to, "Hose him down fast, then undress him. Then I want all his gear hosed again and hung over the side. Then check the men that touched his gear."

After both men were placed in the chamber to start the decompression procedure, Horvath and his gear were found to be clean, and the handlers also checked clean. The "hot" suit was re-hosed with fresh water, then the whole hardhat apparatus was put in a large steel basket and placed over the side to make sure all traces of radiation were removed. The next two divers, warrant officer Ben Tolliver and chief engineman Ray Mitchell were fully dressed, on the stage and headed for the target below. This time the Captain had moved *Whistler* closer so the stage could be lowered to the deck of the submarine for a closer inspection. He also told both men to stay away from any bubbles. Tolliver was given an underwater camera and directed to take close up photos of anything that had letters or numbers on it. Once on deck the reports came promptly to the fantail.

"This is definitely a nuke," Tolliver stressed. "The hull is rounded, there are no diesel exhaust ports. The sail is streamlined, and I'm taking pictures of markings on the after escape buoy that appear to be Russian." Mitchell was up forward and said he could see in the escape trunk.

"Somebody locked out (escaped) from this bastard and it wasn't too long ago. The buoy line looks like new, and I'm going to cut some and bring it up with me. The lower hatch to the escape trunk is shut, and reaching inside I am able to grab some kind of an escape jacket that has some printing on it. I'll bring that up too. There's four upper hatch doors on each side of the deck up here. They look like outer doors to vertical missile tubes." Then from Tolliver, "Topside this is red diver. There are two upper missile hatches aft of the sail. It looks as if the starboard hatch is damaged and pushed upward… I'll get a shot of it."

The Captain turned to Chief Drummond and told him to get both divers to the surface as soon as possible. "We'll Sur D them in the other chamber. I want you to secure from diving operations, stow all diving gear and make the fantail ready for sea. We'll be getting underway shortly…and tell yellow driver to shut the escape hatch before he comes up."

This time, each diver arrived on deck "clean," and as each were swiftly readied for the chamber, the executive officer took the camera. Both he and the captain took great interest in the escape life jacket brought up by Chief Mitchell.

"This is Russian lingo, the exec stated.

"Get those photos developed as soon as you can, Tom. I'm going to the radio shack to call SubFlot Seven on the secure phone."

Captain Frank Kelly was at his desk at flotilla headquarters in Yokosuka, Japan when his chief of staff burst into the room and reported the CO of *Whistler* was on the secure phone in the communications center. "He says it's urgent sir."

"This is Kelly. What do you have, Sam?"

"Commodore (honorary title for flotilla and squadron commanders), we're on routine diving ops down here just off Palawan, and we've come upon what appears to be a bottomed Soviet nuclear submarine. It has no growth on the hull, and looks like it's only been bottomed a short time. Also sir, the forward escape hatch was open with a line hanging out. We brought up an escape jacket from the open trunk with Russian print on it, and we got some photos that are being developed now. The boat is in 215 feet of water on a sandbar, and is about 300 hundred free long and it has three screws. I used the secure phone for this instead of sending a message because it has got to be most sensitive info, and I felt it should be up to you or the fleet commander to decide who to inform and in what sequence."

A stunned Captain Kelly hesitated to catch his breath and then responded.

"You did the right thing, Sam. I can't tell you much now, but this fits into something we've been looking into. I want you to give me the exact position of the bottomed boat and after this conversation leave your anchorage and head back toward Subic. You will shortly receive a message telling you where and when to proceed. By the way, did any other ships see you diving in the area?"

"No sir, only a few small fishing boats, and they were quite distant and too far away for them to see what we were doing. Oh, there's one more thing sir that may be important. One of my divers who went under the stern reported that the nuke left a trail in the sand for as far back as he could see. He said it looked like the sub came straight into the gradually shallowing water without changing depth…We also picked up a little radiation on one diver, but he's clean now."

"Sam it sounds like that sonofabitch came straight in instead of having sunk vertically there. How flat is the ocean bottom where the boat lies?"

"It's a very gradual up-slope to where the nuke grounded. You can go seaward from our position a good mile, and the bottom is only a fathom deeper."

Kelly made very careful notes, and after having Gallagher repeat the position twice and writing it down, he concluded the conversation.

"Sam, you and your ship have done a super job and right now I've got to make a call on this very phone to the fleet boss. You'll get a message within a few hours as to what we will want you to do next, but I imagine a big debriefing is in order, so get all your ducks in line.

"Aye, aye, sir."

Kelly returned swiftly to his office where his chief of staff and operations officer waited anxiously to see if their boss could tell them the gist of the urgent call.

"Gentlemen, you're not going to believe this…but it looks as if *Whistler* has found CHARLIE FOUR…on a sandbar in only 215 feet of water! Get me a blow-up chart that shows the northwest coast of Palawan. I want to look at the position before calling the Admiral. Prepare yourselves for a long night. Morning is still four hours away in Washington, and they haven't gone to bed yet in Pearl."

CHAPTER 11

DANGEROUS UNDERTAKINGS

Deeply involved with his staff aboard the flagship, the cruiser *Aurora,* regarding ongoing operations in and around Vietnam, Vice Admiral Marc Langlois, Commander of the U.S. 7th Fleet, shook his head and grimaced with a "what now?" expression as he was paged for a "most urgent, classified" call on the secure phone net from the Commander of Submarine Flotilla 7 in Yokosuka. Moored to the large "fleet pier" at the Subic Bay base, the *Aurora* was a floating, mobile headquarters for the Admiral and his large staff that had overall control of all U.S. Navy ships in the western Pacific. In the chain of command, Langlois reported to Admiral Dexter Collins, who was the boss of the entire U.S. Pacific fleet. Collins reported to Admiral Geramia, who held the title of CINCPAC, and as such, controlled all U.S. armed forces in the Pacific; army, air force, navy and marines. CINCPAC answered to the Chief of Naval Operations and the Joint Chiefs of Staff who come under the service secretaries and the Secretary of Defense, one step from the President.

Admiral Langlois listened carefully to Captain Kelly's message, which was a near duplicate of what he had been told by Gallagher. Like Kelly, Langlois took down the position of the discovery and instructed Kelly further.

"Frank, I want you to direct *Whistler* into Subic, but have them conduct independent training ops at sea, and not too far from here until we have a date and time for a debriefing. When this occurs, have them anchor in the harbor. Tell the CO to allow no one to leave the ship or to come on board until we get the spooks and whoever else they want out here to look into this. I've got to call up the line to see what the plan will be. In any case, the decision on where we go from here on this one will be made in Washington. Also, Frank, for the time being I want everything that pertains to this development that has to be communicated to be done on secure phones. We don't want any written messages, that could possibly be viewed by those who have no need to know."

"Aye, aye, Admiral. Should I call SUBPAC in Pearl, or will you have Fleet notify him?"

"I'll see that Fleet notifies SUBPAC, and for now keep to a minimum those on your staff who have to know about this. Sooner or later a lot of people will know, but right now keep it limited. I say this because the word is out that the Soviets are missing a submarine in the South China Sea, for it's already been in a few newspapers that they had a big search going on for the missing boat. Now that we know exactly where that boat is, we must keep that position a very closely guarded Top Secret."

The word of the discovery went rapidly up the chain of command, and the Honorable Randolph Beasley, Secretary of Defense, was notified by General Orville Wilson, USAF, Chairman of the Joint Chiefs of Staff, at five in the morning of the discovery.

"So we know where a sunken Russian submarine is located…what is so urgent about that General?"

"I apologize for the inconvenience Mister Secretary, but the Navy, and I concur, feel this is important because the submarine is nuclear. It probably has nuclear missiles and torpedoes on board, and is bottomed in shallow water where she can be reached by salvage personnel. Also sir, this submarine may be hot and present the potential for a colossal environmental disaster to several Philippine Islands and the surrounding waters."

After several grunts into the phone, the Secretary was wide awake and alert to what the General was telling him. "I'm sorry, General, you were perfectly correct to call me, and I'm going to buzz the White House right away. I've got a feeling there will be some sort of meeting right after the President has breakfast, so be prepared. I'll get back to you as soon as I can to let you know about what he wants to do."

The President was awakened at his regular hour of 6 am, and was handed the secure phone by the aide who awakened him. After hearing the brief description of the situation from his Secretary of Defense, the President called an immediate briefing where he could get all the facts.

"Eight A.M. in the War Room over here. I want yourself, SecNav, CNO, ONI and the JCS Chairman to be there. I think the CIA should also be present, and I'll have him notified."

The meeting in the White House War Room lasted no more than 20 minutes, as the President had a tight schedule that day. Air Force One was waiting to take him to the west coast for a series of joint campaign appearances with California congressional candidates to boost his (and their) chances in the November elections.

"Gentlemen, I'm going to play the devil's advocate," the president started. "Tell me why we shouldn't just tell the Russians that we've found a submarine that we think is theirs, and why don't you come and get it? We could say it is a radiation environmental hazard, make political points around the world and put the Soviets on the spot to do something to remove it."

Admiral Bradley Danielson, USN, a submariner and the Chief of Naval Operations (CNO) took a short swig of his coffee, snuffed out his cigarette and addressed the president directly in a slow, calm, but convincing voice.

"Mister President, your advocate proposal certainly has political merits. However, there are other factors we should consider. First, I admit at this early date we do not have a definitive plan to propose to you, and at this point I see no way we could raise the submarine and tow it away to a place where we could get what we want from it. It would probably take weeks to raise it, and we'd be observed doing so. Also, the boat is more than likely full of radiation and as such we couldn't get inside it for years. But, there are some things we could do, possibly without detection, that would be of monumental value to our national defense such as pulling the nuclear weapons out of the hull and removing some of the antennas from inside the sail. None of these items would be in the inside radiated spaces. They are in launch tubes that are isolated from the compartments."

"And why, Admiral, would these things be valuable to us?"

"It would tell us the level of nuclear weapon technology the Soviets have reached and show us whether we've over or underestimated their capabilities and determining whether or not we need to develop something new to go after these weapons in a war situation."

The Admiral in charge of the Office of Naval Intelligence fully supported the CNO and added that the antennas and one of the propellers would also be of tremendous value. Admiral Danielson's proposal was deemed "worth looking into further" by all present, but it was agreed upon unanimously that there were two questions that needed to be answered: (1) How could the removal of weapons and other items be accomplished without detection? And (2) What would be done with the hull of the submarine after the items were removed?

CIA chief Brady Carmichael spoke of the risks:

"Mister President, I don't have all the info on this that our Navy here does, but it seems mighty strange to me that the Russians can't find one of their own submarines, and we come upon it be accident?...We have to be very careful here. The Russians could retaliate in many serious ways if they catch us trying to steal one of their submarines with many of their dead sons aboard. World opinion would also go against us if we are caught. This one scares the hell out of me!"

The President nodded to the CNO who was ready for a response to Carmichael.

"From what we know so far Brady, the Soviets have been searching hundreds of miles to the north of where we found their submarine, and so have we, for there was an underwater explosion in that area several weeks ago, but nothing was found up there. In a nutshell, there is no explanation as to why the sub came to rest off Palawan or even if the explosion to the north had anything to do with the sub we discovered. But I certainly concur that we must be very careful as to how we proceed here, for it we take the wrong road, it could lead to very dangerous consequences."

The meeting concluded with the Secretary of Defense proposing that the Navy come up with a salvage plan within 72 hours, at which time another meeting would be scheduled to consider the proposal and allow the president to consider a fuller range of possibilities before a go or no-go decision is made.

"Whether or not we decide on any kind of a salvage expedition, we should have a plan in 72 hours, and that plan depends upon getting every bit of information from the underwater discovery sight and piece it together with everything we've picked up from our intelligence networks. Right now, the most important thing is that no word of this discovery leaks out. Top secret is an understatement. This information is super-sensitive and the repercussions of a leak of what we've found could be disastrous."

The President nodded in apparent agreement with the secretary's proposal, rose from his chair and shook hands with each official as they left the room. He spoke a few words to each and most wished him to – "Have a good trip mister President."

Immediately after the short White House meeting, Defense Secretary Beasley asked the other attending officials to meet with him at his office in the Pentagon. There they decided the Navy must come up with the plan of action within three days and that in the meantime there would be nothing transmitted in writing about the matter and that anything pertaining to the subject of the discovery be immediately classified *Cosmic Top Secret*. The Navy Secretary stressed security and said that, at this stage, all involved staffs must keep to a bare minimum those considered to have a "need to know." The CNO also made the decision to quarantine the *Whistler* crew for now.

"We just can't take a chance on one of the men getting on drugs or alcohol and letting the cat out of the bag," he cautioned.

During the discussions, Brady Carmichael made a terse remark that startled no one but Beasley, the newly appointed Secretary of Defense (SECDEF).

"Gentlemen, I hope we're not looking at another Russian gift-horse here!"

Letting the comment pass, Beasley instead asked Carmichael to secretly use operatives in the Philippines and

Borneo to probe the Islands and other land areas near where the submarine was found.

"Since there's a possibility that some people may have escaped from this vessel and made it to shore, we'd like to find them before the Soviets do. Also, items from the submarine may have washed up on the beach or been picked up by fishermen. Do you have people who can discretely search the area without anyone suspecting what we're looking for?"

"Mister Secretary, it is our business to take on just such a mission as this one. I have a man who is responsible for the very area you're talking about. He is in charge of our operatives in the Philippines and Malaysia, and will not leave a stone unturned…I also want to suggest sir that we alert our boys in Siberia and Moscow to keep their eyes and ears open."

Beasley didn't know quite how to take the somewhat brusk CIA Chief, but he felt a need to let him know where his orders would be coming from in this matter.

"I will leave it to your discretion as to how you go about obtaining information, but I want to make it absolutely clear that as the investigation progresses, no one in your organization discloses what we've found northwest of Palawan. Also, I want your man in charge of this search to be prepared to meet with the Navy in Pearl Harbor in two days hence. Admiral Danielson is organizing a preliminary plan, and is sending some people out to the Philippines today."

Carmichael nodded, and said he would have his man in Hawaii within 24 hours.

The chief of naval operations also got things moving in a hurry by sending two key naval officers to Subic Bay to gather all the information they could from the *Whistler*. They were Captain James Leominster, the U.S. Navy supervisor of diving and salvage and Captain Murray Gunderson, Soviet submarine specialist from the office of naval intelligence. Flown out to the Philippines in a special high-speed air force courier jet, the two were ordered to "get all the facts" then fly to Pearl Harbor within 36 hours and meet with CINCPACFLEET and SUBPAC, who were delegated to work with both officers to come up with the technical and operational aspects of a salvage plan for CHARLIE FOUR.

Gunderson, Leominster and a Captain Seely from the 7th fleet staff flew by helicopter to the *Whistler* which was preparing to enter Subic Bay from sea. It was now the second day of June, and shortly after the three officers came aboard, the ship made fast to a mooring buoy in the outer harbor. Seely brought a large bag with him that contained the ship's mail, and all three wore work khakis and carried only briefcases and shaving gear.

Leominster, who was called *"soup-sal"* (supervisor of diving and salvage) throughout the diving navy, was an ex-enlisted man and former diver who had well over 30 years service. Arriving on the fantail, he and the other visitors exchanged salutes with *Whistler's* skipper. Placing his hand on Gallagher's shoulder in a friendly fashion he told him they were on a tight schedule.

"We won't be here long skipper, the heavy brass in Washington has us going to Pearl tomorrow…so we need to get all the information we can from your end before any decisions are made as to where we go from here."

As the debriefing began in the *Whistler's* wardroom, the executive officer mustered the crew on the fantail and heard groans when he told them there would be no liberty for awhile.

"You haven't done anything wrong," he told them. "In fact, this whole crew can be commended for what we've uncovered, and for the excellent job you've all done since we've been deployed out here in the far East. But the problem is, what we found last Monday is now a Top Secret, and they're not taking any chance on someone blabbing about it. And this is not just enlisted men. Neither the captain nor I nor any of the officers will be going ashore until this security quarantine is lifted. I must also tell you that until further notice, all mail will be censored before it leaves the ship. I don't know what our schedule will be from here, but I've got a gut feeling that we'll be further involved with what's going on. We will let you know something as soon as they tell us."

The wardroom debriefing took six hours, and involved the close scrutiny of the underwater photographs, testimony from the four divers, examination of everything that was seen and conversations recorded. Captain Gunderson from ONI, was able to translate Russian language stenciled on the escape jacket and also painted on the stern market buoy… "As you know, the Soviets paint no numbers or names on their boats, but we now know that the real Russian name of this one is the SS *Morozov,* and her hull number is 875." But one feature of the *Morozov* puzzled him…

"Everything fits that this is of the new CHARLIE class except the two missile launch doors aft the sail. We've never seen this before, but because of their placement, I suspect those tubes are for nuclear missiles. We believe the other missiles this baby carries are conventional with a fifty-mile range. It also looks as if there was some kind of an explosion in the starboard missile tube that very well could have caused the loss of this boat. It would be of stupendous intelligence value to our country if there is a bird in the port tube and we could salvage it. The forward missile tubes are also interesting along with the torpedo tubes. Getting samples from each would give us a good estimate of the Soviet's state-of-the-art in weapons development. This class boat may also carry nuclear-tipped torpedoes that could be used against a carrier task force. Being able to retrieve and examine such a weapon from this boat would be of monumental intelligence value. When you consider that we've never been able to get our hands on a real, modern Russian missile or torpedo, what we're looking at here is a mind-boggling intelligence jackpot of enormous proportions. But we must cover all our bases to succeed. ONI is also very interested in the antennas, electronics and propellers, particularly the small one that is used for quiet running."

The skipper of the *Whistler* and *"soup-sal"* were questioned by Gunderson about possibilities of removing missiles, torpedoes and antennas without raising the boat.

"All three could be done, with the missiles being the most difficult and the antennas the easiest," Gallagher predicted. "We'd have to do a lot of underwater burning with oxy-torches, which could be dangerous near warheads. We're assuming that all these tubes are dry and free of radiation, but that's something else we've got to find out. We've also got to determine what part of this boat is flooded and what part is not, and is the entire interior hot with radiation or just certain spaces? I also have questions about the forward torpedo/missile compartment. Is it flooded or dry? And if it's dry, is it contaminated? And if it's contaminated, how did anyone escape or attempt to escape? Before any weapons removal is attempted, we must do some probing to find out exactly what we're dealing with here."

Captain Leominster, the head of U.S. Navy diving and salvage, tried to put the whole thing in perspective.

"Gentlemen, first I want to commend Sam Gallagher here for the work that *Whistler* has done so far, and it was a very smart move to close the forward escape hatch before leaving the scene as more of those jackets or other items could have floated up and been found. Now, when the question comes up as to whether we could raise this submarine and salvage it…the answer is yes, but the length of time we would need to do so would depend upon whether the inside of the boat is flooded or not. From the information we have about the trail that CHARLIE FOUR left on the sandy bottom, it appears the boat is not flooded to any great extent, and if this is true, we could easily raise her in a day. But if she's flooded it could take a month. In either case, we could never get away with it without detection. There is no way to hide such an operation as we would need several ships, many divers and special equipment. However, the possibility of salvaging the items described by Captain Gunderson is real, and with good weather, the *Whistler* here, with a minimum of help, could retrieve most of what ONI wants within two weeks. But here again, we'd have to keep what we are doing a secret, and I don't know how we can do that, and I have no idea what the Russians would do if they found out. We may be in international waters, but it's their submarine, and the men entombed within are all Russians. We don't want to start World War III out here."

Before the debriefing concluded, captain Seely from 7th fleet explained how any salvage operation would be organized if one took place.

"We're going to the fleet boss in Pearl with all the information we've gathered here today. The Admiral and his staff and some SUBPAC people will come up with a recommendation to send back to Washington. If that recommendation is to salvage items from the *Morozov* boat, the 7th fleet commander would have operational control of the mission with technical support from Captain Leominster's organization. Logistic support would be from here in Subic. The three of us are now going to make a report of this debriefing to my boss then we'll be underway to Pearl Harbor within an hour or so. At this point I want to commend you captain and the *Whistler* crew for the fine job you've done so far. We've got a wealth of information to go on thanks to your efforts. I can't say for sure what *Whistler* will be doing between now and the onset of any operation, but I think you can probably plan on being at sea for a week or so. You should receive orders shortly."

* * *

News of Whistler's discovery in the South China Sea caused tremendous interest in Pearl Harbor, where the key officers from the fleet and submarine force staffs were directed by the CNO to, "Come up with a plan, but minimize the number of people on your staffs that receive knowledge of this development to only those deemed necessary to work on this project. After the three officers arrive in Pearl, the formulation of a proposal in this matter will be of top priority over everything else."

Those chosen to work on the plan and meet with the three captains were Captain Mobley and Lcdr "stubby" Fusina from SUBPAC, Captain "Ruby" Martinez from CINCPACFLT and a special agent from the CIA. Fusina was in a virtual frenzy when he heard of *Whistler's* find. He went to a chart, plotted the position, and then looked quite puzzled.

"How in the Christ did CHARLIE FOUR get way down there?"

Mobley shook his head in bewilderment, and pointing to the position on the chart where the so-called explosion occurred and asked his assistant, "Stubby, how far is the bottomed boat from the explosion position?" Taking a set of steel dividers, Fusina spread them out between the two positions and then moved them to the latitude markings along the left side of the chart, "One hundred ninety miles sir."

"Maybe it's not CHARLIE FOUR. You'd think that if they took some kind of a hit and were able to survive the explosion that they would have been able to surface and either send for help or abandon the boat and get survivors into the water. Apparently none of that occurred, and now we find this boat with the escape hatch open, indicating that at least one person got out. But there's been no word on any survivors from land or sea. Maybe the sharks got whoever escaped. This whole thing is screwy. Could this be another boat or some kind of a Russian trick? What do you think, Stubby?"

"Well, sir, I don't think it's another boat because we would have detected it somewhere along the line. We kept good track of every nuke that came out of Siberia and every boat that went in and out of the Vietnam area, and nothing has been heard of CHARLIE FOUR since the explosion. If this was another boat, say one that came in from the Indian Ocean undetected, it would be one hell of a coincidence for it to have the exact same characteristics as a three screw CHARLIE class and to sink off Palawan 190 miles from where we lost contact with CHARLIE FOUR. Also, sir, why were the Russians searching along CHARLIE FOUR's last plotted track 200 miles north of the sunken boat?" Then gesturing again toward the spot off Palawan on the chart. "If they thought they had a boat lost down here, they would have searched down there, and they didn't. Like our own boats, the Ruskis have assigned operating areas, and I believe that either intentionally or by accident, CHARLIE FOUR got out of hers. The Soviets never searched below twelve degrees North Latitude, and I'm convinced that was the southern boundary of the assigned area. I don't know why or how this boat got where it did, but I believe, sir, that this is indeed CHARLIE FOUR. As for it being a trick, it seems highly doubtful to me. What would be the purpose? And sir, we found this boat by pure luck. If the skipper of the *Stiles* and the skipper of the *Whistler* hadn't known each other and met by chance at the Subic O-Club, we might not have come upon this boat for years. Some fisherman probably would've found it before we did."

"Those are good arguments stubby, and we'll find out more when the ONI, a man from the CIA and *soup-sal* arrive here tomorrow. We've got to think this one out carefully and come up with a sensible recommendation, and I want you to make sure you've got every piece of paper and detail that pertains to this organized and ready."

"I intend to do better than that sir. I've already got a plan in the back of my head, but I need to do some more research and to fine-tune it. I'm going to work on it here tonight and have something to present to you and the Admiral tomorrow morning first thing. The meeting with the spooks and *soup-sal* won't be until thirteen hundred. Hopefully, everything will be all set by then."

* * *

The Secretary of Defense had a long, hectic day at the Pentagon, but through all the meetings, phone calls, Vietnam operational briefings and the usual wads of paperwork, Randolph Beasley was preoccupied with the Soviet submarine discovery, and was dogged all day by the "gift horse" remark by the CIA chief Carmichael that got little reaction from any of the other officials present.

He decided to talk about it with the CNO, a man he had first met back in the late 1930s playing football when Bradley was a star halfback for the Naval Academy when they played Princeton University, where Randolph Beasley was the team captain and an outstanding tackle. Although they hadn't seen each other since those days, they established an excellent rapport after Beasley became the new SECDEF. Their wives also hit it off, became good friends and frequently played bridge together. The four occasionally got together for dinner where they made a rule never to discuss national defense or the goings-on at the Pentagon. He phoned the Admiral late in the afternoon and he readily agreed to a get-together at the Beasley residence after dinner. "I'll bring Amy along, and the wives can also have a chat," he suggested.

Randolph Beasley was no newcomer to national defense, but most of his past expertise was in the civilian world as a CEO of a highly successful aircraft manufacturing company. The President selected him for the defense post based upon his extensive background in procurement, budgeting, and his overall business management skills which he deemed invaluable assets needed to run the Pentagon. The President told him before his appointment that, "We've got to get the hell out of Vietnam" and that "My predecessors never should have got us involved in the first place. You will have a lot of input from the service secretaries and the JCS on how to accomplish this and how to minimize our casualties and still get out of there with some sort of honor."

Beasley's biggest weakness was that he was not *"Washington-wise"* to the way government really worked, versus how it was supposed to run. His military background came from his defense industrial know-how and as an Army officer in World War II, where he served with distinction in the European theater of operations. But he lacked any expertise in international affairs and the formulation of Cold War strategies. He'd been SECDEF for less than six months and knew there was much to learn, and he wasn't afraid to ask questions. This part of his demeanor was greatly appreciated by the JCS, the three service secretaries and all those he worked with.

Now relaxing over an after dinner drink with Danielson in the den of his home, he asked a question that brought a half smile to the CNO, who suspected what the topic of conversation would be.

"I hate to break our rule about talking shop, Brad, but the girls are in the other room, and there's something that was said this morning that's been puzzling me all day. What the hell did Carmichael mean when he characterized the Soviet submarine find as maybe some sort of Russian gift-horse?"

"To answer that, I've got to tell you a story and bring you back to 1962 and the so-called Cuban missile crisis that almost got another war cranked up. During that era, Brady Carmichael was the CIA's Cuban expert. He also had considerable background with the Russians, whom he hates with a passion. He predicted that after the Bay of Pigs fiasco in '61, which he witnessed in person, that the Soviets would somehow exploit our reluctance to support the invasion. Back in 1960, the military was directed to formulate war plans to invade Cuba. These were just-in-case plans for contingency operations. But they existed, and the Russians and Cubans found out they existed. They were naturally quite nervous over the prospect of defending the island against such an invasion from the world's most powerful nation sitting right on their doorstep. When we back-scuttled at the Bay of Pigs, and left thousands of men in a helpless situation, the Soviets saw this as a colossal display of weakness by a so-called "super power" and they set about doing something about our war plans."

Pausing to light a cigarette, the CNO sat silent for a moment, then decided to go further. "Now as long as this stays in this room, I'm going to tell you what I and most of the senior U.S. military officers, then and now, believe to be true. Carmichael claims to have proof that it is true from what they've learned from a few high-ranking KGB defectors. The Soviets put the missiles in Cuba merely as bait. In chess you must sacrifice something in order to get something, and the Russians are chess masters whose moves in the world political arena are not unlike those practiced on a chessboard. They saw the President as a weak sister who had no idea how to use the power he possessed."

"Christ, Brad, that's one dangerous chess game. How did it change our war plans?"

"The Russians only agreed to take the missiles out after we signed a Peace Treaty with Cuba, promising never to invade. We also pulled our missile forces out of Turkey as part of the deal. The press subsequently made the President a big hero for 'backing down Khrushchev', but the Russians and Cubans got exactly what they wanted, and the Soviet people were never told what transpired. Castro and his communists still rule Cuba, but even if the gift-horse missiles ploy worked for the USSR and Castro, it was an incredibly dangerous move by Khrushchev, and it started his downfall from power. The crisis it caused scared the crap out of a lot of the Soviet brass who nonetheless were surprised that our President agreed to let Cuba alone and tolerate the existence of a communist regime just across the Florida Straits. One of Carmichael's defectors said that an island like Cuba, if located off the coast of the USSR with an anti-communist government installed, would be knocked off like swatting a fly. I'm not saying we should have invaded Cuba, but if communism was the big bugaboo for the politicians, then why would we let it exist right in our own backyard then challenge it half-way around the world? Many here in Washington were subsequently incredulous when the same President quickly forgot about Cuba, then sent us to Vietnam instead! I know since he was assassinated they've made him a hero and a martyr, and we hear from the media all the time now about this *Camelot* bullshit, but I can tell you, sir, that he was not held in high esteem back then by the military, and he was not respected overseas. He was popular with the press and with the liberals. The exact opposite of what we have now…a President who is despised by the press and the liberals but respected overseas as a man who knows how to use the power this nation possesses."

Beasley poured a second cognac and prodded Danielson further.

"But you kept your mouths shut and followed orders!"

"Yes, sir, and we still do, and we don't care about republican or democrat…we'd just like to see some consistency. We shouldn't get involved in armed conflicts we have no intention of winning. The flip-flopping of our foreign policy is what makes it difficult to plan for any future conflict. You see this every day in defense procurement. You and I both know that Vietnam is a no-winner, but it could have been! We should have either gone in there with the intent of driving the VietCong completely out or just stayed home. It is frustrating and disheartening for those of us now in high command to ask our young men to lay their lives on the line in a war we have no intention of winning. In the meantime, sir, you have a Pentagon to run and I must run the Navy and we both must forget that this conversation ever took place." After a pause, Danielson continued.

"But back to Brady Carmichael. I can tell you that he is still bitter about what happened, because he told them that Khrushchev was a crazy bastard and capable of such a gambit, and he was ticked off at that time because his own boss, the CIA Director, was afraid to get involved by backing him up. After the crisis the administration ordered Brady away from the Cuba-Russia scene and he was subsequently assigned to the South African office. All that said, I fail to see how this bottomed nuke can be some kind of bait. But Brady just doesn't believe the Russians have accidents. He's obsessed that there is a hidden agenda for everything they do. That's why his remark surprised no one but *you* this morning. He knows the Russians well, and we shouldn't ignore him when he emphasizes that we are dealing with a very dangerous situation here."

"Admiral, I don't know what kind of a plan your Navy is going to recommend, but right now I'm in the same boat with Brady Carmichael, and I don't want you to repeat this to anyone, for we don't have all the options in front of us yet, but this yes or no salvage situation is one very hair raising gamble that I'm not yet ready to lay my money on."

Knowing the discussion was over, both men rose from their chairs and walked to the living room to join their wives who were chatting over long-stemmed glasses of sherry.

"Well, did you men solve all of the problems of the world in there?" the secretary's wife quipped.

The Admiral winked and replied, "We only talked football tonight, but the big world problems will be tackled bright and early tomorrow morning…and in that regard, we've got to say good night, and Amy and I thank you once again for your kind hospitality."

* * *

Immediately after the strategy session in the Secretary of Defense's office in the Pentagon, CIA boss Brady Carmichael summoned his old friend Jose Roque to his office at the headquarters in Virginia. A favorite of Carmichael's since their Scotland days, Roque had been with the agency for 15 years. He had a reputation in the community of spooks that was second to none. A native of Manila who was educated in Hawaii, Roque returned to the Philippines after his schooling and worked for a major copra dealer who operated out of Zamboanga City, but had business dealings on every main island in the Archipelago. Roque was the "leg-man" and spent 90 percent of his time traveling from island to island as a buyer. In this capacity he learned to speak nearly all the dialects spoken in the Philippines, and as a most personable fellow, he made many friends at all levels of society, including those at the highest level of the republic's government. He was recruited by the CIA in the mid '50s to provide information about the scope of communist and Muslim insurgency in the Philippines. His reports were deemed accurate and extremely important by the agency, but after a failed assassination attempt on his life by a communist agent who sniffed out what he was up to, and with his cover blown, Roque wisely decided to leave the islands and took a full-time position with the agency back in the U.S. He met Carmichael at this time and accompanied him on the Holy Loch look-see mission in the late '50s.

As further troubles cropped up in the Philippines, the CIA, at the urging of Carmichael, decided to utilize Roque's proven knowledge of the islands, its people and groups who were causing problems and put him in charge of all intelligence gathering from there. To do this, they had plastic surgery done to his nose and chin, changed his hairline and had him grow a beard and wear glasses. He then returned to his native land and spent six months recruiting agents and setting up an "information funnel" that he could run from Hawaii or his other desk in Washington. During this time he kept a low profile, and there was never any indication that the enemy factions learned his true identify, which was only known by several of his loyal co-agents from the past. This operation was an overall success and Roque was once again able to regularly provide the agency with a wealth of needed intelligence from his network.

The call came just before lunch, and the chief told him, "Pack clothes for a couple of weeks in a warm climate and meet me in my office around 1700. You'll be leaving shortly after that on a special trip."

Arriving precisely on time, Carmichael greeted his protégé with a wide grin, a handshake and an offer of coffee or "something stronger." Roque opted for the "something stronger" and his boss went to a nearby cabinet and poured them each a generous glass of *John Begg* single-malt Scotch whiskey, the drink the two men had shared on many occasions, both good and bad. "Christ, it's after four isn't it Jose? I think we both deserve this, don't you?"

Roque laughed and with a fair Scottish accent repeated to Carmichael the commercial they had both heard on the radio several years back while doing the Holy Loch job. *"Aye... take a peg o' John Begg...*they used to say, and we sure did that night didn't we, Chief," Roque chuckled.

Carmichael rolled his eyes and smiled with the memory, and after they both lit filtered cigarettes, told him the basic facts about the discovery of the Russian nuke. Also, arrangements had been made for him to take a military flight from Bolling Field at 1900 that would arrive in Hawaii before dawn, in plenty of time for the 1300 strategy session with the Navy. Then rising from his chair to a wall chart of the Philippines, Carmichael pointed to the area northwest of Palawan where the *Morozov* was found and then told Roque some more details:

"Jose, I want you to put the longitude and latitude of this spot to memory, because it is not to be marked by you or anyone else in our organization on any chart or map. The location of the submarine is above and beyond top secret. It is absolutely imperative that the position does not fall into the wrong hands. That is why I want you out there and not one of your agents."

"What the hell am I going to be looking for out there Chief?"

"The Navy will give you the details tomorrow, but one of the things is that it's possible some men escaped from the sub and somehow got ashore. If that happened, we'd want to grab 'em before the Russians did for they could tell 'em where to find the sub. You'll be scouring the nearby islands for any signs of the existence of survivors. You know how to use your eyes and ears as well as anyone in this agency and that's the reason you're the man for this mission."

"What do I do if I locate someone?"

"The ONI will send in people to grab such a person and get him the hell out of the islands in a hurry. The Navy will give you more details about such an eventuality. This is a very dangerous situation, and it could become more dangerous if the President lets the Navy get involved with some sort of a salvage plan. There are two things that could get us into real trouble here. The first is that if the Russians actually know where their lost submarine is, and are just waiting for us to make a move…then there could be a serious confrontation. The other possibility, which is also full of danger, is that if the Russians in fact *do not know* where the sub is but if one or more survivors show up somewhere that *do know*, they could ruin the Navy's salvage plans."

"Does the Navy want to raise the sub? How the hell could they do that without anyone knowing about it?"

"I don't think they'll try to raise it, but they may try and pull some nuke weapons out."

"Chief, that sounds like a problem too."

"As for your itinerary out there, listen to what the Navy tells you about probable places where survivors or flotsam could get ashore and then make up your own scouting plan and utilize your knowledge of the islands, the people and the languages to make a good survey. The Navy will tell you more exactly what to look for, and set up a system for you to report whatever you find directly to the Navy ONI man, who'll probably be in Subic Bay. He'll also tell you what your cover will be. I don't want anything sent to me in writing while you're out there. Use the regular coded secure phone hook-up for reports. If you come across something that has nothing to do with the naval interest, don't tell them about it. But get the word to me using our regular secure system. I must warn you, Jose, that his one could roller coaster into something more serious than it seems, like how marvelous the military told us it was when they discovered missiles in Cuba ten years ago. Be very careful, my friend. The President and the JCS are on top of this and are very interested in what happens from here on out. Good luck, Jose."

* * *

Lieutenant Commander Fusina worked until well after midnight at the SUBPAC headquarters at Pearl Harbor. The plan he devised for the exploitation of CHARLIE FOUR was one he was genuinely proud of, and he anxiously awaited the arrival of this boss, Captain Art Mobley, to run it by him. The Captain arrived at exactly 0700 and found his assistant red-eyed and unshaven and still poring over nautical charts and a wide variety of military manuals.

"Holy cow, Stubby, you look like hell. Have you been up all night?"

"No, sir. I caught a couple of hours, but I think I've got something here you should look at."

"Well let's get a cup of coffee here, and you can show me what you've got. Then you gotta get showered and shaved before we brief the admiral."

Fusina moved to a chart of the South China Sea he had mounted on the wall and explained his scheme briefly, without going into great detail about each phase of the operation.

"First of all, sir, I will zip through what I propose without exact times, which we'll have to work out later."

Fusina's plan called for the following events to take place in order:

PHASE 1

(1) Tow a large steel barge from Subic out to the deep area where the Russians have been searching for CHARLIE FOUR. Assuming they tried to find her in the operational area they told her to stay within.

(2) Sink the barge at night in 1500 fathoms of water and send a survey ship to the spot.

(3) Bring in the bathyscaphe *Starfish* from Saipan, and stage a mock operation simulating underwater surveillance by

the bathyscaphe of the supposed sunken submarine. (The *Starfish* is towed from place to place in a large floating drydock, which is flooded down to launch or retrieve the bathyscaphe. The dock also has special umbilicals used with the *Starfish*). Both could be on station within ten days.

(4) Do not openly publicize the mock search, but make no effort to hide it either, as the purpose is to make sure the Soviets pick up on what's going on, and make them believe we've found their missing nuke. The sunken barge will put a real sonar target on the bottom for the Soviets to detect when they send in ships and submarines and take over the search area. (The Soviets have nothing like the *Starfish* that can explore that deep, but they should detect the barge on their surface ship or submarine sonar).

(5) Hopefully, the Russians will conclude we've found the missing nuke that they failed to come across during their recent search efforts. Once the mock deep-water operation is underway, we start phase 2.

PHASE 2

(1) Crash a military aircraft, right next to CHARLIE FOUR. Crash can be done by remote control.

(2) Put "survivor" in raft to be picked up by a destroyer and witnessed by local fishing boats.

(3) Local news of the crash will be forthcoming without us releasing any information.

PHASE 3

(1) Bring in *Whistler,* another salvage vessel and a barge supposedly to start recovery of the airplane and what's in it.

(2) Pull up some of the plane, but just enough for prying eyes to see.
(3) *Whistler* divers commence weapons removal from CHARLIE FOUR.
(4) Anything removed from sub to be done after dark and kept hidden in barge.
(5) Weapons/equipment removed from CHARLIE FOUR to be taken immediately (in darkness and covered) to waiting aircraft in Subic.
(6) Maintain absolute security during this phase.
(7) Complete Phase 3 within 2 weeks.

Captain Mobley stood for a few minutes, chin in hand, staring intensely at the situation chart as many questions raced through his mind. He walked to where Fusina stood, put his hand on his shoulder and exclaimed:

"This sonofabitch could damn well work! You did one hell of a superb job, Stubby! I agree with you on the security aspect, and I might add that we also have to be concerned with that old bugaboo, the weather, and the possibility of a typhoon coming into the area. But there's one big thing we must do if *Whistler* is involved: We must do our best to disguise her. Sending a submarine rescue ship to pick up a downed aircraft woulnd't be a problem in *our* Navy, as an *ASR* certainly has the capability, but we can't let the Ruskis get suspicious. We should make her look like an ARS. Before *Whistler* departs for the scene, we should want to pull her four huge mooring buoys from the superstructure and the submarine rescue chamber from the fantail. We could have an *ATF* haul a barge for this. Also, have *Whistler* paint out the hull number and the sub rescue symbol on each bow. Paint *RS 52* instead to make her look as a regular salvage ship. The ship's name should also be removed from all the

Whistler boats that may be sighted near the scene. These boats will be used to keep curiosity seekers and fishing boats out of the area. All of the removal and painting must be done after dark and out of sight. The buoys and rescue chamber could be placed in a covered barge and moored out of sight at Cubi Point. All of this should be done before Phase 2 gets started. The only other big question I see is what the hell happens to the boat after we take what we want from it? A plan for phase 4 is needed or we might as well forget any salvage."

Nodding his head in agreement, Fusina remarked, "I goofed in not disguising *Whistler* in Phase 1 and I agree that Phase 4 is a bugaboo."

"What if it's as hot as they say it is with radiation?" Mobley worried. "Somebody higher up than I will have to answer that one. If it's hot and the radiation spills into the sea there will be a serious hazard throughout the area to everything that exists in the immediate sea and the people who live on nearby islands. It would be morally wrong to get what we want from the boat and then just leave it there. The salvage people will have to tell us, but maybe this baby could be raised and towed to deep water where it could be re-sunk in depths where there would be little environmental damage."

Mobley met with his boss, and Rear Admiral Carpenter called Fusina's plan "ingenious," but agreed with Mobley that ingenious or not, there must be a phase 4 as a means of removing the sub after any weapons salvage operations were completed.

Next was the big meeting, which in addition to Mobley and Carpenter, included the three captains just returned from Subic, the Pacific Fleet Commander, the Navy Admiral in charge of all armed forces in the Pacific (CINCPAC), Captain Martinez and Roque from the CIA. All aspects of the situation were presented by Gunderson and Leominster, and before Fusina's plan was discussed, the big question continued to be asked, "How and why did CHARLIE FOUR get to where it was?"

Of the several theories presented, Captain Leominster's came the closest to hitting the nail on the head.

"Gentlemen, after close study of these photos taken by *Whistler's* divers, I have concluded that CHARLIE FOUR came upon the shoal straight in, that is, she did not sink there, and would have gone even further toward the shore if they hadn't come up on the shoal." Holding up the enlarged 8x10 black and white photo where all could view it, Leominster pointed to a long crease in the sand astern of the bottomed boat and explained his theory of how CHARLIE FOUR ended up where it is.

"This is of extreme importance," he emphasized, and went on. "This crease, or shallow ditch, was caused by the ship's keel, and in fact it appears this submarine virtually glided in to where it is, and did not strike the bottom violently from a sudden flooding or explosion. This leads me to believe the boat was probably under some sort of automatic pilot for depth and course, and they could have been on the system for a long time to bring CHARLIE FOUR to where she now lies. This auto system could be similar to those in use on aircraft and merchant ships. I say this, because if they went aground because of a navigational error, they should have been able to blow up to the surface, and if that couldn't be done, a lot of people could have escaped, and we would have found some of them, dead or alive, and a lot of flotsam. But in this case, I believe that the only men alive in this boat when it went up on the shoal were in the forward torpedo room, and how many there were and what happened to them are questions still to be answered. The major point here, gentlemen, is that in all probability this submarine is not extensively flooded inside. She is more than likely full of radiation, but it could be easily raised and taken elsewhere… and that is something that should be considered in any plan, and it is also something we can confirm once we get divers and equipment to the scene. The weapons you're after should not be radioactive, as their launch tubes are outside the pressure hull. These are ripe for plucking, and by the way, we determined the Russian name of CHARLIE FOUR. Holding up the escape jacket brought up by *Whistler's* divers, he pointed to the Soviet print on the collar, "What you see here on this escape vest translates to the *SS Morozov*."

Admiral Carpenter questioned the automatic-pilot theory, but called it "certainly possible." "As you know, our nuclear boats all have such a system, but we only use them occasionally. The polaris boats probably utilize the system more than the attack boats."

The Pacific Commander (Admiral Geramia) made the crucial point:

"Gentlemen, regardless of how good a weapons salvage plan we come up with, the crux of this whole thing boils down to whether the sub can somehow be pulled undetected to deep water after the weapons salvage is complete…the moveability of *Morozov* must be determined before any salvage ops begin…" Then to Leominster, "How will you do this Captain?"

"As soon as *Whistler* arrives on the scene, we'll put down divers, and utilizing the ship's main boom, hook a cable to the bow of the sub and take a gradual strain to see if we can lift it off the bottom. Then we'll do the same thing to the stern. Both hauls will be observed by the divers, and if we are able to actually, one-at-a-time, lift both ends of the boat with the boom, then she is probably not flooded and near neutral buoyancy. If this is the case, she could be easily moved to deep water without blowing her to the surface by using a special air tank. There are other ways to find out if she's flooded or not, but it would take much too long a time and require many hull penetrators to make a determination. Therefore I say sir that if we can't budge her with the boom then we abort any salvage operations."

Gunderson considered maximizing the situation: "If we find out that this submarine can be easily towed submerged, why don't we go for the whole bowl of wax? Why not tow her undetected to a remote and secret location where we could have the biggest intelligence catch of all time? We would not only get the weapons technology, we'd get their communications machines and break their codes. We'd also learn how good their sonar, radar and countermeasures are. There is a tremendous intelligence opportunity here"

Geramia being the senior officer present and in full charge of the proceedings nodded to his fleet commander Dexter Collins who appeared anxious to respond to the ONI man.

"I think we're getting way ahead of ourselves here. So far we have no assurance we can salvage anything from this sub without the Russians finding out what we're up to. This whole salvage operation is laced with risk. No matter what we end up doing here, think of the hundreds of men who will know what's going on. Even if we find a way to grab some of their weapons, how long could we keep it a secret? As for towing the whole submarine submerged for a long distance, I don't think we'd stand a prayer of getting away with it, and furthermore, there would be a strong possibility of losing the *Morozov* entirely while towing her due to weather or other complications. I say Captain Gunderson's wish list is real and certainly has huge intelligence possibilities, but is it worth the chance of our being caught or losing everything during a tow? Playing the devil's advocate, I say we just tell the Russians to come and get their boat. We could make them look bad and show our good will to the rest of the world. Of course on the down side, they may try for a propaganda gain by accusing us of sinking it. But if they catch us trying to steal it or take things from it, there's going to be all hell to pay. I know the President and the JCS have only asked that we come up with a salvage plan and did not ask our opinions about the political ramifications of detection, but I strongly feel that such possibilities be included with any plan we send to Washington. This plan should have pluses and minuses but leave the final decision on how we proceed up to them. We must try our best to include all the risks we're talking about here to make sure that whatever they decide upon is based on real and complete information, both positive and negative. All I can tell you gentlemen, is that what I've heard so far, I'm glad that I'm not going to be the one to say yes or no on this one."

Admiral Geramia agreed that this was a serious situation, and that he wanted to hear everything from those present.

"Admiral Collins is correct. Before I send any proposal to Washington, I want to hear all the facts and possibilities, whether positive or negative. Now on the positive side, SUBPAC has a plan to pull some weapons without detection from *Morozov,* and Captain Mobley will now show us what they came up with."

Before he started, Mobley credited his assistant with coming up with the scheme. The plan was received with keen interest, and after many questions about logistics and who would be in charge of what and a timetable, Geramia asked where they would get the aircraft to be ditched from?

Admiral Collins suggested an old Navy P4V could be used and that such a plane could be found at Cubi Point.

Finally, Jose Roque from the CIA was asked his opinion of the plan and how he would fit in.

"I see certain risks here," he said. "The main one is the possibility of the word getting out in Palawan, in Subic or anywhere in the Philippines for that matter about what you're really diving on out there. The islands are full of communist sympathizers and others who buy and sell information like gumdrops at the corner store. The downed airplane ploy sounds like it will work, and the deep water diversion is an excellent idea, and any other way you can distract the Russian navy's attention elsewhere in the Pacific would also be helpful. They have a vast intelligence network throughout the Pacific. They have eyes and ears in Hawaii, Japan, the Philippines and anywhere we have military bases or activity. Intelligence gathering and snooping is a way of life in the communist world, and that is why this operation…if it goes - must be done swiftly, secretly and with a minimum of personnel informed as to what is transpiring off Palawan. It is interesting that you have uncovered the name of this submarine. If you desire to find out more about where it was built, based, or any other facts that could contribute to this venture, we have operatives in Moscow, Leningrad and Siberia that from time to time deliver valuable Soviet naval data to both my office and on the ONI, and perhaps they could uncover something that would be useful to you. The director would have to approve such delving and with the concurrence of the ONI and the JCS."

Admiral Collins asked Roque where he would be when, and if, the operation gets underway.

Roque gave a rundown of his schedule, the areas of the western Philippines he would cover and how he would communicate with a Navy ONI representative in Subic. He also told the group that he and his chief were the only members of the CIA who were informed of the ongoing mission and the discovery of the Russian submarine off Palawan.

"My boss intends to keep it that way," he concluded.

After an intense in-depth, three-hour session and a short break for a meal, the group re-convened and after two more hours came up with a tentative plan to send to Washington on a swift Navy courier jet that was waiting at Hickham Field for captains Gunderson and Leominster, who were designated to convey the goods eastward. The plan was given the code-name *OPERATION PEGASUS.* As two specially selected Navy yeoman began typing the first phases in an adjoining room, Admiral Geramia told the officers of his personal recommendation that would accompany the salvage plan:

"After hearing and reviewing all this, I am going to recommend to the JCS and the President that, after the aircraft crash, if our salvage ship cannot budge the sub off the bottom with her main boom and we determine that *Morozov* is extensively flooded, that we cancel all operations and tell the Russians to come get their submarine."

After a few moments of silence, Geramia called for final contingency options brought up earlier by Admiral Collins.

"We must have plans as to what we do if the Soviets find out what we're diving on off Palawan, and we've also got to have a plan as to what we do with *Morozov* after we've taken what we wanted. These are both questions that the JCS and the President will ask."

Admiral Carpenter answered the first part of the question by stating his opinion as to how a Russian discovery would be handled. "First of all sir, they should really be watching the phony deep operation with *Starfish*, and we can stage a pretty good show up there to keep their attention. And as you know sir they follow the *Starfish* every time we send it on a mission. The last time, they had two of their intelligence trawlers near the tender-dock for a month while *Starfish* dove to pick up a spy satellite that fell in the ocean just east of Midway, and right now there's one waiting off Saipan, just to see where we go next. But if for some reason they find out their boat is off Palawan, and our decoy operation fails, we should simply announce that while our divers were picking up parts of our downed aircraft that they were "astounded" to find a bottomed submarine nearby and that we are attempting to identify it. Then we should immediately, under cover of darkness, tow it submerged to deep, unsalvageable water using *soup-sal's* special gear and drop it. Such depths are only 30 or 40 miles west of where the sub lies. We can tell the Russians we moved it because it was exuding a lot of radiation, creating an environmental threat to the coastal area."

"We should do the same thing after we've pulled what we want from it. Tow it submerged using the same gear to deep water."

Captain Mobley made another suggestion:

"Sir, if we really want to keep their attention on the deep operation, maybe we could let them find out surreptiously that we recovered the marker buoy or the jacket out there with the name of the boat and hull number on it. That may help to convince them that the deep ops are for real."

"That may be worth a shot, Art," Admiral Geramia said, and then stated he agreed with both options proposed by Admiral Carpenter and ordered them to be included in the PEGASUS operation order.

The final questions were directed to *soup-sal* by Geramia:

"Captain Leominster, in your opinion, how long after *Whistler* moors over the sub will you know if the boat is light, that is, easily raised?"

"Within four hours, Admiral."

"What are these special devices that have been mentioned for towing submerged?"

"They are tanks that fit to the hull and contain compressed air that is controlled by a small computer to maintain depth. Divers can fit them to a submarine hull in two hours time."

"And where are these tanks?"

"They are here in Pearl Harbor, sir. We keep several of these special tanks pre-positioned for use in this ocean and other sets are stored in Norfolk for Atlantic use."

"I ask about these things because these are questions that will come up in Washington. My guess is that they will only go for PEGASUS if they are convinced we can get the boat the hell out of there if we get caught or when we are done. Otherwise, they'll either wait six months or so before we do anything, or like admiral Collins' "devil's advocate" pitch, they'll announce to the world that we found the boat and then make political hay out of it by condemning the Soviets for contaminating the South China Sea and the Philippine Islands. I don't like the wait option because it allows a greater opportunity for the word to get out about the sub's location and additionally, what we can learn from the weapons and antennas on board is information we need now...not six months from now! And also it could be discovered accidentally by fishing boats or amateur divers if we wait. On the other side of the coin, if we take what we want from the boat and then leave it there, we will do a great disservice to our friends in the Philippines, and the Russians will make political hay out of us! They could also go to the scene and learn what we took. That is why we've got to know if we can move *Morozov* out of there before we start pulling the weapons." Then looking up at *soup-sal* he gave a final instruction:

"If Washington approves the plan, see to it that the special tanks are immediately flown out to Subic, just in case we need them."

CHAPTER 12

OPERATION *PEGASUS*

Despite objections from one member of the JCS, a "lets wait" from the Secretary of Defense and a "beware of a trap" warning from the CIA head, on the 10th of June, the President of the United States approved OPERATION PEGASUS. The mission was classified *Ultra Cosmic Top Secret* and was ordered to begin immediately.

The operation started with the floating drydock carrying the bathyscaphe *Starfish* being towed from Saipan by the fleet tug (ATF) *USS Mohican* and the oceanographic survey ship (AGS) *USS Northwind* was sailed from Sasebo, Japan. Designated TASK FORCE TWELVE, the ships were slated to rendezvous on June 20 at the fake bottomed submarine position 200 miles north of Palawan. Another ATF, the *USS Sioux*, under the cover of darkness, was set up to tow a 250-foot steel barge full of metal wastes from the base at Subic and sink the entire rig at the same position on June 15.

This barge and its contents were a key facet of the operation. Sonars in 1972 could not discern the shape of a steel object in deep water, and identify what it was. A sonar echo would merely appear as a blip, or a bump on the bottom if marked on a fathometer trace. It was hoped the Soviets would show up in the same area after the *Northwind* and the *Starfish* commenced their "deep discovery" façade and perhaps pick up the trace themselves and conclude it is *Morozov*.

Logistics support for the operation was also put into motion with extra diving gear, oxygen, helium and special underwater radiation detection equipment flown into the

Naval Air Station at Cubi Point, adjacent to the base at Subic. Two of *soup-sal's* special tanks were also flown in. Arrangements were made for additional Navy divers and the assignment of the ocean salvage ship (ARS) *USS Engage* to assist *Whistler*, the ship officially designated to carry out the main thrust of PEGASUS, the removal of weapons and antennas from the *Morozov*.

Steaming off the western coast of the Philippines and still awaiting orders, the *USS Whistler* continued under a no-liberty quarantine while the operation was being organized. Realizing that something should be done to raise the morale of the crew, the skipper requested that the ship be allowed to proceed to an uninhabited and nameless island just east of Mindoro to allow the crew a few days of recreation. One of the old-timers on the ship told the captain that he'd been there several times in the 1950s when two or three ships would anchor nearby and bring the men ashore in the ship's boats for swimming, softball and beer drinking. The captain liked the idea, and sent a message requesting such a visit, and that 20 cases of beer be included with the ship's mail and supplies that were due to be brought out by another vessel in two days. The request was approved, and in the same response message, *Whistler* was given a schedule of events that included a return to a Subic Bay anchorage on 22 June for briefings on the forthcoming operation, the loading of supplies and the departure date for its part in OPERATION PEGASUS. The ship was also told that Captain Leominster would be in charge of the salvage work and would be embarked in *Whistler* for that purpose.

"They're sending *soup-sal* and we finally get going on the twenty-third," Gallagher remarked to his exec.

"It's about time we got this show on the road. The beer ball game on the island will be a good break for the crew, but getting back to work is what we need to do right now," Lieutenant Ramos said.

As *Whistler* headed for a few days of rest and recreation on a deserted tropical island, the fleet tug USS *Mohican* with the large floating drydock (ARD) containing *Starfish* in tow astern, departed the Mariana's Island of Saipan for the fake deep water position west of the Mindoro. Aboard the drydock, only the skipper of the bathyscaphe and the captain of the ARD were informed of their role in PEGASUS, while on the *Mohican,* all they knew about the operation was that the bathyscaphe would be "diving to investigate something classified on the bottom of the ocean." Their job was to tow the mother-ship ARD to and from the scene and to stand by her (to keep the ARD in a set deep water position) while the diving was taking place.

With a good following sea from the northeast, the *Mohican* was able to get her speed up over eight knots, which was about as fast as they could expect to go with the heavy rig they were towing astern. Passing near the island of Guam as they headed down the Mariana Trench with more than 30,000 feet of salt water under their keels, the two vessels were inauspiciously joined by another, which was identified as a Soviet "*Elint*" (electronic intelligence collector) trawler of the *Okean* Class. The 150-foot vessel took up station two miles abeam to port of both ships and settled in on a parallel course at the same speed.

"Here we go again," the ARD skipper Lieutenant A.J. Clark chortled, as he raised his binoculars to view the spy ship on his port beam. "Looks like the same one that tailed us to Saipan," he said to *Starfish's* pilot Lieutenant John Humphries, who was standing next to him on the bridge and also scrutinizing the Russian.

After observing the maze of electronic antennas protruding from the top of the large, after deckhouse and the yellow hammer and sickle painted on the bright red band that encircled the stack, Humphries noticed two Russians on the bridge of the *Elint* looking back at them with binoculars of their own. "Look at those bastards on the bridge…they're both doing the same thing we are. Christ one of them's even waving at us," he laughed.

Fitted with state-of-the-art electronic intercept and sonar systems, the Soviet spy ships were used around the world to keep tabs on U.S. naval ships, missile launchings and to gather electronic intelligence from the airwaves or the depths of the ocean. These ships were manned by Soviet naval officers and civilian engineers and technicians. Once the captain of the *Elint* trawler *Hydraz* noticed the two American ships were underway, he sent a message to his command in Vladivostok giving the time, position, course and speed of the two American ships. He immediately received a message in reply to "Stay with them."

The ARD skipper also sent a message, and this one was well received at PEGASUS headquarters aboard the U.S. flagship *Aurora.*

The coded message was short and sweet: SOVIET ELINT TRAWLER OF OKEAN CLASS NOW IN COMPANY.

The 7th Fleet Commander, Admiral Langlois, nodded with a smile when he read the message and commented to his intelligence officer who pointed to the position of the three vessels on a chart. "So far, so good. For once we can say *welcome aboard* to a snoop trawler!"

* * *

As American naval forces continued to set the stage for Operation PEGASUS, life in Zamboanga City for Alfredo Gabizon, his daughter Maria, and Alexei rolled along nicely. Alfredo found out from the two that he was to become a grandfather, and that the pair planned to wed as soon as Quintal returned to the city and was able to provide Alexei with a bogus Polish birth certificate and other necessary papers required for him to marry in the Philippines. Alfredo clung to his "fate" theory and was not unhappy to hear the plans. That evening he treated them to a night on the town, and after a big meal and much libation, put his arms around both and told them his feelings.

"I have a wonderful and beautiful *Mestiza* daughter, a big, strong son and soon a grandchild that will be a combination of both of you...I pray happiness for each of you."

Alexei was starting to turn heads in town. At the *Club Sulu* "Ski" became virtually unbeatable at chess, where challengers lined up each evening for a match. He would play three and sometimes four matches at once, and was rarely defeated. "Are you sure you're not Russian?" one loser remarked to him after being check-mated in less than a dozen moves. Alexei also gained considerable attention on the soccer field, where he astounded the locals with his speed and skills. He played each Saturday for the semi-pro Zamboanga team, and his coach and several other followers of the sport told him "he was wasting his time playing for Zamboanga and that his talents could easily get him a high paying job with a professional team in Hong Kong, Singapore or Australia." Alfredo and Maria went to all the games and celebrated at the club with Alexei and other members of the team after each match.

Upon returning home after one such celebration, a well inebriated Alexei told Maria his real identity, and of the submarine disaster. "I just had to tell you. Since we're getting married you should know everything…there shall be no secrets." After he muttered a few other statements in incoherent Russian, a shocked Maria put her hand over his mouth and told him to be quiet about it now.

"Go to sleep now, my darling. You can tell me the whole story in the morning."

While Alexei had little trouble following her suggestion and dropped off instantly into a near coma-like sleep, Maria lay wide-eyed for several hours considering the implications of what Alexei told to her. She wondered what would happen if the Russians found he was here? Would they take him away from her and send him back to the Soviet Union? What about the baby? Could they still get married? Would Quintal help them or betray them? And why is Alexei not living out of sight instead of making a name for himself playing soccer and showing how good he is at chess? Somebody will find out who he is and where he came from and I will lose him…"Where God, would all this lead," she anguished.

North in the capital city of Manila, Emilio Quintal continued to wheel and deal with a number of contacts he maintained for a wide variety of enterprises he was involved in. One of those contacts arranged to meet him in *Rizal Park.* This man was a Filipino KGB operative who occasionally purchased information from Quintal. The usual barter was U.S. armed forces movements and other data gleaned from his informants at the Subic Bay Naval Base, Cubi Point Naval Air Station and the city of Olongapo, where many of his prostitutes learned of U.S. Navy ship arrivals and departures, and in some cases provided him with sensitive, classified technical items that the KGB agent would pay good money for. Quintal would dole out a minimum of pesos to his informants, depending upon the importance of what they reported, and then he in turn would sell the same information to the KGB contact for a hundred times or more than he paid for it. On this occasion, and after considerable quibbling over the price, Quintal told the agent of several new ship arrivals at the navy base and others that had just left for the Vietnam area or were headed back to Hawaii. After the intelligence was passed and Quintal paid, the agent advised him that the Soviets had lost a nuclear sub in the South China Sea.

"My orders are to find out if anything from the sub ever washed up on the shores of Mindoro, Palawan or any of the small islands down that way. The last I heard, they haven't found a trace of the submarine, but if the sub broke up and sank, there may be some flotsam that washed up or even some survivors on the islands. Have your sources check around the fishing villages and see if anybody found anything on the sea or the beaches."

Squinting his eyes while lighting a cigar, Quintal posed a question, "When did this submarine disappear?"

"Sometime in April," the agent advised.

"I will look into it," Quintal said as the two got up from the park bench where they met, and walked off in opposite directions without speaking another word.

Quintal took little time connecting Walewski to what he had just heard. That Polak with Maria is really a Russian, he concluded. The hell with sources, I will go alone to Palawan and the fishing house on Busuanga to see what I can see. If this Walewski is really a Russian seaman, he could be worth a small fortune, for the Soviets would not only want him to find out what happened to the submarine, they could also find out where the vessel is now. If this guy is who I think he is, I will not only get paid nicely, I can get rid of him for good and have the *Mestiza* all to myself, he connived.

* * *

CIA special agent Jose Roque was also in the Philippines talking to contacts and asking them to find out if anything unusual had washed ashore or been picked up by fishermen. He had to determine that no one in the islands knew of the existence and location of the *Morozov* prior to the commencement of phase 2 of PEGASUS. Once he was convinced, he would make a prearranged, coded phone call to the ONI man in Subic on June 22, just prior to the planned plane crash that night and the sailing of *Whistler* and *Engage* on the 23rd, with the buoyancy test and salvage work scheduled to start the night of June 24. Roque arrived in Manila on June 13. He had a brief discussion with one of his confidants and instructed him to keep his eyes and ears open in the capital city and in and around Subic Bay. He then flew to Mindoro where he met with another loyal informant for the same purpose. The next day Roque took a short ferry trip to Coron on Busuanga Island, where he contacted a man he had known for many years. This man, Antero, was flabbergasted at the changes the facial surgery had made to Jose's appearance. When they met at a waterfront bar for a drink, Antero, who hadn't seen Roque since the 1950s, questioned him over and over in *tagalog* to make sure it was really him, and not an impersonator. Finally convinced after asking him some old stories that only Jose would be able to recall, he gave his old friend a vigorous handshake.

"Christ man, you don't have to worry about anyone recognizing you. They did a fantastic job on your face. In fact, you look better than before. You were an ugly bastard, you know!" He quipped.

Jose went over the same things, but Antero said he couldn't provide any information at present, but that he would keep his eyes and ears open. He also asked when the Russian sub was lost, and Roque told him, "The last week in April, well north of here." Roque ordered another round of *San Miguel* beer for them, and they moved outside in the cool of the evening and sat at a table near the water's edge, sipping their beer and watching the fishing boats come in as they talked about old times. It was well into the night before they parted and a well-lubricated Antero asked to meet Jose the next morning for coffee, "Just in case I think of something when my head clears," he stammered.

* * *

That night the U.S. Navy fleet tug *Sioux* towed a large, 250-foot steel barge crammed with heavy steel scrap, to the prearranged northern decoy position and sank it and its cargo without incident or detection. Prior to the drop, the U.S. nuclear submarine *Mullet* patrolled the area to ensure there were no Soviet nukes, elint trawlers or any other vessels in the area to witness or hear the sinking on sonar. Upon a coded radio signal from *Mullet* to *Sioux* that "ALL IS CLEAR," the barge's sea-cocks were opened and it slipped below the waves in less than three minutes and crashed to the bottom of the South China Sea shortly after midnight.

* * *

The next morning, two hung-over pals met at a small, outdoor café in Coron for a final confab before Roque departed for Zamboanga City on the 10 o'clock ferry. With a shaking hand, Antero lit Roque's cigarette and then his own while they drank black coffee. Antero told Roque he may have something interesting for him.

"Sometime in early May my wife and I saw something that we didn't consider unusual then, but after last night's discussion, I think it may be something to look into. There's a nice big beach house up the coast that's owned by a suspicious character from Zamboanga named Quintal. He goes up there occasionally to meet with all kinds of shady people. But a couple a times a year he lets a fellow named Alfredo Gabizon, also from Zamboanga City, use the house. Alfredo usually brings his daughter, who is an exquisite *mestiza*, with him and they stay two or three weeks at a time. Alfredo fishes every day and brings his catch here to town to sell. He is a nice, friendly man and on each occasion he comes up here, he and I drink beer and play cards several times a week at the same bar where we talked last night. He and I know each other well, and he's told me a lot about himself, his auto repair business and his daughter Maria, who's a talented painter. Now one day my wife sees them in town in a car with another man, a young, muscular European-looking guy sitting with the *mestiza* in the car while Alfredo drove. Then a week or so later, I saw the three on the ferry pier, with bags, ready to leave for Zamboanga. Alfredo didn't see me, but the tall young man and Maria were hand in hand and quite cozy. I saw the three board the ferry, and thought no more about it until this morning."

"Why did you think it unusual for the man and daughter to have company?" Roque asked.

"Because Alfredo would've told me all about this big Caucasian that was so friendly with his daughter, and must'a stayed with the two at the fishing house. He never said a word to me about this guy, and I dunno if he arrived on the island with them or not. Now if you want to check further, for a few pesos I can get my friend at the customs office to let me go over the ferry logs for the past few months. From that I can get the young man's name and where he's from. I can also find out when and if he arrived in Coron by ferry."

"How many pesos do you need?"

"A hundred will do nicely."

"How long will it take you?" Roque asked, as he handed the bills to Antero.

"No more than an hour," Antero replied as he rose from the chair and headed down the pier…"I'll meet you back here," he shouted while walking away.

Roque thought about what Antero told him, and considered it a long shot that what he had related could be significant. But it's worth looking into, he concluded and decided to check out the fishing house if Antero turned up something interesting from customs. Then while staring out at the harbor while waiting for him to return, Roque racked his brain to remember where or when he had heard or read the name Quintal, but he could not place it. He decided to call Manila when he got to Zamboanga. My man up there must have heard of this guy, he figured.

Antero returned a little over an hour later and somewhat breathlessly told Roque what he uncovered. "Listen to this Jose! I checked all the way back to March, and there is no record of the white stranger arriving on this island. The ferry log lists his name is Alexei Walewski, and lists his country as Poland and that he's from Warsaw."

"Well, I don't know what all this means, but I'd like to borrow your car and go check out this fishing house," Roque proposed. Antero recommended against it.

"Quintal arrived up there yesterday with some whores, and from what I hear he's a dangerous sucker to mess with."

"Let's go together," Jose suggested. "Bring your binoculars. I just want to get close enough to see what this guy Quintal looks like. Then we'll come back, and I'll take the ferry tomorrow instead of today." Antero shook his head, but begrudgingly agreed to go.

Despite Antero's apprehensions, the trip to and from the house was uneventful. A well-hidden Roque was able to get a good look at Quintal through the binoculars as he sat on the veranda drinking rum with two scantily clad women and another Filipino man who had a pistol on his belt. He also noticed a dock with a boat tied to it, a small waterfront boathouse and Quintal's car. Roque memorized the license plate as well as the entire beach and house scenario.

* * *

After his business and entertainment acquaintances left the fishing house, Emilio Quintal's thoughts returned to Walewski and the Russian submarine. He decided to search the house and the premises for anything left behind when the Gabizon's and the stranger left the place that would add credence to his hunch about where the man came from. Finding nothing in or under the house, Quintal searched the car and the fishing boat without success. Finally, he entered the dank boathouse and looked among the fish nets, crab traps and various lines, hooks and devices used by Gabizon when he used the place. Just before leaving the shack, something red and white, partially buried under a pile of old anchor ropes caught his eye. Pulling away the ropes he saw that it was some kind of a float. "It's just one of Alfredo's fucking fish floats," he said out loud as he tossed it aside.

But then he saw some black print stenciled on the end of the red and white striped buoy. Squatting down to examine the print up close, he immediately recognized the lettering as Russian!

"This is it...I've got that sonofabitch now!" he hissed. Then contemplating what to do with the evidence, he decided the buoy was too bulky to take with him, so he went back into the house, retrieved his camera and took several close-up shots of it with a yardstick alongside it to depict the size of the object while making sure the photo also showed the Russian print. He then wrapped it in plastic and buried it far in the jungle.

Quintal still was not one hundred percent sure that what he found would prove Walewski a Russian. As he couldn't translate the language, maybe the buoy had nothing to do with a submarine. Maybe it was just an object from a Russian fishing boat that washed up on the shore or was picked up by Alfredo out to sea. He vowed to find out in Zamboanga if Walewski and the buoy both came from the missing Russian submarine. The photo will be convincing proof to the KGB that I can produce a real-live survivor for them if the price is right. Quintal congratulated himself for keeping a copy of Walewski's passport and photo which would now be used as "final convincers." As further proof, he contemplated contacting another "friend" in Manila who could check with the Polish Embassy as to any missing seaman or ship passengers in the South Pacific.

* * *

Jose Roque – *now known as Rafael Tausaga* – left the Island of Palawan on 17 June and arrived the next morning in Zamboanga. Prior to leaving Coron, he pumped Antero for everything he knew about both Gabizon and Quintal. His old friend was able to tell him the name of the garage that Alfredo Gabizon operated and one of the clubs that Quintal ran in Zamboanga City.

"The only one I've heard mentioned is called the *Club Sulu*. It's the biggest, the most expensive, and it's right on the main street," Antero told him.

Antero also made a major slip-up. Returning home after the night he and Roque got pleasantly drunk in Coron, he was greeted at the door by his angry wife Corina, who with arms folded across her chest demanded to known *where he'd been?*

"I been with my ol' pal Roque," he slurred, not remembering that Roque was under cover with a new name and that his presence in the islands was to be kept a secret.

"What's he doing back here?" she asked.

Now realizing he'd better shut up, Antero said, "Just business…old business."

The next morning while Roque and Antero looked over the fish house, Antero's wife met and chatted with other women in the marketplace, and as the usual gossip and banter went back and forth, Corina blurted out…"Guess who Antero ran into last night?" The word was now out that Roque, who was well known to several local ladies, was back, and such information would not take long to fall into the wrong hands. The word also went out that Roque was disguised, as several locals had seen him and Antero together drinking in Coron. Roque's cover was blown.

After arriving in Zamboanga City, Roque checked in to the *Lantaka Hotel,* one of his favorite places in town. He called Manila on a pay phone from the lobby, and explained to the Manila operative that he wanted a rundown on Quintal. He was told an agent would contact him in person that evening at the hotel's *Talisay Bar.* The agent, who did not identify himself, found Roque at the appointed time sitting on a stool at the colorful outside waterfront bar, that was built around the trunk of a 300-year-old tree. He related to him what he knew about Quintal.

"The Philippine government believes he is involved with the MNLF (Moro National Liberation Front), but they can't prove it. Quintal is a slippery one who is suspected of selling arms, women and information to the highest bidder. But, he also has legitimate businesses and is well connected with politicians and police here on Mindanao, who he probably pays off, and they have formed a protective ring around him."

Roque was curious about the gun-running operation.

"If he's running guns to MNLF, then why doesn't the government take him out?" he asked the agent.

"Right now they only have scant evidence, and also some of the provincial politicians are protecting him, but sooner or later he'll get nailed."

"Where does he get weapons for the MNLF?"

"It is believed they come from Arab countries, but most of the arms are manufactured in eastern European countries such as Czechoslovakia and also in the Soviet Union. As yet, they haven't intercepted any of the arms shipments coming to Mindanao, but they believe most are coming in at night by *Kumpits* (small cargo boats) from Brunei (Malaysia-Borneo)."

"What about a man named Gabizon who runs an auto repair shop in town? Is he involved with Quintal?" The agent shook his head no.

"As far as we know, the only connection between the two is that Quintal owns the building and equipment at the shop that Gabizon runs. We don't believe Gabizon is involved in anything other than the auto shop. He's a happy-go-lucky man who is well liked and respected here in Zamboanga City. It would be a big surprise if he was in on any of the bullshit Quintal is dealing in. If anything Gabizon is most probably pro-American and Quintal uses him for a show of legitimacy."

Roque sipped his beer while considering what the agent told him. He was still confused about the Gabizon/Quintal connection and how it fit into the situation at hand. He thought about the Caucasian stranger that left Palawan with Gabizon. His instincts told him it was not a good time to mention this man. He would follow up on this development on his own.

"Is Quintal known to deal with Russian or eastern bloc operatives?" he asked the agent next.

"As I said, he sells information, and we know he has people in Subic who probably feed him U.S. Navy ship movements that are of interest to the Vietcong and the Soviets. It's conceivable he's selling this info to a contact who works for Moscow. As you know, there are plenty of sympathizers in the islands, and particularly here in Mindanao."

Jose nodded in understanding to the man whose name he did not know. He told him what kind of information he was seeking. Shipboard objects washing up on the shore, or anything else pertaining to Russian ships in the area.

"I'll be staying here at the *Lantaka* for a few more days. Contact me if you hear anything. Remember, this is passive. Don't interrogate people. Just keep your eyes and ears open." The man gave Roque a nod and left the bar, quickly disappearing among early evening shoppers milling all around the vicinity. Roque finished his beer, flipped a tip on the bar and walked to his rented car to seek out the *Club Sulu*.

After he was out of sight, a small man took Roque's stool at the bar, and while the bartender was facing in the opposite direction, he quickly took Roque's empty beer bottle from the bar and put it in a shopping bag at his side, from which he took a duplicate bottle and put it on the bar in its place. When the bartender finally served him he never knew the difference as he took away the empties from in front of the small man.

* * *

The latter part of the first phase of Operation PEGASUS commenced at noon on June 20, when the *Mohican*, with the ARD and bathyscaphe in tow, rendezvoused with the survey ship *Northwind* near the position of the barge drop. The U.S. nuclear submarine *Mullet* was also in the area and in contact with the ships that commenced an elaborate simulated search pattern designed to get the attention of the shadowing Soviet intelligence trawler *Hydraz*. The trawler was picking up radio signals between the ships and UQC (voice sonar) signals between the *Mullet* and the *Northwind*. Convinced that he was a witness to something of great intelligence value, the *Hydraz* captain sent a *Top Priority* dispatch to Vladivostok describing the situation.

U.S. BATHYSCAPE WITH TENDER, OCEAN SURVEY VESSEL NORTHWIND AND SUBMARINE ALL OPERATING WITHIN A CLOSE RADIUS OF POSITION 13-22N, 118-30E. BELIEVE THEY ARE PREPARING TO LAUNCH BATHYSCAPE FOR BOTTOM SEARCH. WILL ADVISE WHEN THEY COMMENCE TO DO SO.

The message received immediate attention in Vladivostok where Captain Kursky plotted the position on his wall chart, then went to the Admiral's office where a plan was devised to closely observe the Americans.

"They may have found the *Morozov* Admiral," Kursky stated. A visibly angry Admiral Gusev stood suddenly from behind his desk and moved right in front of Captain Kursky and several other staff officers.

"Tell me, comrades, why in the hell the Amerikanskis have apparently found something down there when our own task force with *Lebedev* and *Komsomol* turned up absolutely nothing?! Is it equipment or is it technique?! Is it both or is it neither?! I am very disappointed, comrades. They are finding things before we do, and this is unsatisfactory. Just last year they found our satellite that fell to the bottom of the North Pacific Ocean with that bathyscaphe, and even though we as yet do not have such a deep diving vessel, we should be able to detect things with sonar…now in this case, all we can do is watch and wait, and then maybe we can try for a few deep-ocean photographs from *Lebedev's* special cameras to maybe see what the Yankee bastards found down there!"

Regaining some composure, but still red-faced, the chain-smoking Gusev sat down and lit another cigarette from the still burning butt of the one he left in the ashtray on his desk before he went into the tirade. Inhaling deeply, he glanced over the top of the officers who were staring at their shoes, and spoke in a deep but steady voice.

"Comrades, the one and only positive aspect of this turn of events is that if in fact the Amerikanskis have found the *Morozov* at the position sent to us by the *Hydraz*, then at least she was lost in waters too deep for any kind of salvage, as the charted depth at that position is near 3,300 meters. The best the Amerikanski Navy can hope for would be some close up photos from the bathyscaphe, which our intelligence office tells me is incapable of bringing anything to the surface from that depth. Therefore, I propose we send a group of ships to the area to pinpoint where the bathyscaphe dives and then go there ourselves when the Amerikanskis leave the area."

"Comrade admiral, what ships do you want to send there at this time?" Kursky asked.

The Admiral ordered another intelligence vessel to work with *Hydraz,* one nuclear submarine and the *Lebedev* to head down to the location and to send recon aircraft to conduct as many fly-overs as necessary to get photos, particularly of the inside of the dock-tender which carries the bathyscaphe as the only way this can be viewed is from the air.

Gusev also ordered that the *Hydraz* be told to be aware that prior to launching the bathyscaphe the dock-tender must flood down to bring sea water into the dock prior to floating out the bathyscaphe.

"Tell them to notify us immediately when this flooding down begins."

The Soviet response plan also called for a helo-equipped destroyer, an oiler and re-supply ship to be immediately dispatched. The helo to bring supplies and personnel from ship to ship, and the destroyer to work with the submarine to detect other submarines and also to use their sonar to see if we can find what the Amerikanskis detected.

"I will check out these plans with Moscow, but I see no problem in getting approval." You may commence writing the orders now, and I will give you a final go-ahead within a few hours."

"Sir, the *Lebedev* is still in the shipyard and can't sail for at least ten days," Kursky reminded the Admiral. She's in dry-dock now here in Vladivostok for hull repairs and the installation of new sonar equipment. The earliest we could sail her would be the fist of July, and it would take her seven days to transit to the position in the South China Sea."

"We will have to live with the delay," Gusev said with a shrug. "The Amerikanskis will probably be there until then anyway, but I want top priority put on the work taking place on *Lebedev*. Perhaps we can sail her sooner if we expedite repairs and go with three shifts round-the-clock. That is all comrades."

* * *

While the Soviet Navy made plans to send ships and planes to the South China Sea, the U.S. Navy at the Cubi Point Naval Air Station on Subic Bay was also making plans. Theirs were to send a P4V Naval Aircraft on a one-way mission to the bottom of the ocean northwest of Palawan. Phase 2 of PEGASUS called for the crash to take place during daytime when it would be witnessed by distant fishing vessels. A destroyer would drop a small radio-beacon buoy 100 feet from the bottomed *Morozov's* position. This buoy would emit a signal for the plane to home in on after the pilot bailed out. The destroyer would pick up the pilot and use its helicopter to conduct a bogus "search for more survivors", hopefully to be witnessed by fishermen or people on board other coastal shipping vessels that may be in the vicinity. Other helicopters would be sent from Cubi Point to continue the search. The following day, the *Whistler* and *Engage* would go to the scene to start the buoyancy test, begin Phase 3, and hopefully salvage operations.

Other preparations were taking place at the Subic Bay naval base where Captain James Leominster, known to all in the diving world as *soup-sal,* assembled the men and tools he would need to pull the valuable weapons from *Morozov*, and then hopefully take the submarine to deep water to eliminate the radiation hazard from the shallow water where the submarine lay. The salvage operation would involve *Whistler*, where Leominster would take overall charge, the *USS Engage*, several barges for equipment and for placing the aircraft parts and 20 hand-picked U.S. Navy hard-hat divers to supplement those already aboard *Whistler* and *Engage*. A navy diving medicine specialist doctor flew to Subic to be embarked in *Whistler*, where he would supervise the treatment of any diving accidents or other injuries. Extra supplies of helium and oxygen along with the special buoyancy tanks, explosive devices and diving tools ordered by Leominster were stockpiled at the base and ready to be loaded.

On June 21, the 7th fleet commander received the report that all was in readiness for both Phase 2 (plane crash) and Phase 3 (salvage). The next day the ONI man (Capt. Gunderson) in Subic received the phone call from Jose Roque in Zamboanga City to go ahead as planned. The pre-arranged signal “Silence is Golden” was taken by an excited Gunderson who in turn notified Admiral Langlois of the message.

At exactly 1300 hours (1 pm) on June 22, a four-engine navy ASW P4V aircraft crashed in spectacular fashion not too far from the Philippine Island of Palawan. Witnessed by at least seven fishing boats who were within ten miles of the crash site, the big prop plane exploded as planned when it hit the water at 250 miles an hour, sending smoke and spray hundreds of feet above the calm sea. The U.S. Navy destroyer *Dracut* picked up the one “survivor”, Commander R.L. “Rusty” Sewell, USN, who floated out of the clear skies from an altitude of 5,000 feet, where before bailing out, he set the aircraft on the automatic homing device that locked in on the signal from the buoy. The crash was so accurate that the buoy was destroyed by the explosion of the aircraft on impact. As the *Dracut* conducted the bogus search for survivors, three Filipino fishing boats sped to the scene to have a look and offer to help in the search. Within an hour, news of the crash was the talk of Coron, and word soon spread to Puerto Princesa, Zamboanga and Manila. The Manila newspaper reported the crash the next morning and it was also announced on many Philippine radio and television stations.

"As the result of the fiery crash of a U.S. Navy Patrol Aircraft Northwest of the Island of Palawan yesterday afternoon the Americans are hoping to recover most of the aircraft and the bodies of four crewmen who went down with the plane. There was one survivor who parachuted and was picked up by a nearby U.S. warship. The cause of the crash is under investigation and salvage ships are expected to be sent to the scene today from Subic Bay, a Navy spokesman said."

The downed aircraft off Palawan drew little attention from the Soviets, but an intelligence trawler on station just off Subic Bay reported the departure of the salvage ships on June 23.

> TWO U.S. NAVY SALVAGE SHIPS WITH TWO BARGES IN TOW DEPARTED SUBIC TODAY AT 0800 HOURS. CRS 195 x SPD 10 KTS. HULL NUMBERS 21 AND 52…

At the Soviet Fleet Headquarters in Vladivostok, the ships were duly plotted, and the staff operations duty officer determined by plotting the course in the message that they were heading for the aircraft plane crash scene off Palawan. With the U.S. Navy bathyscaphe being readied for launch in the South China Sea and the ships and aircraft operating off the coast of Vietnam, the salvage ships leaving Subic were all but ignored when the morning briefings took place.

Jose Roque was sitting at the *Talisay Bar* in a scorching hot Zamboanga City when he saw a report of the plane crash on TV. News of the crash caused little attention from the dozen or so bar patrons, most of whom were waiting for the evening sports bulletins to come on. Reflecting on what he had learned the past several days, Roque was convinced that Alexei Walewski was a Russian, but as yet he had no proof he was a sailor or officer who survived the sinking of the *Morozov*, and thus saw no reason not to send the "silence is golden" message.

He made the positive Russian determination on his third visit to the *Club Sulu*, where he closely observed the bouncer playing chess with bar customers. Then pretending to have had a few too many, he challenged Walewski to a chess game for a small wager. An excellent player himself, Jose knew all the 'sucker moves' an experienced player could put on a neophyte that would result in a quick checkmate. Desiring the opposite result and wanting the game to go on long enough for him to learn what he could about the young man, Jose played it smart, carefully setting up a formidable defense to counter the initial aggressive moves of his opponent. After 15 minutes with only a pawn taken by each player, Alexei realized that despite the drink, the man he was up against knew the game well, and he would have to use all his concentration in order to win. During the match, Jose asked questions about Poland and Warsaw, slurring queries about geography, politicians and other trivia that any legitimate Pole would know. Alexei was evasive but quite ignorant of some things he should have known. Jose also detected a Russian accent with the fairly good English they both spoke in. After an hour and a half, the match ended in a draw. A surprised Alexei vigorously shook Jose's hand, who got up from his stool, nodded politely and expressed his enjoyment of the match.

"Thanks for the game, Ski…but the next time we play I will be sober and whip your ass!" Alexei just smiled and shrugged as he helped Jose to the door.

Roque went one hot afternoon to watch Alexei on the soccer field and was amazed at the speed and ability the foreigner possessed. He thought the man looked out of place competing with the smaller and less skilled Filipinos. "He's in a league all his own," he said to himself.

The CIA man also took the time to conduct a surveillance on the auto repair shop, the house where the Gabizons and Walewski lived, and learned all he could about Alfredo and his beautiful daughter Maria by observation and what he gleaned from his local contact. Finding nothing unusual in the lives of the father or daughter, Roque was still confused about the Gabizon/Quintal relationship, but more convinced than ever that Alexei Walewski could very well be a Soviet. But he certainly did not fit the stereotype of a common conscript sailor from the oppressive Soviet Union. Here was a tall and superbly conditioned man of 21 who was a professional level athlete and a gifted chess player and spoke excellent English. This guy fit neither the Russian navy enlisted nor officer mold and his pleasant, easygoing manner was downright un-military…just who the hell is this guy? This was the question that Roque realized was of extreme importance, for if Alexei was from the *Morozov*, it was imperative that he be prevented from being grabbed by someone and turned over to the Soviets, who would learn from him the real location of the submarine. PEGASUS would go down the tubes. The suspicion that Quintal might know something also haunted him, and he decided to become better acquainted with the suspected Russian in order to learn more about him and put himself in a position where he could monitor the whole situation, and if need be, prevent the knowledge of Walewski's existence from falling into the wrong hands…if, in fact, he *was* a Soviet Navy man who survived the sinking of the *Morozov.*

A few miles to the north of Zamboanga City, another man had already made up his mind that Walewski was in fact an escaped Soviet submarine sailor. Emilio Quintal had just received word that the Polish Embassy had never heard of such a man and, "They were not missing anyone who goes by any name from any ship in southeast Asia." With this news, Quintal was ready to take the next step, contacting his Russian mole in Manila and arranging a meeting where he would barter for a "piece of intelligence information of monumental importance to the Soviet Union." After two days of trying, the call was finally completed, and the mole promised to meet with Quintal in Zamboanga within 48 hours.

Quintal planned to tell the mole that he had information about the missing Soviet submarine, and that he knew where an actual survivor was. For proof that he was telling the truth, he would give the mole the passport picture of Walewski and the photo of the escape buoy with Russian print on it. For this he would demand 50,000 pesos, with another 50,000 to be delivered before telling where Walewski could be found.

* * *

Far out at sea, the U.S. Navy was on a roll. The bathyscaphe *Starfish* made sporadic dives deep into the South China Sea over a nondescript surplus Navy steel barge and scattered steel junk some 10,800 feet under the surface, while curious Soviet vessels circled two miles distant. Having finally detected something on the bottom with their sonars, the Soviets were now convinced the Amerikanskis had indeed found *Morozov* and were taking photographs from the bathyscaphe. All of this info was spontaneously sent by top priority messages to the Russian Vladivostok headquarters who forwarded such information to Moscow and to the Soviet ships that were now en route to the scene.

The shallow-water part of PEGASUS was also on a roll, and within a day *Whistler* had determined with the lifting boom test that the *Morozov* was not seriously flooded internally and that it could easily be raised or partially raised and relocated. *Soup-sal* sent an immediate message to Subic with this news. Using special explosive probes, it was also determined that the sub was indeed hot, as it had radiation levels well above the lethal level in every compartment of the boat. Next, the divers from *Engage* brought up a few pieces of the P4V aircraft and placed them on the barge that was moored between both salvage vessels. This wreckage was left in plain sight for any snoopers to see. Once this was done, the serious business of weapons and antenna removal began in earnest. After two days of diving around the clock, while hard-hat divers toiled to cut the upper hatch from the after missile tube, other divers managed to cut away the thin sail fairing-steel with underwater oxy-torches and removed four communication antenna heads and one ECM (Electronic Counter-Measures) mast. These were hoisted aboard *Whistler,* and after dark flown to Cubi Point aboard Navy helicopters. There they were carefully packaged, then flown to Hawaii aboard a Navy jet transport where eager ONI representatives took charge.

Four days into the operation and another of *soup-sal's* gadgets was put to use when the four-inch thick, upper door over the sub's after missile tube was cut through and opened to provide access to the huge missile within. After radiation checks to the external launch tube showed *negative traces*, a cable with Leominster's special gripping device, consisting of two locking loops of heavy wire on a cylindrical frame was lowered with the *Whistler's* main boom to the deck of *Morozov*. Divers slid it down over the missile head as far as it would go. They then set the lever that would cause the apparatus to cinch tight around the missile when the cable was pulled up by the ship's capstan through the ship's boom. Once the divers were clear, a huge strain was taken on the cable, as it had to put enough torque on the missile to break the holding rods and connection tubes that held it in place and also provided for input for guidance before the missile was launched. After several tense minutes and a heavy strain on the boom and cable that caused the *Whistler* to heel over, Captain Leominster spoke quietly but with a grim expression to the *Whistler* skipper as they both watched the evolution from the fantail.

"Keep your fingers crossed, Sam," he said.

After what seemed like an eternity, but was in reality just a few minutes, the *Whistler* righted herself, and the chief boatswain controlling the hauling operation hollered loudly:

"AVAST HEAVING."

Then master diver Drummond, while controlling the divers, asked if the missile was free of the tube. Then the answer that they all were waiting to hear came out through the speaker, and was greeted with a loud cheer and some back-slapping when yellow diver shouted into his helmet from two hundred feet below:

"THE SONOFABITCH IS FREE AND CLEAR TO COME UP. THE TIP OF THE BASTARD CAME UP FOUR FEET ABOVE THE DECK."

"Lets not bring it all the way up until after sundown, and until the next barge gets here tonight," Leominster ordered.

"Yes, sir," Gallagher said. "We're now ready to put another set of divers in the water to get to work on pulling one of the torpedoes out, but it's going to be guesswork as to which of the eight tubes we cut into, because some or all the tubes may be empty. The torpedoes may all be in the room."

"Try one of the lower most tubes first. They're usually the toughest to re-load, and most likely we'll strike pay dirt there."

At PEGASUS headquarters aboard the flagship *Aurora*, anchored in Subic Bay, 7th Fleet Commander Vice Admiral Marc Langlois was delighted at the attention TASK FORCE TWELVE was receiving. Two *elint* intelligence collecting trawlers were already at the scene and a Soviet nuclear submarine had been detected, and was now being tracked by the U.S. nuclear attack submarine *Mullet*. Long range Soviet BEAR recon aircraft had twice overflown the bogus search area, and two surface ships, a *Kashin* class guided-missile destroyer and a *Chilikin* class fleet replenishment ship were being tracked east of Japan, where the ships were on a southwesterly course, making 18 knots, and presumed headed for the same location. Conferring in his cabin with ONI's Gunderson, Langlois expressed surprise that the Soviets had yet to send one of their big survey ships to the search area.

"I'm not complaining, Murray, for you know those survey ships have a deep photo capability, and we don't want one of them to get close enough to get a shot of the barge and junk pile down there, but sooner or later they're going to send one in, and we've just got to hope that the salvage operation is complete by then."

"Yes, sir, Admiral, I agree. Two weeks ago we tracked the *Lebedev* returning to Vladivostok, where we believe she remains. But I wouldn't be surprised to see her heading south again within a few days. In any case, we will have at least five day's notice before any of their oceanographic survey ships, no matter what direction they are coming from, can get to the vicinity of TASK FORCE TWELVE."

* * *

After the initial report from 7th Fleet that *Morozov* could easily be raised by *Whistler* but that it was rife with deadly radiation, the brass in Washington submitted a proposal to the President for Phase 4 of PEGASUS. Another high level meeting was convened at the White House, where the President wanted to hear all the details. The Chief of Naval Operations stood in front of a large blow-up chart of the Palawan/South China sea area of interest and explained Phase 4.

"This plan sir, which goes into effect after pulling the weapons and electronics from *Morozov,* calls for *Whistler* to raise the sub no higher than 50 feet below the surface and tow the submarine to a deep spot located 40 miles northwest of where the salvage operation is taking place. We selected the drop position because it is well marked on all wreck charts as the scene of a big World War II battle, where Japanese warships are virtually piled one on top of another. The ships are in 660 fathoms (3,960 feet), where the radiation would be rendered virtually harmless. The tow will utilize special computerized buoyancy tanks, that when attached to the sub's hull and activated will keep it at the same depth."

"What if the sub breaks the surface while under tow?" the President asked. "Won't we have a big risk of it being sighted?"

"The whole procedure will be timed so the tow will not begin until after sunset, and they have seven hours to go 40 miles to the drop spot. We're also going to tow a barge astern of *Whistler* to disguise what's going on. The barge will be towed directly over the *Morozov* and piled high with material that would prevent anyone from getting a good glimpse of any of the submarine if they lose control and it comes up to the surface."

"How will they sink her when the spot is reached?"

"Pre-positioned plastic explosives will be set off electronically from *Whistler* and cause the amidship compartments to flood and start her down. The divers also cut off the bow and stern planes to prevent the sinking sub to plane out away from where we want her to make her final resting place."

The President looked around the table. "Questions, gentlemen?" then nodded to the ONI Admiral.

"Now let's just say, sir, that the Soviets find out in a few weeks that they've been had. Say they eventually bring in a survey ship that gets a photograph of the old barge and scrap-iron all over the ocean floor and realize that the search by our TASK FORE TWELVE was an ingenious diversion and that they foolishly went for the bait. Next, some sharp Ruski staff officer does some back-tracking and remembers that the downed aircraft salvage is near Palawan. My bet is that the Soviets will then make a major effort to find the exact spot where that salvage took place and scour the bottom for anything we left there. Even though the horse has already left the barn, so to speak, it would be extremely important that every trace of *Morozov* is removed before we leave the scene. It's of great importance to my intelligence office if the Russians believe *Morozov* went down in unsalvageable waters and we never found her. By the way, my assistant suggested we tow the boat to the vicinity of TASK FORCE TWELVE and re-sink her right there, where the Russians would eventually find and photograph it. Was this ever considered?"

"You have raised good questions," the CNO responded, "and here is what the scheme is: First, we did consider re-sinking *Morozov* over the bait location, but the 7th fleet boss and I recommended against it for three reasons. One: the submerged tow transit time is too long, and the risk of the tow-trick being detected would increase as the tow neared the position because of the Russian ships all around the scene. Two: even if we got the sub to the spot without detection, when the boat is re-sunk in water that deep, the inner hull will implode and make a hell of an underwater noise that would surely be picked up by the snoop. And three: Let's say we got away with all of the above. When the Russians eventually find it and take photos, it's entirely conceivable they could get close-ups that reveal where we cut into the vessel and what we got away with, as the implosion of the compressed inner hull would not necessarily cover the work we did on the outer skin and weapon hatches of the boat. Now as far as cleaning up the inshore salvage scene, I completely agree with you, and the *Engage* has been ordered to perform this task and to get to it immediately after *Whistler* takes *Morozov* out of there. All of that said, here is what we want the Russians to deduce from all of this…That the bathyscaphe diving on the barge and junk was merely a training exercise, conducted in an area where both navies were looking for a lost Russian nuke. We want them to finally conclude that we trained people and equipment in bottom search and also gained intelligence by getting the Soviets to respond, giving us an opportunity to observe and monitor the operations of their surface ships, submarines and aircraft. Then if they investigate the Palawan spot and find nothing, we will be home fee. That is if no one talks. Quite a few men have now been involved with PEGASUS, and I'm afraid it's just a matter of time before the word gets out…but let's just hope it's a *long* time, and let's just hope the rest of this operation proceeds as smoothly as what's been accomplished already."

The President then spoke to the CIA chief. "Mister Carmichael, what do you make of all this?"

"Mister President, so far my agent in the Palawan, Mindanao region has reported nothing to indicate the position of the sunken submarine is as yet known locally. Apparently the crashed aircraft ploy is working. But I say sir, that time is of the essence. The sooner we dispose of this nuke the better. The Russians will not be fooled much longer, and as the Admiral just stated…hundreds of men now know where *Morozov* lies, and it won't be long before the word gets out. My man out there says the islands are loaded with all kinds of groups and individuals who are unfriendly to us. Also, since we've never notified the Philippine government what's going on in their territorial waters, there's gonna be hell to pay when they find out. At some point our ambassador should be made aware of the situation, for he will have to deal with a very angry Marcos before this is over!"

With an "excuse me gentlemen," the President's Naval Aide entered the meeting room and handed the CNO a piece of paper.

"This just came in from the pentagon, and I believe it's important," the aide said.

"So far so good mister President," the CNO announced after reading the short but sweet communiqué.

"*Whistler* has pulled the big nuke missile out of *Morozov* and it will arrive at Cubi Point before dawn. Once there, a special plane will transport the first Soviet missile ever captured back to our secret air base in the Arizona desert, where all the weapons will be delivered.

"Do we have the scientific people lined up to study this missile?" the President asked.

"Sir, I have a list of key scientific people to send to the base. These people have been on standby, but I will now order them immediately flown out there," the ONI Admiral replied.

CHAPTER 13

FATAL INVOLVEMENTS

In Zamboanga, it was the calm before the storm. Jose Roque, using the name Rafael Tausaga on this mission, played chess twice more with Alexei, winning one match and losing another. The two developed a liking for one another and during a visit to the auto repair shop, Alexei introduced him to Maria and Alfredo as Mister Tausaga…"who is in town for a few weeks as a copra salesman, and this guy also plays a little chess!" Maria invited Roque to the house one evening for a meal, and Jose reciprocated by treating the three to a sumptuous dinner at the *Hotel Lantaka*, where he was staying. The friendship that resulted from this casual socializing was soon to become more important than any of the four realized.

The next day, several miles northwest of the city of Zamboanga, Emilio Quintal was getting impatient and irritable as he anxiously awaited the arrival of the Soviet agent. Pacing back and forth on the wide veranda of his waterfront house that faced the Sulu Sea, he was drinking heavily and had put away five, tall rum and cokes since lunchtime. He was mixing the sixth when he felt a carnal urge to make a call on Maria. Aware that Alexei was at the soccer field for practice and that Alfredo was at the garage, he deduced that the opportunity was there to get her alone and resume doing the things to her that he used to do before the Russian sonofabitch showed up.

There was something about the *mestiza* woman that filled his head with thoughts of sex. Despite having access to any number of whores, who indirectly worked for him and were readily available, visions of Maria's body dominated. Swiftly draining the drink, Quintal called loudly in *Cebuano* to his driver who was fishing on the long pier that jutted out from the front of the house into the adjoining waterway.

"Come to the house. We leave in five minutes," he hollered while struggling to buckle on his shoulder-holstered .38 caliber pistol. Next he went to the bedroom where he took the envelope with Walewski's photo and the shot of the buoy and placed it in his shirt pocket. Then glancing at his dresser, he grunted an "Aha" as he saw the envelope containing Maria and Alexei's forged wedding papers lying there. Then as he stuffed the envelope in the same pocket he resolved to use it to get what he wanted from Maria. This wedding ain't gonna take place anyway for we should be rid of *mister ski* within 24 hours.

Now staggering drunk, he poured the last of the rum into a big glass and took it with him to the waiting car that immediately sped him down the dirt road toward the city.

Maria was enjoying and afternoon nap when she heard the front door open. She sleepily surmised it was either Alexei or Papa arriving home early. Then her door, which was half closed, suddenly opened with a slam against the wall. Startled, she raised her head from the pillow and was shocked and horrified to see a drunken Quintal swaying in her doorway with a hideous expression on his bloated face. Now fully awake, Maria raised to a sitting position, gasped and put her hand over her mouth. Then she remembered that Quintal might have come to see her about the wedding license. But when he lurched toward her on the bed, she knew he had other things in mind. Grasping the bedpost with one hand as she squirmed away from him, he spoke to her in a slurred *Tagalog.*

"I'm pleased to see you on the bed today Maria, because that is what I want to see you about," he stammered, as his cruel, bloodshot eyes ran up and down her sheet-covered body.

A scared and repulsed Maria tried to get off the bed and leave the room, but Quintal half sat on the side of the bed and held her shoulder so hard she screamed in pain.

"Leave me alone…I don't want you ever to touch me again…get out of my house, you have drank too much."

Undeterred and brimming with lust, Quintal grabbed the sheet, pulling it from her naked body. Maria whirled forward and struck him on the side of the head with her fist.

Fully enraged, Quintal backhanded her across the face, breaking her nose and causing it to bleed all over the bed sheet as she cried out in pain.

"What the hell do you mean YOUR house? The last I heard this fucking place is all mine, and you better damn well do what I want you to do, or you won't be living here any more…and neither will that Russian sonofabitch. Do you hear me whore?…I said Russian!…and I can tell you that he is dead meat and will be long gone from here in a few days time."

Reaching into his shirt pocket he took out the pictures and thrust them toward Maria's bloodied face. Then he showed her the second envelope and shaking his head back and forth scolded her again, "I waas gonna give you these wedding papers…but no, you had to be a bitch…didn't you?"

Both envelopes and the passport picture of Alexei fell to the floor when gagging and choking on her own blood, Maria swung a free arm toward the grotesque and heavily breathing intruder who now unzipped the front of his trousers and climbed upon the bed in an effort to get on top of her and pin her down. With a desperate twist of her body, Maria was able to wrest herself away, and she fell off the far side of the bed where Quintal grabbed her by the throat and stood her up.

"You are a stupid bitch," he hissed while cruelly slamming her head against the wall. "You and I can make a lot of pesos, and that Russian boyfriend of yours is going to make us hundreds of thousands to start with…don't you understand?"

A delirious and helpless Maria now believed she was about to die and that her worst nightmare was coming true as a raving and panting Quintal threw her to the floor and started to kick her in the stomach.

Neither of them heard a panicked Aflredo run into the house after hearing his daughter screaming. Running to the bedroom, he yelled, "What the hell goes on here?" The interruption caused Quintal to stop the brutal kicking. He turned with glazed eyes to face the horrified and unbelieving Alfredo, who immediately realized what he must do. He wheeled toward the kitchen for his large fish-cleaning knife. He grabbed it and ran back to the bedroom where his bleeding, beloved daughter was wailing, "Papa, Papa, Papa…" from the floor alongside the bed.

Alfredo lunged toward the crouching Quintal unaware of the automatic pistol Quintal had aimed at his chest. The shot knocked him backwards onto the floor, as the bullet pierced his heart, killing him instantly. Quintal then stumbled toward the small man and shot him three more times in the chest as a helpless Maria tried to crawl to help her father. "Oh my God, my God, oh my God, Papa…" she screamed. Quintal blurting obscenities, stumbled backwards out of the bedroom into the living room. Now completely out of control and wheezing like a pig, he squeezed off his last two shots at the prostrate Maria, then pulled the trigger three more times before realizing the gun was empty. He crawled to the front door, and once outside, the petrified driver wrestled him into the back seat, slammed the door, jumped in the front and roared from the scene with screeching tires.

In full shock as well as pain, Maria could not tell whether the two shots had hit her. All she could think of was Papa, that maybe he was still alive. She pulled herself up by holding onto the side of the bed and worked her way to the telephone on a small table near the head of the bed. With bloody fingers, she managed to dial the operator, begging for help in her native *Tagalog.*

"Please send ambulance…my Papa has been shot…send police, too…"

Then Maria instinctively moved toward her father, but when she dropped the phone she saw Alexei's photo and the other papers Quintal had thrown in her face, lying in her blood on the floor. Despite her injuries she scooped them up and buttoned them in the pocket of her blouse. The police and medics found her sitting in the middle of a huge pool of blood on the bedroom floor bent over her father, cradling him in her arms, begging for him to come to life and speak to her.

As Alfredo's corpse was covered with a sheet and loaded into the rear of a police jeepney, a screaming Maria yelled at the police while she was being placed in an ambulance by two medical emergency men…"Quintal did this! He is a murderer! He has killed my Papa and my baby…you must get him…he is a pig and an animal! He-he-he m-m-must pay for this…"

After being told of the commotion, Alexei ran the half-mile from the soccer field to the hospital, where he found Maria being wheeled from the Emergency Room to a private room on the first floor. Looking up at him as he raced to her, she started to cry all over again, and gripping Alexei's hand tried to tell him what happened, but the emotion of having him at her side caused her to sob uncontrollably and the words would not come out. The attending doctor motioned Alexei to the side as a nurse eased Maria into a hospital bed.

Realizing that the big Caucasian probably didn't speak *Tagalog,* the doctor spoke to Alexei in broken English, and explained to him that the woman had been beaten and kicked, but fortunately her injuries were not serious. The doctor then gave some bad news.

"But unfortunately, and I don't know if you were aware that she was pregnant, she has miscarried. She also suffered a fractured nose, badly bruised ribs and minor skin damage to her left arm where a bullet grazed her. Our x-rays show no other internal injuries. She's still quite shocky, not only from her own experience, but also from what happened to her father."

"What happened to him, doctor?" Alexei interrupted.

"He was shot to death."

Alexei could only utter an incredulous "What?" before putting his hands to his face and shaking with sobs for the first time since he was a child when he learned his mother had died.

"May I see her now, doctor?"

"Just for a few minutes, we are going to sedate her for she must rest overnight. If all is well tomorrow, we can probably release her the next day."

Still moaning when Alexei reached her bedside, Maria pulled his head next to hers on the pillow and feverishly patted his shoulder while he asked her how it all happened.

"Quintal did this to me and he killed Papa, and also tried to shoot me after he beat and kicked me." With tears streaming down her cheeks and over the bandage that covered her nose, she gripped Alexei with both arms and told him of the miscarriage. "He also murdered our baby. Papa tried to save me but he didn't have a chance against the gun…Quintal tried to grab me and he told me he knows you came from a Russian submarine, and he would make a lot of money from something he showed me about you…but he forgot them when he ran away." Then pointing to a pile of her bloody clothes on a chair in the corner of the room, she told Alexei to take the pictures and papers from the pocket in her blouse.

Alexei stared in disbelief at the photo of the buoy and realized he made a big mistake by forgetting about the buoy when he was at the fishing house. "I destroyed the raft but forgot the buoy," he said out loud. "But darling woman, I promise you that one way or another, Quintal will pay dearly for this. I must go now. The doctor says you must now rest. I'll go back to the house and then come back here in case you need me but in any case, I'll be here when you wake up. Good night now, and remember my love for you."

"I love you, Alexei."

Alexei walked from her room as the doctor entered and went down the corridor to the waiting room with a burning inner rage that caused his heart to pound and his fists to clench as thoughts of Quintal's atrocities pounded and re-pounded through his brain. Reaching the waiting room, he was startled out of his vengeance mindset when he was greeted by many of Maria's, Papa's, and his friends, who came to him one by one to express their sympathy and to ask of Maria's condition.

"She will be okay, but the police had better get their hands on the bastard who did this before I do," he vowed.

The last friend to approach him was Jose Roque, who put his hand on Alexei's shoulder and voiced his concern, "I am very sorry for what happened my friend. Let me give you a ride home so we can talk about it."

"Yes, lets leave now," Alexei agreed.

Although still not 100 percent sure that Alexei came from the *Morozov*, Roque had considered laying it on the line and telling him who he really was and who he believed Alexei really was, but he realized the risk of doing such a thing was great. If warned, Alexei would probably flee and it would be up for grabs who finds him first; but on the other hand, perhaps he should alert his boss and have him grabbed right away, without telling him anything first. There's no guarantee he'd go to the states voluntarily, so if he's who I think he is, we'd better zip him out of here now rather than take any chances. We cannot risk anything that will threaten PEGASUS, he resolved.

Still hoping to learn a little more while riding to the house, Roque asked why Quintal assaulted Maria and killed her father.

"The bastard tried to rape Maria. He brought some papers for a marriage license, and I think he tried to use 'em to bribe her to have sex with him but she said no and fought him off. About this time Papa came in the house, saw what was going on, went after him with a knife, but got shot dead before he could use it. He not only killed Maria's father, he also made her miscarry…he murdered two people. Maria told me that he forced her into sex when she was young by telling her that if she refused, her father would lose his job and his house. He is one evil sonofabitch who must be done away with."

"I agree with you that this is one beast of a man, and that he must be taken care of, but it's a tough problem because even the police are afraid of him. Now I know you want to take care of Quintal yourself, and I don't blame you, but he is not worth spending your life in jail for. Now I believe I can help you in this matter, but you and Maria have got to lay low till the job is done."

"Why won't the police do anything? And why should we lay low?" Alexei asked.

"Because he owns them. Most of them are corrupt and receive payoffs from him for shutting their eyes and ears to illegal things such as gambling, drugs and prostitution. As far as laying low for awhile, the big reason is for you and Maria to stay alive. Despite his influence with the police, he knows Maria witnessed the murder, and he also knows you are a threat to him. He may try to get the both of you out of the way. The best bet is to lay low and let my friends and I take care of this."

Turning into the street where Alexei and Maria lived, they saw police cars in front of the house, and as they parked the car, a man approached and spoke through the window.

"I am with the Zamboanga police. Is either of you Mister Walewski?"

After Alexei replied, the policeman told him the Chief wanted to see him in the house. He then looked at Roque and asked who he was.

"My name is Rafael Tausaga, I am a friend," he answered.

As Alexei and the policeman entered the house, Roque noticed the bloodstained envelopes Alexei had left on the seat. Quickly removing the contents, he was astounded when he saw the photo of the *Morozov* labeled buoy stapled to a small snapshot of Alexei. Then after glancing at the perfectly forged documents that would allow Maria and Alexei to wed, he tried in his mind to put the whole story together. The bastard obviously knows who Alexei is, but why would he bring the evidence to Maria's house? He reasoned that

Quintal must have unknowingly dropped the photos during the fracas for he could not figure why he would show such a thing to Maria. He'll be back for these, he predicted, correctly determining that Quintal was going to sell the evidence and hoping that he hadn't already done so. In any case, neither photo tells where the sub is located. Only a live Alexei could provide that. Putting things in order, he told himself that first he must hide Alexei and Maria. Next make the call to Carmichael and have Alexei picked up. Then lastly, he knew that he must take out mister Quintal and there were no doubts that Carmichael would agree to this as a necessity. PEGASUS is definitely in jeopardy now.

Alexei returned to the car shaking his head and Roque asked him what the Chief wanted?

"He asked me about Quintal and Papa's relationship. After I told him what I knew, I asked him if they had arrested Quintal yet? All he told me was that they're looking for him but he thinks he's left the island."

Roque convinced Alexei that he and Maria must go in hiding for a few days, and with the realization that Quintal, and maybe others knew his true identity, Alexei thought it a good plan. He also knew that he and Maria must now arrange a scheme to leave the Philippines at the earliest opportunity.

"I agree with you about the hiding for awhile, but tell me about who you really are and why you are interested and capable of taking care of Quintal."

"Let me just say that I work for an organization that would like to see Quintal erased for good. Now we have a good excuse to get it done. I have a police background here and in America and will be in contact today with associates of my business who will sniff out the rat. I'll arrange to take the both of you to a remote beach house up the coast that belongs to a friend of mine who's out of town for a month. I suggest we go as soon as Maria is released and Alfredo's funeral has taken place. But between now and then you must watch over her and try to keep as many people around her as you can. I have another man who will be around the hospital here to watch for any of Quintal's goons, who may be sent here to get Maria. Believe me…right now we cannot trust the police or any other law enforcement agency around here. We must protect Maria ourselves until Quintal is gone…and once that is done, the biggest part of the problem will be over."

"And what do we do then, my friend?"

"You two should get married and start a new life together," Roque deceived, as thoughts of what he was going to do haunted his mind. He truly liked the young Russian as a friend. He liked Maria also, and decided to propose to Carmichael that they take her along with Alexei and maybe get them into something like the witness protection program.

Jose Roque's plan to protect Maria at the hospital worked. She was released after two days, just in time for her father's funeral, which she attended with more than 200 family, friends and a grief-stricken Alexei. After the mournful ceremony, Roque drove both to a small, but modern beach house, two miles from Zamboanga City and took elaborate precautions driving there to ensure they were not followed. While Maria was under care at the hospital, Roque had stocked the house with food and written down the telephone number of the place so he could call if necessary. As he dropped the two off, he warned them to "stay out of sight as much as you can," and then handed Alexei a .45 caliber pistol and two clips of ammunition. "Just in case the wrong person knocks on the door," Roque told him.

"Good hunting," Alexei called out as Roque waved goodbye.

"Just sit tight, I'll call you in a day or two," Roque responded.

After he left, Maria asked Alexei about their friend.

"Who is he and what does he know?" she asked.

"I don't know, but if he was a danger to us he wouldn't have given me a gun. And he's given us the opportunity to make plans for a quick wedding and then let's get the hell out of this country and try another...Quintal's the guy we've gotta worry about, and we don't know who he's told about me and the picture of the buoy."

Maria put it in perspective, "When he threw those pictures in my face and said how much they would be worth, he was talking about the future...in other words, as of the day he murdered Papa, he hadn't done anything with them...and now WE have them, don't we?"

"Not for long sweetheart. Let's go outside and burn them right now," Alexei suggested.

While the photos smoldered, the two talked on and on about their plight before making the decision that their move from the Philippines should be undertaken within a week.

* * *

While Alexei and Maria were spending their first night together in the beach house, the U.S. navy was reaching the critical part of operation PEGASUS. With good weather, good diving skills and the innovations of *soup-sal* the salvage guru, *Whistler* and *Engage* had accomplished a spectacular underwater feat by removing all the antennas, one nuclear missile, one nuclear-tipped torpedo and one propeller. All of the booty was now either en route to the United States or already there. Additionally, one small barge with aircraft parts had been towed to Subic Bay, and another remained on the scene with part of the fuselage and an engine, to convince any onlookers that the salvage of the P4V was still in progress. All that remained now was the ticklish task of making *Morozov* light enough so she could be towed to deeper water. This final phase was taking considerable time, as divers had to "tunnel" under the submarine using high pressure water hoses prior to running cables under the boat to support *soup-sal's* special trim tanks that would be used to control the depth of *Morozov* while under tow in a submerged condition.

At a meeting the next morning with the officers from both salvage ships, Leominster emphasized the importance of preventing *Morozov* from coming to the surface while being towed.

"Gentlemen, this job would be easy if all we had to do was blow this boat to the surface and tow it away. But as you know, and unlike most submarine sinkings, this one is not flooded to any extent internally, and with the ballast tanks still full of sea water, all we would have to do to bring this baby up is give the port and starboard amidships ballast tanks a few shots of compressed air and up she comes! But in this case we must keep her underwater when we move her. This boat must not reach the surface where it could be detected."

Now a new challenge faced PEGASUS…Fleet Weather Center warns of a typhoon that could threaten part of the South China Sea.

"This storm could be here in 48 hours, so we must be ready to tow this Ruski out of here before then," *soup-sal* warned. "It's going to be tricky enough towing her submerged in fair weather. I don't even want to think about what it would be like in a typhoon. What this means, gentlemen, is that we must continue to work the crews and divers around the clock. We must have the special trim tank in place by tomorrow morning, and I want to commence the tow with the dummy barge in place by tomorrow at nightfall. Once *Whistler* starts the tow, *Engage* will remain here for the bottom clean-up. If the typhoon comes near, you may seek a lee behind Palawan or any of the islands north of there. Once the storm passes, go back to this location and finish the job. And I want to emphasize that the bottom here must be immaculate. I don't care if there are a few aircraft scraps down there, but I want absolutely no trace that this Ruski submarine was ever here. Does anyone have any questions? If not, let's get on with it…and, oh, I promise you all that when this operation is completed I am going to make sure that your ships get some quality time in a prime liberty port for some well deserved R and R."

* * *

Jose Roque changed his mind and decided not to make the call that would cancel PEGASUS. He now looked to take care of Quintal first. He knew that locating him wouldn't be easy. He figured Quintal would avoid his house on the water and stay in hiding elsewhere for awhile, and this could be just about anywhere. But he had a hunch that he'd stay reasonably close to Zamboanga City because he'd want to keep track of Maria and Alexei, especially if he found out that Maria was alive and would surely alert Alexei that Quintal knows about him. He'll most likely try to eliminate Maria at the first opportunity. Roque knew what Quintal's car looked like. So he put two operatives to work scouring the city and rural roads for any sign of the thug. On a special phone he also called Antero on Busuanga Island, asking him to check out the fishing house for the fat man and Antero knew immediately who he was talking about and agreed to do it immediately. He then told Roque that U.S. navy ships were working offshore picking up pieces of a downed airplane.

"I heard they must've had some special bombs or secret gear on board the plane, for all the work that's going on. They say only one man was able to parachute. The rest of the crew went down with the plane."

Smiling, and relieved to hear the diversion was still working and that there were no Russians snooping around, Roque thanked Antero for the info and told him to call back immediately if "*you know who*" shows up.

In Zamboanga, the search went on for a day and a half with no success, and there was no call from Antero. Finally, one of his informants notified him of some interesting information. He reported spotting a small jeepney outside a house in the north of Zamboanga City that had been parked in the same spot for two days.

"What's so unusual about that?" Roque asked.

"I have a pal who lives across the road who told me a big heavy guy was helped from the vehicle a few days ago, but nobody's come out of the house since. My friend says this house is usually unoccupied, but sometimes he sees men bringing women in and out of there."

"Did you get the license number of the jeepney?"

"Yes, it's a Zam City place number KJ 752."

The number hit Jose Roque like a bomb going off in his head. It was just one digit off the KJ 751 that was on the car Quintal used at the fishing house. He knew that people in the business of Quintal would probably register their vehicles in someone else's names for various purposes, but they would get the places from a stack numbered in sequence.

"Stay within sight of that vehicle. I'm on my way. If I find neither of you when I get there, I'll assume you're on his ass, and I'll find you somehow. But be real careful not to let on he's being tailed...You've done a good job."

Emilio Quintal did not awake from his murderous binge until the following noon, and was puzzled to find himself in a strange place. "What in the hell am I doing here?" he yelled at his driver who sat in the next room reading the daily newspaper.

"You had some big troubles yesterday, Mister Quintal, so I hid the big car in the jungle and had another brought from the garage so we couldn't be tailed."

Trying to sort out what had occurred. Quintal finally remembered the girl and shooting Alfredo. He also vaguely remembered getting off some shots at Maria, but had no idea if he killed her too.

"What does the paper say?" he asked the driver.

"It said Alfredo Gabizon, was shot dead during an altercation with an unknown assailant, and that his daughter Maria Gabizon, received a broken nose and bruises and was taken to Zamboanga Hospital."

"That fucker Alfredo tried to stab me. I had to defend myself," Quintal retorted, not telling him the real reason he went to see Maria. Neither did he reveal what next he had in store for her.

Unable to remember anything about the two important photographs, Quintal believed he must have left them at his main house, and that the KGB man should be in town now and looking for him. He knew he had to get the items and make contact.

"We will sit tight here for another day or so. Then I must go alone to the big house and get a few things done," he told the driver.

"Yes, sir, Mister Quintal."

With a break in the monsoon rains and clearing skies, Jose Roque opened a fresh pack of *True Menthol* cigarettes and stepped outside his steaming rented car for a smoke. After releasing his assisting agent and telling him "I'll take it from here alone," he parked the car off the side of the road just below the house where he believed Quintal was. Completely hidden by lush bougainvillea and a closely packed stand of coconut palm trees, Roque could see the place through a break in the shrubbery. He still wasn't sure anyone was inside, but he kept watching for any sign of activity. He decided he could wait until dark, and if no lights came on he would give it up.

While waiting, thoughts of PEGASUS operation went through his mind and he wondered how many more days the Navy would need to get what they want and drag the *Morozov* out to deep water. But whether they wrap it up in the next day or two or not, Quintal knows too much and must be taken out, he reasoned.

Roque's patience was rewarded shortly before four in the afternoon when he saw two men, one he immediately identified as Quintal, appear in the front door, where they talked for a few minutes. The stranger went back into the house while Quintal went alone to the car.

"This is a break," Roque realized, and although assassinations were distasteful to him, he knew that Quintal was a dangerous threat to the whole operation, and after what he did to Alfredo and Maria he felt no sympathy for such a corrupt monster.

He watched Quintal turn the small jeepney around in the narrow, dirt road and then pass right in front of him. Waiting until the vehicle rounded a bend and was out of sight, Roque started his car, eased it out from where it was hidden, and followed the other vehicle at a safe, maximum distance. After several turns, Quintal turned on to the beach road and headed north. Now, with several other vehicles on the wide graveled roadway, Roque was able to follow without being noticed. Soon, Quintal made a left turn onto a small road that led to his house on the water. Suspecting all along that his quarry was going there, and knowing that the road to the house was short and dead-ended, Roque drove past the turnoff, pulled his car into the undergrowth, checked that his compact *Walther PPK* pistol was fully loaded and cocked before slowly moving through the tall grass toward the side of the house. Quintal's vehicle was parked outside.

Roque waited in ambush for 15 minutes or so when he heard a commotion on the water out near the far end of Quintal's pier where his driver fished and sea-borne visitors tied up their vessels. He cursed under his breath as he saw two small dugout canoes filled with juveniles moving up to the pier, where one scantily clad waif of no more than 11 years leaped from the canoe and ran up the pier. Quintal also saw the youth and realized they were bent on stealing a fishing rod and a life cushion that had been left on the dock by Quintal's driver. Running out the door while hollering threats and curses in *Cebuano*, Quintal picked up a piece of pipe and waddled red-faced and puffing down the pier as the young thief ran in front of him and jumped in the little canoe with the loot, barely escaping the fat pursuer with the pipe.

Roque watched Quintal reach the end of the pier and toss the pipe in frustration at the fast-paddling boys. Then just as he threw it, the end of the pier collapsed with a loud crack from his weight, and a fascinated CIA man saw Quintal tumble head first into the water and get swept seaward by the ebbing tide. The youths in the canoes also saw him, and laughed and hollered obscenities in his direction as the big, sputtering swimmer attempted to turn around and head for the shattered end of the pier, which was now way out of his reach. Suddenly one of the lads pointed at the water and hollered, "SHARK! SHARK!" in his native tongue. Roque then came out to where he could get a better view and felt chills go up his neck when he saw two huge dorsal fins heading straight for his adversary.

Emilio Quintal never saw the fins until it was too late. Then with his eyes bulged in terror, he screamed and tried to flail his arms when the first Great White tore into his leg, ripping if off at the knee. The enormous, sharp toothed jaws of the second shark slashed into his neck and head, then with a shaking action, dragged the rest of Quintal's bloody body underwater, where both behemoths fought over the grisly remains, bits and pieces of which floated to the surface amidst a large blood slick. Roque's hands were shaking as he witnessed the end of the hated Quintal and watched the two canoes, with four terrified youngsters paddling wide-eyed at a frantic speed southward toward Zamboanga City.

Those kids will really have something to tell their grandchildren, Roque predicted to himself, but first they will tell the story in town, where the word will spread swiftly of Quintal's demise. They don't know how lucky they are, for those sharks were probably ready to knock over one of the canoes before Quintal fell in. He couldn't have shown up at a better time.

Still dazed and with visions of the gruesome scene he just witnessed spinning through his head, Roque decided to leave the scene immediately and get his thoughts together. He knew he must tell Alexei and Maria right away the news of Quintal's demise. He also determined that Brady Carmichael would have them both picked up once he made the call to Manila revealing Walewski was actually an escapee from

Morozov. His duty demanded he make the Manila call, but the thought of turning in his friends bothered him deeply. Not willing to face them, Roque decided instead to call them from the hotel, as there were no pay phones in existence on Mindanao. He drove swiftly to Zamboanga City, parked the car on a side street next to the hotel, went into his room and called the couple at the beach house with the news.

Maria answered the phone, and Alexei saw her smile and let out a big sigh of relief as she just said, "Thank you, thank you, thank you…yes, yes, yes."

After she hung up, and knowing it was good news, Alexei didn't have a chance to ask her who had called, for she ran right to him, put her hands on his shoulders, looked him straight in the eyes and told him that Quintal was dead.

"He will bother us no more, my darling. Rafael says he died an appropriate death and that he will tell us about it when he returns tomorrow night from Manila, and asks that we stay here until then. He also said something strange…he said, *don't buy any shark meat!* My God, do you think a Great White got Quintal like the woman up north I told you about?"

"I hope so," Alexei flatly declared. "He deserved to die that way."

Then grinning from ear to ear, he gently pulled Maria close and whispered in her ear. "Things are looking up for us, sweet woman. Now don't you think it's safe enough for us to venture to that beautiful, sandy beach right outside the back door and get some of that sunshine?"

Jose Roque next tried to reach his contact in Manila, but was unable to get through. After trying for 15 minutes or so without success, he felt an urge to drive somewhere for a quiet drink and let his nerves settle down after the events of the afternoon. Now facing the possibility that he would be directly involved with the most unpleasant task of picking up Alexei and Maria and shuffling them off to wherever the CIA wants them located, Roque left the hotel deep in thought, and headed for his car as night fell upon the city. Then as he started to unlock the door, a small man crept up behind him and squeezed off 3 shots from a 9 mm pistol, fitted with a silencer, onto the back of his head. Jose Roque fell dead without ever realizing what had occurred. The small man, who was the same one who had obtained his proof of identity fingerprints with the bottle-swap ploy at the *Talisay Bar,* grabbed Roque's wallet, put it and the gun in a shopping bag and disappeared into the darkness. The Philippine communists thus took revenge on the CIA man who had caused them so much trouble in the past. The loose talk on Busuanga and the fingerprints lifted from the beer bottle had sealed Jose Roque's fate on America's birthday…the 4th of July.

His body was recovered and turned over to the police who made out a report that appeared in the daily newspaper: *In an apparent robbery, a 35-year-old man was found shot to death in an alley outside the Lantaka Hotel. The man was identified from the hotel registry as Rafael Tausaga of Manila…*

The same day, on the same page, the paper contained the report of another death: *Local businessman Emilio Quintal was killed by Great White sharks while swimming near his residence north of the city…*

The news of Roque's death traveled fast to Manila, where Captain Gunderson, the ONI rep for PEGASUS had the unpleasant task of calling Brady Carmichael on the secure phone to notify him of the loss of his special agent.

"How the hell did this happen?" Carmichael demanded to know. "Was it related to PEGASUS?"

"We don't think so. Some of his agents say that one of his old friends on an island up near the salvage site blabbed that he knew the man from the past as Roque, who used to be well known around there, and the word got around to the wrong people. It may just be a coincidence, but one of his agents in Zamboanga says a man Roque was tailing was also killed the same day, close to where Roque died. Only this guy was whacked in the sea by Great White sharks!"

"I'll have my people in Manila send me a file on the guy. Now tell me how is PEGASUS progressing?"

"Unbelievably well so far, and so far no sign of detection afloat or ashore. We hope to have everything out of the area within two days…Brady, I'm truly sorry about Roque, I know you and he go way back and that you had a lot of respect for each other."

"Thank you Captain, I think I'm gonna take a little break from what I'm doing right now. This one really hurts, for I probably shouldn't have sent him out there in the first place. Now tell me Captain, as you're a day later than us out there, did Roque die on the 4th of July?"

"Yes he did."

Carmichael walked to the window, stared at the endless stream of vehicles moving along the highway below and slowly shaking his head cursed the loss of his very good friend…"This one was not for free…it had a cost, just like I knew it would…" He then turned and went to his filing cabinet and withdrew a bottle of *John Begg* single malt Scotch whiskey. Then calling in his secretary, he told her, "That will be all for today Mary."

CHAPTER 14

A JUST FINALE

Maria and Alexei had no way of knowing that the only two people besides Maria who knew of Alexei's true identity were now dead. Hearing the news of Tausaga's murder on the radio soon after experiencing the relief from the knowledge of Quintal's demise caused them both to feel that doom was closing in on them. Maria was further alarmed when she also heard on the radio of the American aircraft salvage operation off Busuanga.

"We've got to disappear from the Philippines as soon as possible," Maria decided. "I think they found the submarine, and who knows what people Quintal informed about you. And what about this Tausaga? Was he really who he said he was? Word from Coron is that his real name was Roque and that he was probably some kind of an agent."

"If they found my sub and see the open forward escape hatch, they'll know somebody got out, but they won't know how many, or if they made it to the surface or were killed by sharks, but if the bodies are ever recovered from *Morozov* and turned over to Russia, they will find one man missing… Now as far as who Tausaga really was…I don't know, but I now believe he was working for either the Americans or Marcos here in the Philippines. In either case, I can't figure out for sure if he knew who I was. I made a blunder the day he gave me a ride from the hospital to the house. When I went in and talked with the police chief, I left the bloody pictures and papers on the car seat. If Tausaga looked at them and he was a U.S. agent, he would have seen the photo of the buoy with my sub's name on it attached to my passport photo. Now with knowledge that the sub may have been found, this would tell them about me."

"But maybe Tausaga didn't know about your submarine, for if he did, the Americans surely would have been after you by now. But whatever, I think we both could be in danger, and we should make a plan to vamoose. Papa was thriftier than I thought…he left us enough money to go from here to Manila, get married, leave the country and still have some left over to live a few months on. We've talked of Australia before. I say let's fly to Brisbane, where my grandmother lives. We can change our names after we get there."

* * *

Operation PEGASUS was nearing a successful completion, and was given a further break when the big typhoon veered to the northwest, allowing the *USS Whistler* to secure two special trimming tanks to the bottomed *Morozov* in preparation of taking the wrecked submersible on its final voyage. The tow was finally hooked up and ready to go on the evening of July 6, and as soon as darkness set in, the slow, tedious procedure of lifting *Morozov* from the bottom got underway. The control unit for maintaining the depth was strapped to the amidships deck of the *Morozov*. The tanks allowed *Whistler* to reasonably control the depth of the towed submarine at a speed of five to six knots as both vessels plied through glassy calm seas toward the drop point, 40 miles to the northwest. The depth of the sub was monitored by a fathometer mounted under the diversionary barge that contained more aircraft parts. The barge was towed 600 feet astern of *Whistler* and positioned directly over the *Morozov*. Depth readings from this echo-sounder enabled the men to send signals to the depth control unit to make the submarine rise or sink, as required. Thanks to the calm ocean conditions, they were able to keep the sub between 75-150 feet from the surface.

Prior to leaving the inshore salvage location, divers had attached plastic explosives at several key places on the towing rig. Remotely actuated from the fantail of the *Whistler,* these charges would blow away the heavy gauge cable towline attached to the submarine's bow. Simultaneously, charges would blow out the tops of two of the submarines ballast tanks where medium pressure air was used to make the boat slightly buoyant to initially get her off the bottom. These huge tanks, which gird the hull, are open to the sea at the bottom, and once the vent connections at the top of the tanks are blown off, they rapidly re-flood, causing the sub to obtain negative buoyancy. To ensure she sank rapidly, another charge blew open a hole in the forward torpedo compartment causing it to immediately flood and send *Morozov* rapidly to crush depth at the designated position.

Shortly after midnight, communications were established with the U.S. nuclear attack submarine *USS Orca*, which awaited the arrival of the tow at the pre-arranged position over the multiple-shipwreck site. *Orca's* mission was to guide *Whistler* to the precise drop point where the tow would be brought to a complete stop. Then, on signal from *Orca,* all the pre-positioned charges would be set off electrically and the Soviet submarine would make its last descent.

At exactly 0445 in the morning of July 7th, the *USS Orca* reported to *Whistler* that the area was clear of all contacts, and that the tow was in exact position for the drop. At this time, Captain Leominster, who hadn't slept for two days, turned to the skipper of the *Whistler* as both stood on the ship's darkened bridge and gave the order to release *Morozov*.

"Let her go, Sam, then maybe we can get some shut-eye before returning to Subic."

Gallagher answered with a "aye, aye sir," then gave the short and sweet order that all hands had been anxiously waiting to hear.

"FANTAIL, THIS IS BRIDGE, EXECUTE THE DEMOLITIONS."

Within seconds, a series of *thumps* were head from astern of *Whistler* indicating the plastic explosives had done their job, and after the main towing cable to *Morozov* was blasted off its bow, *Whistler's* towing engine was switched to the *haul in* position and the now slack, four-inch diameter towing cable was hauled aboard. Then after a few minutes, as *Morozov* dropped slowly, straight down through the depths, sonarmen on both the *Whistler* and the *Orca* heard the eerie, groaning sounds of the pressure hull crushing inward as the submersible passed her collapse depth at 1,900 feet.

Gazing with a far away look at the chink of light on the eastern horizon that signaled the first signs of dawn and a new day, Sam Gallagher seemed to speak directly to the flat, calm, black surface of the sea as he broke the hushed silence on *Whistler's* bridge.

"Lord above, there are many of our brother sailors in that graveyard down there…I ask you to bless their souls."

As the bridge again became quiet, several men crossed themselves and said a silent prayer of their own as the Russian submarine, with Captain Second Rank Boris Stepakov and 93 other seafarers aboard, slipped to the bottom of the South China Sea and came to rest at a depth of 3,960 feet, within 20 feet of a Japanese cruiser that had been there for 28 years. The cruiser held more than 1,000 men who had perished when the big ship was sunk in a raging WWII sea battle.

After *Whistler* completed the drop and *Engage* finished cleaning the ocean bottom at the salvage site, both ships were returned to the Subic Bay Naval Base for an upkeep period to repair and replace equipment worn or damaged during the grueling salvage part of PEGASUS. At the end of this period, with both ships completely refurbished and freshly painted, Admiral Langlois addressed both crews and commended them for their outstanding performance during PEGASUS. He also cautioned never to reveal to anyone what transpired these past three weeks.

"If anyone asks you, tell them you were only salvaging a downed aircraft," he said.

Before the Admiral departed he told the men that they had earned some R and R and that upon the recommendation of Captain Leominster, he would authorize both ships to make a liberty port on the way back to Pearl Harbor.

* * *

Maria and Alexei were still looking over their shoulders, but managed to leave Zamboanga, wed in Manila and fly to Brisbane, Australia, where a lawyer friend of Maria's grandmother found a way to change their names to Galanz, after they became citizens of the country based upon Maria's birth rights. Mister and Mrs. Galanz had no trouble settling into a new life in a strange country. Maria's grandmother was delighted to have them both around, and the couple were able to find a comfortable cottage not too far from her house, and both found ample opportunity for employment...Maria as a commercial artist, and her husband "Karl Galanz" found work in an automobile repair shop.

A month after their arrival, Karl Galanz had a tryout with the *Queensland Tigers* soccer team and was signed to a contract the next day. Celebrating his selection, the pair went out on the town for dinner, drinks and dancing. Noticing some uniformed sailors sitting at a nearby bar in the restaurant, the new striker for the *Tigers* asked the waiter if they were Australian.

"No, they're *Yanks*," he replied. "They're from a submarine rescue ship named the *USS Whistler.*"

The End

ABOUT THE AUTHOR

The author is a retired Navy Lieutenant Commander who came up through the ranks. He served on submarines in the Atlantic and Pacific oceans both as an enlisted man and as an officer. Barrows also was a deep sea hard-hat diver and commanded the submarine rescue ship USS *COUCAL* in the far east during the Vietnam war.